A Singles Cinderella Story

(Or How to Find Love Without Losing Yourself)

a novel

Laura C. Browne and Jill L. Ferguson

In Your Face Ink LLC

A Singles Cinderella Story (Or How to Find Love Without Losing Yourself) is a work of fiction. Products and companies mentioned within the story are to lend reality, not to endorse any item or business.

© 2020 by In Your Face Ink LLC and Laura C. Browne and Jill L. Ferguson

Published in the United States of America by In Your Face Ink LLC.

Cover design and book design by Rick Schank of Purple Couch Creative

The Library of Congress has established a Cataloging-in-Publication record for this title.

ISBN: 978-0-578-63179-0 paperback

ISBN: 978-0-578-63188-6 e-book

www.inyourfaceink.com

Printed in the United States of America

For anyone who has searched for love

Chapter 1

The ring on Teresa's finger sparkled as she held out her right hand to show her best friends, Leticia and El. "What do you think?"

"Oh honey, that is gorgeous," said Leticia.

Teresa smiled and pointed out the two small diamonds on either side of the center sapphire stone. "This was his great-grandmother's engagement ring." She moved her hand around so her friends could see the old-fashioned setting. "I'd much rather have this than a new ring. It means so much more to me." Teresa beamed. The blue of her dress enhanced the sparkling ring on her finger.

"To Teresa and Jordan," said Leticia holding up her martini glass.

"To Teresa and Jordan," agreed El lifting her glass filled with tonight's special, a Bourbon Lemon Drop martini. The sweet and sour taste was just what El needed for this occasion.

When Teresa had called Cinderella Casey, whom almost everyone called El, two days earlier on Sunday morning with the news that Jordan had proposed, El was genuinely excited for her friend. She listened as Teresa explained how he had surprised her with the ring.

El's excitement lasted until she got off the phone. She was happy for her friend, really she was. Teresa had struggled after her last relationship had ended when her boyfriend surprised her by saying he needed more "space" after almost four years.

El wanted the best for her friend, but this engagement also made her a little sad. What about her? Where was her ring?

It's not that El wanted to get married soon, but she did want to be with someone special. It had been six months since she'd broken up with Derek, after he had assumed she'd be thrilled to give up her career and her life and run off to Asia where he was working. The thought of it still angered her. But the fact was that even thinking about going online to meet someone was also a painful thought. She sighed and unconsciously twisted her auburn hair around her index finger.

The rest of her life was going well. She had gotten a promotion at her company, and she finally felt like she was seen and respected. And while the new job was challenging, she felt great about it. The additional money made the monthly bills much easier to handle, and she didn't feel as stressed. She stroked Mr. Fluffy, who sat beside her on the living room sofa. There was just one thing missing: she wanted to share her success with someone besides her best friends.

Two days later, at happy hour at the martini bar, El's excitement had returned and she happily toasted Teresa, who looked radiant. Her long brown braid hung past her waist and swung back and forth as she shook her head while laughing.

"Now, what exactly happened on Saturday night? I want to hear it all from the beginning. I could barely understand you when you called with all that screaming," Leticia teased her friend.

"Excuse me, I was not screaming. That was just my happy voice..."

"Your loud happy voice," said El.

Teresa laughed. "Okay, maybe. Maybe I was a little loud. But come on..." She wiggled her fingers. "Look at what I'm happy about. I couldn't help it!" Teresa grinned. "Oooh, he was soooo cute."

"Tell us, tell us," said Leticia. Her short dark hair was cut into a wavy cap, accentuating her high cheekbones and almond-shaped brown eyes. Her grey striped suit was simple and elegant and was paired with a cream silk blouse and plain black heels. El had joked when Leticia arrived at the restaurant that she looked "appropriately lawyerly."

"Wait. Before you tell us, let's order food. Without a rumbly tummy, I can better concentrate on the happy couple," El joked, looking down at the menu. She was clothed in an emerald dress today, one that accentuated her green eyes.

Teresa looked as though she was going to complain, but smiled at the last part of the comment. "How about some bruschetta? I really like the fig and pear."

"Sounds good. Let's add some roasted peppers and goat cheese," said Leticia. "What about you, El?"

"Prosciutto for me," El said, silently acknowledging to herself that she had ordered something that the vegetarian Teresa would not eat. She wondered if her choice was ornery, then decided it was more about what she wanted.

Leticia waved at the waitress and gave their order. Then she turned to Teresa and held up her drink. "Details. All of them."

Teresa giggled. "Okay, okay. So I told you that he took me to the restaurant that we like to go, the one that his friend's family owns. He seemed kind of nervous, but I wasn't really thinking about it because I'd had a tough day at work and I was telling him all about it. Oh, and we sat all the way in the back, sort of out of the way. I even made a joke about it." She took a sip of her drink and smiled again. "So he was just really sweet that night. And he was listening to my complaints and we had our hands on the table, and he was holding my hand like he normally does and sort of stroking my fingers." She paused for a minute and took a deep breath like she was remembering. "And he said some sweet things about what a wonderful time he has with me and I thought it was funny to say that then but really nice to hear. And after we finished the entrees, they cleared them away and we were waiting for the dessert menu. It seemed like it was taking a long time and his friend was there that night because he works there sometimes and he seemed to be looking over at us a lot, but I didn't really think about it at the time." She took another breath.

"Go on…" said Leticia with a big smile.

"Okay, so then he sort of dropped his napkin and he stood up to get it, which I should have thought was strange, but I wasn't thinking about it at all. And then suddenly I realized that he was on one knee. And he said 'Teresa' in a really serious voice and I looked at him and it still didn't register. Then I realized that he had a ring box in his hand. He told me that the last few months were the best of his life and he felt so lucky that he had met me." She blinked a few times as if to hold back tears. Her voice got lower and she said, "And then he said he couldn't imagine his life without me and 'Teresa, will you marry so we can spend our lives together?'" She paused again.

"Whoooh! So awesome!" said El.

"I was in shock and realized that the whole restaurant had gotten really quiet and I said 'yes, yes, yes' and went to get down to kiss him as him as he was getting up and we kind of bumped into each other and started laughing. Then he gave me a big kiss. And it seemed like everyone in the restaurant was clapping and his friend was there standing by him and clapping, too." She paused again, her eyes wide. "It was so crazy. Oh and then they brought a special dessert that said 'congratulations' on it. He had planned it all in advance."

"And the ring?" prompted Leticia.

"Oh right, right. I hadn't even really seen the ring. So he took it out of the box and slipped it on my finger and then told me that it was his great-grandmother Cecily's ring." She stretched out her hand to show it off again.

"It's gorgeous," admired El. "How did he know it would fit?"

Teresa shook her head and laughed. "He didn't." She turned her hand over and showed the back of the ring which had some tape wrapped around it. "He was soooo worried about that but he wasn't sure how to find out my ring size so he decided to take a chance. He was really afraid that it would be too small and then I'd have to wear it on my pinky until I could get it adjusted. I'm going to have to take it to a jeweler to get it resized."

El shook her head. "And you had no idea?"

Teresa's eyes got big. "No, not at all! I was shocked! I didn't expect it. I mean we've only been dating for six months. This was such a surprise." She smiled again.

Leticia exchanged a look with El. "Yeah, about that. I am so happy for you. I think Jordan is great." She picked her words carefully. "It does seem a little, uh, fast. I just want to make sure you're really happy."

Teresa tipped her head to the side. "I know. But when it's right, it's right. I know he's the guy for me. And I have you ladies to thank for that."

Leticia laughed. El thought back to the night when Teresa told them that she had met Jordan at her cousin's wedding but was too nervous to call or text him even though he had put his number in her phone. They made her text him while they were out at happy hour the week after the wedding, and they forced Teresa to ask him out for dinner and dancing, her two favorite things to do on a date.

"Good thing we made you do something instead of just waiting around for him to call," said El.

"Thank you. You were so right." She raised her glass. "To my friends. You are the best."

The truth was El didn't feel like she was the best. She and Leticia had been on the phone the night before questioning if Teresa was moving too quickly. They liked Jordan and compared to anyone that Teresa had dated before, he was certainly the best match for her. Jordan had fit into their circle as easily as El's brother Jack did, though he lacked Jack's sharp wit and easy-going attitude. Jordan was friendly and quick to offer a hand, an ear, or even dating advice the one time they asked him; he was kind of like a male version of Teresa. Plus it was obvious how much he adored her. But El had dated Derek for almost two years before realizing he cared more about his career and money than about her. She would hate for Teresa to find a different side of Jordan AFTER they married, but when she said this to Leticia, Leticia said, "Girl, Derek was that way from day one. You just didn't want to see it."

Ouch, El thought, but she silently acknowledged Leticia was correct. His parents had even joked upon meeting her that Derek was probably attracted to her because of her almost emerald eyes, Derek's favorite color since preschool when he understood green was the color of American currency.

Leticia interrupted her thoughts by saying, "I just don't understand what the rush is." Leticia was intentionally uncoupled. During the past six months she had had a very steamy thirty-six hour date with Jackson Troy Huber III, a Taye Diggs' look-a-like, who wanted to make them into a regular thing, but whom Leticia said no to more often than she said yes…and yet he still kept trying. And she had four other dates, but she was most loyal to her lawyering and her friends.

El's brother Jack had joked with Leticia that if the guys presented her with legal briefs instead of boxer briefs, she'd show more long-term interest.

El had completely been on board the Teresa and Jordan dating train, even though Jordan gushed through John Legend's "All of Me" to Teresa at a karaoke bar one night. Teresa thought it was the most romantic thing ever to be singled out of the crowded bar with the popular love song about appreciating one's partner's imperfections as well as the perfections. But El and Leticia caught each other's eyes behind Teresa's back and feigned barfing, and then ordered double Bacardi shots, downed them, and led the bar in a sing-along for the last refrain on stage with Jordan.

After he and Teresa kissed and the whole bar cheered, Leticia grabbed the mike and belted out Destiny's Child's "Independent Women" as her own inner protest against giving herself over to love and a man. A few women in the bar did throw their hands up when asked who identified as independent and which honeys made money, but many didn't react. El thought that was because most of them looked like they were either on dates or trolling for a hook up.

When Leticia climbed down from the stage, half a dozen guys approached her, offering to buy her drinks. One impeccably tailored, six-foot something guy with a slightly South African accent offered Leticia a "Mercedes SL convertible or any other Mercedes" she wanted if only she'd go home with him that night.

Leticia laughed and said, "Didn't you listen to the song? 'The car I'm driving, I bought it.' I don't need another. Thank you." And then she offered to buy him another of whatever he was drinking.

El, a tad drunk from that double shot, watched the scene with awe and wonder. Would she ever be as smooth with strange men as Leticia was…Though the more she thought about it, Leticia was smooth with everyone. El made a mental note that she hoped she'd remember to ask Leticia the next day how she did it.

Chapter 2

Instead of El's alarm blaring at 6 a.m. like it usually did—in her drunken state, she forgot to set it—her cat woke her. Mr. Fluffy was not happy and he meowed loudly into El's ear to protest that she had forgotten to put out dry food for him the night before. She put a pillow over her head and ignored him. Mr. Fluffy stepped on her stomach and continued to protest. "Ugh," she moaned and turned on her side, pushing him away.

She needed aspirin. She crawled out of bed and gingerly walked over to the bathroom sink and swallowed some pills. She slowly followed the annoying cat into the kitchen and poured some dry food for him, wincing at the loud noise of the pieces hitting the metal bowl. The cat gave one more loud wail then started to munch.

Even though it was Wednesday and she should be headed into the office, El went back to bed and pulled the covers over her head. "Ugh," she said again and thought about the night before. After all of their toasting to Teresa's happiness, El went back to her apartment and drank Absolut Citron while looking at old pictures of her and Derek.

She grimaced as she thought about the rest of the evening. She had searched for Derek's name and company name online to find out what he was doing. She had defriended him on Facebook soon after they had broken up so she couldn't look for him that way. The search pulled up multiple articles about him, and it looked like his company was doing well. She obsessed over an article and picture she found of him and a woman at a charity event. They were smiling way too much.

El squeezed her eyes shut, trying not to think about the time she'd wasted searching for any information about him. After finding those pictures, she wondered what she was doing wrong. Why couldn't she find someone special? It looked like even stupid Derek had found someone.

Upset about Derek, she had made the mistake of click-stumbling through some ads. They said, "Find out why guys don't call," "Secrets to getting the second date," "What men really want," and "Want the man of your dreams?" They all promised to help her become more desirable and attract men. She groaned as she remembered clicking on the "Be A Man Magnet" ad that promised men wouldn't be able to stay away. Not only was there a convenient e-book, there was also an online class that she could purchase that would give her all she needed to know. This was from a guy who promised that he would share the amazing but simple secrets he learned from interviewing lots of other guys. His video was very convincing. He understood her frustrations. He could help HER. He knew the answers that she really needed, but no one had ever told her. And if she would just click the button…

Her head still hurt so she opened her e-mail to let the office know she was taking a sick day, her first ever at this company. And instead, what caught her eye like a beacon in her inbox was the course that she had bought the night before. "Shit," El said aloud. Without the haze of alcohol, it looked terrible. The class creator promised to share the secrets of the perfect words to get your man to fall in love with you, and the kissing techniques that would have him begging for more.

She groaned when she thought that she had spent $495 on the five-part course (a big discount over the $995 that it normally cost because she acted NOW). Fortunately, she noticed the fine print of a money-back guarantee so she requested a refund. She felt so stupid that she had drunk-purchased it.

What was wrong with her? She never did things like that. She felt awful mentally and physically. She debated whether plain cornflakes would make her feel better or would make her want to throw up.

She decided to give the cornflakes a try—no milk, just cereal. She slowly ate them, trying to chew quietly, the crunching sounding loud in her head. And she sent that e-mail to her boss Kate, the other manager Carl, and her team members, letting them know she was taking the day off.

As she ate the dry cornflakes, she thought more about her life. She missed Derek. No, cancel that. She missed being in a relationship; she didn't miss Derek. She knew that she just needed to get out there and start dating again, but it was scary and she didn't know where to start. She didn't want to go through that misery of meeting and trying to connect with guys again. Why was dating so hard? She thought back to her other boyfriends before Derek and wondered why they hadn't worked out either.

She needed answers and needed them from someone she trusted. She thought about Leticia and Teresa. She already knew what they would say about relationships. Leticia would be cynical and say men were nice but not necessary, and Teresa would be starry-eyed and talk about how you have to wait for love to find you. She didn't agree with either approach.

She felt embarrassed that she thought some dude she found online could fix all her problems by helping her to understand how guys think. Though it would be nice to understand guys—sometimes she felt like they were from a different planet. How could she figure them out? Who could help her? An idea pushed its way through her fuzzy brain. Why don't you ask one? Yes, she could ask her brother, Jack. He could be annoying, but he had been there for her when she had broken up with Derek, and she could count on him.

She grabbed for her phone and winced from the pain in her temple. Maybe she'd call him later.

She started to think about the other people she could talk to and remembered what her mentor and friend PJ had told her about taking charge of her education. PJ had wanted to get a Master's Degree in Business Administration but couldn't afford it, so she decided to design her own personal degree by doing research and learning from people to find out what they had done to be successful in business.

Maybe that's what El could do. She could design her own Master's Degree in Romance. She frowned and her head hurt again. No, she thought to herself. Not romance. She didn't want to know how to get a guy to give her flowers. She wanted to understand relationships, how to have a meaningful and satisfying partnership with a guy. She'd get her Master's Degree in Relationships. Now she just needed to figure out how to do that. She winced again at the light coming through her window. She'd think about it after the headache went away.

During a hot shower, El decided that the day would be much better if she spent part of it somewhere she could be pampered, in low lighting and with soft music. She dressed in comfortable yoga pants and a loose T-shirt, and then she looked at the local spa's website and booked herself a two and half hour package that included a facial and a massage. She knew they offered complimentary detox tea at the spa and she felt she needed a gallon of it.

She checked her e-mail to ensure that the how-to-understand-men guy had confirmed her withdrawal from the course and a refund. And that's when she realized she had downloaded the course workbook during her drunken state and that it was still on her hard drive. Curious, she clicked it open.

The table of contents said chapter one was titled "Why Men Are Like Dogs." Dogs are controllable, El thought. Men are more like cats. Demanding, only want you when they want you, and then would love to cat around the rest of the time. She smiled at her stupid joke, then started reading the chapter to find out why this relationship genius thought men were like dogs.

Three-quarters of the way through the chapter, El pushed a button on her phone to automatically dial Jack.

"Yo, Rella, what's up?"

"Are you always so cheerful this early?" El's aspirin hadn't kicked in fully.

"It's another glorious day in the bay. Why not be cheerful?" Jack asked. "We're halfway through the work week and it's rocking."

"Glad it is for you," El said. "I took today off to pamper myself through the effects of too much celebrating last night. You heard Teresa and Jordan are now engaged?"

"Good for them. Do you need me to bring you one of our after-alcohol elixirs?" Jack owned a chain of food trucks and had recently added a smoothie van to his fleet. All of its ingredients were locally grown and sourced in California, and in addition to the fruits and veggies, a variety of protein powders, herbal teas, and powdered vitamins and minerals could be added to each drink.

"Thank you for the offer, but a walk and some fresh air might do me good. Do you want to meet me there in thirty minutes? Is it parked in the Marina District this morning?"

"Yes." Jack said, even though El could have checked the app to locate the truck. Jack's company's app was widely used by what seemed like half the city. The lines at his trucks were so long and people actually drove from the South Bay and East Bay and Marin.

"Great, that will give us plenty of time. I have a spa appointment at 10:30. I have some questions for you about men."

"Hmm. About men, huh? I'm not sure I'm qualified to speak for the whole species, but I'll do my best, Rella. Is one in particular on your mind?"

"Not really. I'm over the hate-myself-for-loving-you part of being angry with Derek—"

"Great tune," Jack interrupted.

"True. And I've started reading a book from some guy who claims he knows how men think, so I'd like to get your perspective as a representative sample." El laughed, and added, "One of the few samples I trust right now."

"Way to add to the pressure," Jack joked. "See you in 20." He disconnected.

El added a few more bits of kibble to the cat's empty bowl and gave him some fresh water. "I'll be back in a few hours, Mr. Fluffy. Enjoy your nap." She ruffled the fur atop his head, which he pushed up against her hand. And then she grabbed her keys, phone, and a light jacket, since she knew the area's fog could be fickle, and headed out the door.

Twenty minutes later, El found her six-foot-four ginger haired "little" (by two years) brother standing ten feet from the truck bearing a rainbow created by fruits and veggie images, with Casey's Crazy Concoctions, your loCAL source for smoothies painted above. He handed her a frothy green after-alcohol elixir and nodded to his crimson drink. "Berry Bright Blend for healthy skin, a sharp mind, and healthy digestion," Jack said. "You don't look bad for someone who tied one on."

"Very funny." El said. "Your drink looks good. Let's walk." She directed them toward the sidewalk that followed the water's edge and to benches about fifty yards away from the truck and its line of customers.

When they were seated, she said, "So the book says men are like dogs—"

"Like dogs in heat?" joked Jack.

"No…well maybe. But that's not what the book says. The book says men are like dogs because they respond better to positive reinforcement than to punishment or pain." El took a long pull from her cup.

"Doesn't everyone?" Jack asked.

"Maybe." El thought about Derek's constant—or maybe it just felt that way, El acknowledged—comments regarding her lack of money, his criticism of her gym membership that in his mind was an unnecessary expense since she wasn't there daily, his calling her apartment "a dump" since it wasn't in a luxury area but was what she could afford.

"I mean think about it," Jack said. "If parents get excited over a kid's A's, doesn't that make the kid want to get A's, as opposed to if the kid has mostly A's and a B or a C and the parents berate him for getting the B or C without mentioning the A's. Then the kid just feels bad and kind of resentful that the parent didn't notice how well he did in the other classes. It's the same with dating."

El watched a sailboat in the distance and said, "You mean that if Derek would have complimented me on how toned I was becoming or how flexible from the yoga, I may have been more inclined to go to the gym? Instead, his anger at the way I was wasting my money by having the gym membership but not going for an hour or two each day made me not want to go at all. Each time I'd enter the building my chest would tighten. I felt like I was going there for him instead of me. How stupid is that!" El faced Jack.

"It isn't stupid. It's just an example of how we let others control or taint our perspectives." Jack took a deep breath and audibly exhaled. "You know, sis, you can get past him. You have so much to offer someone."

El's eyes filled with tears. "Thank you. I'm trying."

"Yeah well you know what Yoda says," Jack smiled.

"I do," El said. "Thank you for the reminder. And that's why I started reading that book. I don't want to make the same mistakes in the next relationship or even with a casual date for that matter. Remember when I first told you about PJ and how she created her own PJ Master's Degree instead of enrolling in an MBA program? Well, I've decided to create my own Master's in Relationships, a tailored degree just for me. And this conversation with you is part of my first class, so tell me, wise bro, what else do you know? And do you think men might be like dogs and like cats?"

Jack laughed. "No way. If you scold a dog, it pouts and tries to get you to show it love. If you scold a cat, it is like F-U. I'm king of the castle. Take that, my slave." Jack mimicked a dog lifting its leg and spraying a sofa, complete with pissing sound.

El laughed. She knew Jack was right. Mr. Fluffy considered himself the master and her the serf.

"So, Jack, what online dating platforms do you recommend, and how do I even get started? I don't want to just be on a site where every guy just wants someone to play with his beanstalk."

"Funny," Jack said, running through a list of the dating apps and their pros and cons.

"Wait, wait, wait," El interrupted. "Can you start from the beginning again? I need to record this as it's so much info." She pulled out her phone and turned on the voice memo, and Jack started from the top.

Chapter
3

El's head no longer ached and she felt almost light and airy after talking to Jack. She still had some concerns regarding her dating future, but co-mingled with those concerns were the golden rays of resilience and hope. She sighed and smiled at strangers as she walked the last few blocks to the spa.

She felt guilty about calling in sick. Even when she didn't feel well, she normally managed to make it to work. Maybe she'd explain her "24-hour bug" as a stomach virus or food poisoning the next day, though she wasn't sure about lying. She certainly had been worried about keeping things down. She could tell them that it was something she had eaten. And, of course, it was also something she had been drinking but she wasn't going to mention that.

She took a seat in the reception area and quickly sent a message to PJ letting her know that she'd like to meet with her. Then she switched off the phone and quietly listened to the soft chime music. She closed her eyes and breathed in the scents. Was it vanilla? There was also a hint of spice. She was still trying to identify what she was smelling when her name was called.

Two and a half hours and three cups of detox tea later, she left for home feeling much better. PJ had invited her to an online meeting that evening and El quickly accepted. She checked her work e-mails to make sure that there were no emergencies and she found messages from her colleagues hoping that she felt better soon. That made her feel guiltier but she pushed that thought aside by saying to herself that everyone needed a mental health day at some point.

She considered what to do for the rest of the day. There was laundry and vacuuming and general cleaning. Or there was a delicious new cozy mystery novel. She had been saving it for the weekend but it seemed like the right time to pull it out. El enjoyed reading several series with female main characters and a little romance in addition to the sleuthing. She ordered them from the local bookstore as soon as a new one was available. She loved the convenience of online shopping, but she wanted to make sure that her favorite bookstore, The Ink Spot, stayed in business.

This book was from her current favorite series from Jenn McKinlay and featured two women with a cupcake business in Arizona. She loved the characters, and the stories transported her to adventures far away from her life. She enjoyed following the characters change from being single through dating and now engagement. She envied how even though the characters had issues and their relationships were tested, they had found nice guys who loved them.

Mr. Fluffy joined El on the couch as she opened the pages of *Wedding Cake Crumble* and stepped into the action at the Fairy Tale Cupcakes bakery. The wedding theme seemed particularly appropriate after Teresa's announcement. After spending half of the afternoon lost in the book, she sighed and closed it to take a break. If only she could meet a guy like one of the boyfriends in the series. Someone kind, caring, and fun. That's what she wanted. She petted Mr. Fluffy and said, "But life isn't like that, is it, buddy?"

Dinner was a plain but tasty meal of chicken, spirals, and veggies that El cooked from frozen; then she quickly cleaned up and got ready for her meeting with PJ. She had met Patience "PJ" James on a plane the previous autumn. PJ's card said that she was an "Empowerer of Women", and when El finally got up the courage to ask her for some mentoring, PJ quickly agreed but there were two requirements. First, El needed to take action on what they discussed, and second, she had to promise to help other women by sharing the advice. El was happy to agree to both terms and used what she learned to get a raise and promotion at her job.

The screen on El's phone lit up and she smiled as she answered it. PJ looked relaxed in a bright yellow T-shirt with her short dark curls pulled back with an orange headband.

"Hi El, how are you? Great to hear from you." PJ waved.

"Good, good," said El. "Thanks so much for meeting with me. What's up with you?"

"You know the usual, busy at work, starting some new fun projects, and getting ready to take a vacation."

"Oh? Someplace fun?"

"Yes, Shayla and I are going to Hawaii for a week. Some friends are having a destination wedding on Maui so we decided to make a vacation out of it."

El smiled at the thought of Shayla, PJ's partner, who had also given her some great career advice. "That sounds great. Please say hi to her for me."

"Will do." PJ nodded. "But what's going on with you? How's the job? Something new happening?"

El put her hands up and said, "No, no, nothing like that. Everything's great there. Working for Kate is wonderful. I'm learning a lot from her."

"And so?" asked PJ.

El hesitated. She knew she wanted PJ's help but she suddenly questioned whether this was a good idea. She decided to plunge ahead. "Actually, I need some relationship advice."

PJ grinned. "Not what I expected, but I'm intrigued. What's going on?"

El sighed. "You remember that I broke up with Derek months ago?"

"Mmhmm. As I remember that was a good thing."

"Well I haven't wanted to date anyone since then, but I've started thinking that maybe it's time. Though I don't want to date another Derek. I want to date someone special. But I just don't know how to do it." El started talking faster and said, "So I started thinking about how you had put together your own PJ MBA and I thought it might be a good idea for me to understand relationships better so I thought maybe I could learn more about what really works and put together my own Master's of Relationship degree sort of like yours."

PJ nodded again. "I like it!" She ran her fingers through her curls. "That could work. Tell me more."

El felt the tension leave her shoulders. "Well Teresa just got engaged and..."

PJ interrupted her. "Oh that's awesome! Please congratulate her for me. Jordan right?"

"Yes…"

"Wait, didn't they just start dating a few months ago?"

El sighed and immediately felt bad. "Yes, but they're in love…"

PJ laughed. "And that makes everything perfect, right?"

"Actually, it made me think about what makes people fall in love. I want to know what really great relationships are like."

"Hmmm. What have you come up with so far?"

"Nothing. You're the first person I'm telling. And I was wondering how you put together your curriculum. What books or other information do you think I should start with?"

PJ laughed again. "I'm honored. I'm no relationship expert, but I'd be happy to give you some ideas. Let's see. First, you need to embrace that a degree usually has the following components: readings for background and research, original research, and then a kind of culmination project or event. For my PJ MBA, I read everything I could, listened to podcasts, interviewed experts, and then started to apply what I learned and noted what worked for me." She looked up and tapped her nose with her finger.

El resisted the temptation to interrupt her. PJ continued, "Here's what I would start off with for your master's degree. It's not exactly a book about relationships but it's one of my favorites. It's called *Mindset* by Carol Dweck. It talks about how some people have a growth mindset and some people have a fixed mindset. If you have a growth mindset, you learn from your past mistakes and are willing to try new things. You know that in order to grow, you need to take some chances and sometimes stumble. That could help you to review your past relationships and think about what you've already learned, good and bad."

El nodded and jotted down the title. "Mostly bad," she mumbled.

"But without those experiences, you wouldn't be here today and ready to tackle the subject."

"True," said El.

PJ looked up again and paused. "Okay, there is one relationship book I do like. It's called *Attached*. I don't remember the authors but you should be able to find it. I think it will give you some things to think about."

El made a note of that also. She and PJ spent a few minutes talking about ideas for starting the research for her degree. At the end, El thanked PJ and said she'd keep her updated on progress.

As soon as El was off the phone, she called The Ink Spot and asked if they had both books in stock. They did, so she headed over to pick them up. When she walked into the bookstore, she felt at home. Normally, she spent more time browsing and sitting at the tiny café, The Ink Link, but she wanted to get started so she quickly went to the front counter and picked up the copies that had been held for her.

When she got home, she made herself a cup of chamomile tea and opened the *Mindset* book. Mr. Fluffy joined her as she officially started the literature review for her degree. She had almost finished the first two chapters before starting to yawn. The book made her think about her relationship with Derek in a different way. How could she learn from the problems in that relationship? How did her time with Derek help her grow? She yawned again and reminded herself that this was going to take some time.

The next morning at work, her colleagues asked how she was feeling and she vaguely let them know that it was probably something she had eaten that didn't agree with her but that she was feeling much better.

Carl, who once was her most annoying colleague, but who had grown into her favorite co-worker and strongest ally, popped by her office. He had on an exquisite royal purple shirt and a solid yellow tie, and somehow managed to find black wool trousers textured with subtle nubs of purple, yellow, and green. "Wow, great outfit," El said, thinking her old navy suit and white blouse paled in comparison.

"Thank you. So glad to see your smiling face in the office again. Feeling better?"

"Absolutely."

"I'm sure Mr. Fluffy took good care of you," Carl joked.

"He was good company, but not much of a caretaker. More of a my needs, my needs kind of cat."

"Aren't they all? Though, granted, I've never had a cat." Carl sat in the chair next to El's desk. "Anyhoo, I know it is short notice, but I wondered what you were doing tomorrow evening."

Though El hated to admit it, she had no plans.

"Well now you do," Carl said. "Garrett and I have decided to tie the knot at city hall tomorrow afternoon, and we want to celebrate with our friends afterwards. Nothing fancy. Champagne, appetizers, cake. Come after work."

"What!? Congratulations!" El stood up and hugged Carl. "That's so exciting."

"Thank you. You're welcome to bring a plus-one."

"Yeah, I'm not really seeing anyone…" El frowned as she said it.

"He's out there, El," Carl said. "I just know it." He patted her arm.

"Maybe," El replied. "Thank you so much for inviting me to your celebration. I can't wait to raise a glass to your happiness." And El really meant it, though she was starting to feel like everyone else had someone and she was the only one who didn't.

After Carl left her office, she texted Leticia. "You busy tomorrow evening?"

"Might hook up with Jackson. Why?"

"Carl's getting married and invited me to their reception. Tomorrow at six."

"No shit. You asking me to be your plus-one?"

"You or Jack. Lamer if I have to bring my bro."

"LOL. Anything for my BFF."

"Thx."

El opened a project file on her computer but couldn't concentrate on the words and graphs in front of her face. Carl and Garrett had lived together for four years. They seemed perfect together the few times El had seen them together. She wondered how they met. At lunch time, she decided to ask as it seemed like more research toward her relationships advanced degree.

She found Carl just as he was boarding the elevator. "Hey, El, want to come to Starbucks?"

"Sure. Or I'll buy you lunch anywhere else, if you'll allow me to pick your brain a little."

"You can always pick my brain. You don't have to buy me lunch though," Carl said as he pushed the button for the elevator to go down to the lobby.

"Can we go for Chinese food?" El asked. Starbucks was in their building. The Chinese restaurant was a couple of blocks south, and less likely to be filled with their co-workers. She didn't want others overhearing their conversation.

"Sure. Anywhere you want." Carl held the door of their building open for El to pass through.

After ordering cashew chicken and Mongolian beef to share, Carl asked, "What do you want to discuss?"

"I wondered how you and Garrett met." El sipped some tea.

Carl smiled. "It's not a very exciting story, I'm afraid. I was doing a First Thursday Art Walk by myself, and he managed one of the galleries where I stopped to see their exhibit. We got to talking, and he asked if when the art walk was done at nine, I would meet him for a drink. The rest, as they say, is half a decade of history."

El smiled. The waitress put the platters of food in the middle of the table and handed each of them a plate. "Enjoy," she said.

"Thank you," El said to the waitress, before turning her attention back to Carl. "But how did you know he was the one?"

"I'm not sure I did, or at least I'm not sure I thought of it like that." Carl scooped some food onto his plate. "I mean, we had a great time talking that first night. And then we spent more time together, and got along well. After a few months, we took our first weekend trip together. That went well, so we took a couple more. We both love to travel. Eventually, we were spending almost every night at his place or mine and realized neither of us was seeing anyone else."

El interrupted, her forkful of food halfway to her mouth. "You never discussed if you were exclusive?"

"Not exactly. I mean between our jobs and the amount we saw each other, there wasn't much time not to be, unless one of us messed around while at the gym or something. But no, we hadn't really discussed being exclusive until we decided it was stupid that both of us were paying for places. You know how exorbitant housing is in this city. He owned his condo so he suggested I move in there with him, and I agreed. And then we redecorated it to make it ours over the course of that first year or so. You'll see it tomorrow. It's a big loft with a great view."

"I can't wait," El said. "Oh, and I'm bringing one of my best friends with me. I hope that's okay."

"Absolutely," Carl said. "I look forward to meeting her...or is it a him?"

El laughed. "Her. Leticia. She's a lawyer but don't hold that against her." She grinned.

They ate and drank in silence for a few moments before El asked, "So you've been together for five years. What made you decide to get married now, if I may ask?"

Carl smiled. "You can ask anything, El. I consider you a friend." He took a sip of tea. "We are getting married because a) we can and b) marriage has tax benefits and inheritance benefits. But we are also getting married because though we know we are a couple, we want to declare to the rest of the world that we are. We're committed and in it for the long-haul. And besides, we think Blue should have legally-bound parents," he joked. Carl's new puppy Blue was a grey and white Australian shepherd and his photo was Carl's iPhone lock screen and his work computer background photo, and like any parent with a new baby, Carl had Garrett bring the baby by the office for a meet and greet one Friday afternoon and was eager to show photos as the "baby" had grown over the past three months.

"I love Blue," El exclaimed, finishing the last few bites on her plate. "I can't wait to see him at the party."

"He's going to be the best dog at the ceremony." Carl grinned.

"Nice."

"We debated between that and ring-bearer but he's still at the stage of putting things in his mouth that don't belong there."

"Good move," El said, putting enough cash on the table to cover the whole check. "Thank you for talking to me about your relationship, Carl."

"Thank you for lunch."

As they parted by the elevator after it reached their floor, Carl promised to text her the address to his place. He was taking paid time off for tomorrow to prepare for the wedding and the reception. El walked back to her desk while wracking her brain trying to think of a great gift she could get on short-notice.

That night as she prepared a spinach salad with strawberry dressing, she wondered why it seemed like everyone she knew was getting married. First, there was Teresa and now Carl. Last week her mom had told her that one of her cousins would soon be sending out invitations for her wedding. Was it one of those things where once you start thinking about something, it seemed to pop up everywhere?

El thought about what it would be like if she was bringing Derek to the party instead of Leticia. She shook her head and told herself to get over it. Derek was gone and she was happy about that. She needed to get him out of her brain.

She went to get the *Mindset* book but then decided she wanted to look at the other one, *Attached: The New Science of Adult Attachment and How It Can Help You Find – And Keep – Love.* There was a quiz in it to help her determine her attachment style or how she would act in a relationship. She absent-mindedly munched her salad as she answered the questions.

She came up strongly on the anxious style which meant that she tended to worry about relationships and felt sensitive about possible rejection.

She found another questionnaire that she could answer about the other person in the relationship so she thought about Derek as she started it. The first question about sending mixed signals made her sigh. Yes, she thought, he certainly did that. She continued and felt worse and worse. She had scored Derek high in the avoidant style with needs for space and independence. As she read more about the avoidant style, she thought that there should be a picture of Derek as a textbook example. It described perfectly how he pulled away when she seemed to be getting too close and how he made fun of her and criticized her for being too needy.

Remembering those conversations stung but it helped her to realize that it was a typical pattern, which made it feel a little less personal.

She brought the salad bowl to the sink, rinsed it, and shoved it and the fork in her small dishwasher. The book had also mentioned a third style, secure, and said that people could change their styles. People with a secure style were most effective. They communicated well; they weren't afraid of commitments and didn't play games. That's what she was going to do. She was going to learn how to be more secure. That seemed like a good place to start.

And she was going to figure out how to meet a secure guy. No more Dereks.

As she got ready for bed, she idly wondered how she could give out the quiz to guys she met before she decided to go out with them. It would save a lot of time and trouble, she thought with a smile.

Chapter 4

The next day of work went by quickly. She was still trying to catch up from her mental health day, and she covered for Carl since he was out. She hoped that everything was going well for him.

She rushed home between work and the party to feed Mr. Fluffy, who met her at the door with loud meow demands of more water, kibble, and affection, and she changed into a form-fitting evergreen dress that Leticia had talked her into buying. She paired it with nude strappy sandals, and fake pearl drop earrings. She had decided not to buy a wedding gift until she got an idea of what to buy from their décor. El knew etiquette dictated that she had one year to buy the newlyweds a gift, but she figured she'd come up with an idea after being surrounded by their style (and maybe poking around their kitchen, if it came to that).

El got to Carl's place shortly after 6 p.m. Leticia said she would meet her there since she was running late with work on a case.

A smiling guy wearing a T-shirt that looked like a tux answered the door and introduced himself as Carl's cousin, Randy. El had only been to Carl's place once before when he and Garrett had sponsored a game night to raise money for their favorite charity. She'd gotten the full tour at that time and had marveled at Garrett's ability to design a room. It looked like something from a catalog but better. The living room walls were painted a deep blue with splashes of complementary color accents on the furniture and accessories around the room. Just standing in the living room gave El a serious case of room envy. Maybe she'd ask Garrett for some suggestions when she decided to actually decorate a place.

She saw some co-workers and said hello while several people rushed in and out of other rooms. A few people remarked on how stunning El looked in her dress. Carl came into the living room wearing a shiny black jacket, a turquoise shirt, and a magenta and turquoise silk square protruded from his jacket pocket. "You came!" he said and hugged people one by one as he made his way around the room. Then he showed off his left hand with his new gold band. "We did it!" The doorbell rang again and Randy greeted more visitors.

Carl hugged the new arrivals and introduced them. "This is my friend, Bernie," he said indicating a brown haired man with glasses, "and my friend, Stu," he said, indicating the taller blonde man wearing a cap, a white collared shirt open at the neck, and black jeans.

"We're here," responded Stu. "Let's get this party started!"

Carl laughed. "Yes, let's get my better half out here."

"Did someone call my name?" Garrett emerged from the kitchen followed by Blue. Garrett was wearing a black tuxedo jacket, a magenta shirt, and sported the same silk pocket square as his now-husband. Around Blue's neck was tied a magenta, turquoise, and black silk bandana. Stu gave Garrett a big hug and Garrett laughed when Stu told him he was "a boring old married dude now."

Randy answered the front door to Leticia as Bernie asked Garrett how he could help. Carl quickly put him to work in the kitchen as he ushered other guests into the dining room where appetizers had been set out.

Leticia had come straight from work and looked exhausted. El greeted her friend and said, "You okay?"

Leticia brushed it off and said, "Just the usual, lots of work. Come on, let's have some fun."

El met Carl's sister, Ginny, and his brother, Ken, as well as his mom, Catherine, and from her El could see where Carl got his looks. Garrett's parents lived in Philadelphia and hadn't been able to make it so his cousin Sadie was going to video chat with them for the toast.

Bernie and Stu passed out champagne flutes as Ginny shouted, "Speech, speech!"

Carl grinned broadly and Garrett looked a little embarrassed by all the attention. "Come on," said Stu, "tell us all about it!"

Carl launched into an entertaining story about waiting their turn at the court house to get married and having to wait for two other couples "including another Carl!" he said.

"There's only one Carl for me," added Garrett, kissing him on the cheek. Carl blushed and continued telling the tale. When they got to the part where they wrote their vows, the group demanded to hear them so Carl and Garrett recited them again.

As El listened to them say their commitments to each other, she felt her eyes tear up. At the end, the new husbands kissed and the room cheered. "To Carl and Garrett," called Stu as he raised his glass. "To Carl and Garrett," the room responded as they raised their glasses to toast the happy couple. Blue barked and people laughed.

As they devoured the chorizo stuffed mini-potatoes, the carrot-harissa hummus and lentil chips, and many other gourmet delights, El made sure to introduce herself to the other friends and family that she didn't know. She then edged over to the dessert table to investigate a delicious looking chocolate cake and turned around quickly, knocking into Bernie. The pinot noir in her hand splashed his cobalt blue shirt and spilled on the floor. "I'm so sorry," she gasped. "I didn't see you there. Let me help you." She grabbed some napkins. They both bent over at the same time to wipe up the spill and she knocked him onto the floor.

Bernie threw back his head and laughed as El apologized and helped him up. "I am soooo sorry," she said as she started to laugh.

"You don't sound sorry." He grinned, as he wiped off his shirt.

"Oh I... I just... really I am, really, really," she gasped between laughs. "And I'm happy to pay for the dry cleaning to remove that stain."

"I don't think I've introduced myself. I'm Bernie, the guy you knocked over." He put out his hand. "And you are?"

"Unbelievably sorry," she said as she shook his hand. "I'm El, a friend of Carl's from work. I'm not normally this clumsy."

"It was me," said Bernie, still smiling. "The sight of the chocolate cake made me swoon. I couldn't help myself."

They cleaned up the spill on the floor and decided to try the cake. Leticia had come over by this time and introduced herself and took a small slice. She promptly tore off the point of her piece and popped it in her mouth. "Divine," she declared.

Carl, passing by, heard her and told them that his sister, Ginny, had made the cake. Bernie said that El had wanted it so much that she had pushed him out of the way to get to it first. As El was about to protest, Carl burst into laughter and said, "I would never believe that of El. If anyone rushed to get to the cake, I'm sure it was you. Bernie. You're a beast."

"Takes one to know one," Bernie taunted like a child on a playground.

Carl laughed. "*Touché.*" And then he extended his hand to Leticia. "I don't believe we've met."

El swallowed a bite of cake, and before Leticia could answer, she said, "This is one of my best friends. Leticia, Carl. Carl, Leticia."

"*Enchante,*" Carl said, and instead of shaking her hand, he kissed it, which made Leticia, Bernie, and El laugh.

"Always a smooth one," Bernie replied. "I'm Bernie." He stuck out his hand to Leticia.

"Nice to meet you," Leticia said.

"The abstract art on his shirt is compliments of me," El admitted.

"How very Pollokesque," Leticia joked.

"Seriously," Bernie said, staring down at the now-drying purple splotch, and then he looked up at El and grinned. Carl had turned his back on them to greet more guests.

Leticia eyed the two of them and grabbed El's empty glass, and without a word, headed towards the kitchen to get El a refill.

"I need the recipe for this cake," Bernie declared.

"Oh, you bake?"

"Only on special occasions and not well. Though I'm a bit better than those contestants on Nailed It!"

El laughed. "I love that show. Have you seen the Mexican version?"

"I've seen them all, El. And I have an idea. Let's get the recipe for this cake from Carl's sister and recreate it next Saturday morning. I can come to your place or you can come to mine...as long as you aren't allergic to cats."

"You have a cat? Show me a picture." El put down her cake plate in preparation for holding his phone.

"I have two. Remington and Qwerty." Bernie's iPhone displayed a blue Scottish fold with almost orange eyes and a green eyed Scottish fold with grey and black tiger stripes.

"Incredible," said El. "They are gorgeous." She couldn't stop staring at them.

Leticia returned with El's wine and said, "Cool cats," which from her was a huge compliment. She loved Mr. Fluffy because he lived with El, but otherwise, she was indifferent to cats…or basically anything that demanded constant attention and care.

El pulled her own iPhone from her purse and showed her Mr. Fluffy lock screen.

"Ah, the love of your life," Bernie said.

"You could say that," El said, a wistful smile on her face as she stared at the screen.

"Let me see if I can nab that recipe. Be right back." Bernie set his empty cake plate next to El's and went off in search of Ginny.

"What'd I miss?" Leticia asked.

El recapped in two sentences, and Leticia responded, "So is this a date?"

"Oh, no. I don't think so. He came here with Stu—she pointed to him through the living room archway—so he's probably gay—"

Leticia cut in. "You don't know that. I'm here with you, and I'm not. Not even bi."

"True…" El took a sip of wine. "But—"

"No, buts. No assumptions."

"Spoken like a lawyer," El joked.

"Don't rule out anything without evidence. And did you agree to bake with him?"

"I won't and no, I didn't but I didn't not agree either. We got swept away with cats."

"Which could make it a perfect match for you. He's attractive in a slightly nerdy hipster way. Where's he live?"

"Don't know. We didn't get that far yet."

Bernie popped up next to El again. "Success! The recipe is on Ginny's blog so she texted me the link. See?" He held out his phone to show El the text. "So are we on for Saturday?"

El glanced at Leticia before responding, "Sure."

"Your place or mine?"

"Where is your place?" El asked. She really wanted to go there and meet those cats. She had only seen Scottish folds at a county fair when she was a child, but she had never petted or played with one.

"Near the Marina. I'll text you the address if you give me your number. Is ten o'clock good?"

"Yes. What would you like me to bring?"

"Well I'd say you could bring Mr. Fluffy, but since he's a cat, I'm guessing he doesn't like carriers or to go for a ride." Bernie smiled.

"Exactly, hates it with the power of a thousand suns."

"*10 Things I Hate About You,* huh?"

El laughed. "Guilty…of plagiarism."

Leticia interrupted their banter with, "Bernie, you look like you could use a drink. I know I can," and she reached to grab his glass from his hand.

El was momentarily stunned by Leticia's uncharacteristic curtness, but instantly realized this was the first time Leticia wasn't the center of male attention…even if the male might be gay.

"I loved that movie," Bernie admitted.

"Me too," El said. "I've probably seen it a dozen times."

When Leticia returned with Bernie's glass, he raised it towards El. "Rest in peace, Heath Ledger."

El clinked glasses with him and Leticia did too though she had no idea what the hell was going on.

Stu walked towards them, his cap slightly askew now. "There you are," he said to Bernie. "Who's your new friend?" He tilted his head towards Leticia.

"Stu, you met El, and this is her friend Leticia."

Stu shook Leticia's hand and said, "Channeling my Japanese friends, Leticia, what's your blood type?"

"O positive," Leticia said, not even pausing for a split second.

"Outstanding," Stu said.

"Huh?" El didn't understand. "What does being Japanese have to do with blood types?"

"It's kind of like a version of what's your sign," Bernie explained.

"Yes," Stu said. "Kind of a personality and compatibility indicator. Check out a site called Tofugu.com for what is called Japanese Blood Type Personality Theory. Positive and negative traits are assigned to each blood type. Leticia said she's O, so in Japanese culture, that means she's optimistic, outgoing, a strong leader, flexible, resilient, and often sets the mood in groups of people. Does that seem about right?"

Stu looked from Leticia to El as he asked the question. El chuckled. "She certainly is outgoing and a strong leader and resilient."

"Me too," said Stu. "I'm also an O but a rare O negative. What are you, El?"

"I'm an A, but don't know my rhesus."

"Rhesus doesn't matter as much as the type itself," Stu explained. "A is what much of the Japanese population is. And the primary personality type is well-organized. A's are also described as sensitive, tactful, kind, reliable, diligent, and conscientious, but they can also get stressed easily, be stubborn, anxious, and act withdrawn. Does that sound like you?"

El thought back over the last year of her life. She certainly was well-organized; this trait made her a great project manager. And her kindness, tactfulness, and conscientiousness were things her team members commented on and said how much they valued in her, their leader. But she had to admit, she felt stress more easily than Leticia and Teresa did, that was for sure. And the whole thought of delving into dating was making her anxious.

She smiled at Stu. "Some of it," she said. She turned to Bernie. "And what are you?"

"The rare AB."

Stu said, "Yes, Bernie's a complicated AB, or basically all of the good and the bad of blood types A and B rolled into one. He's super talented and creative, but a bit eccentric and occasionally indecisive."

"Hey now," Bernie fake punched his friend in the arm.

"Don't you think it is all a bit generic?" Leticia asked. "It's like astrology. I saw this thing once where everyone in a room was handed a slip of paper with the same personality description on it and asked if it described them. And every single one of them said, 'yes, this is me'. We are all each of those descriptors you said, Stu, depending on the day, our moods, etc. Pretty difficult to determine compatibility based on that."

"And yet people have written whole books on marriage compatibility based on blood types," Stu said.

"People have written books or published studies on lots of topics. But it doesn't mean they have merit. Lots of shaky science and bad information out there," Leticia added.

El silently agreed but made a note to check out the website Stu mentioned as soon as she got home. At this point, she was keeping an open mind on any dating and relationship information she came across. She figured the more things she could learn, the less risk she had of finding another Derek or any other guy who wanted her to change her life to suit his needs.

Chapter 5

The hosts were in no hurry to end the party and continued to offer drinks and food. Leticia finally said she had to leave and El decided it was time to go also. As Carl thanked them both for coming, Bernie waved to El and said, "See you next weekend."

When El woke up on Saturday morning, she realized she needed to make a quick trip to the store. In the pharmacy, she headed straight to the tampon section. She passed the condoms and briefly wondered if she should pick some up just in case. She laughed at herself and thought that was something she really didn't need to worry about...yet.

As she waited in line to pay, she recognized the song by Michael Buble playing over the speakers called "I just haven't met you yet..." She sang along in her head. She remembered how the singer in the music video met his special person in a store when a band suddenly appeared along with dancers and confetti. She looked at the bored teenager and mom with a carriage in line ahead of her and thought, that's not happening to me today.

At home, she pulled up the blood type website that Stu had mentioned. It was interesting and the description did sound accurate, but she remembered Leticia's skepticism. She texted her friend to see if she wanted to grab some dinner later. She was in the mood for a stir-fry and it would be fun to share it.

El spent the day running errands and cleaning up the apartment while Mr. Fluffy slept. She dreaded Saturday nights because being alone felt like failure. Teresa and Jordan often asked her to join them but she didn't want to tag along every weekend.

Leticia came by at seven with a bottle of wine just as El had started to cut up the vegetables. El grabbed glasses and Leticia poured. Leticia's hair was pulled back with a headband and she wore a plain gray sweatshirt and navy leggings. She seemed more quiet than usual, and way underdressed.

"What's new?" El asked.

"Since last night, not much. Just spent the day trying to get caught up on work."

"You always seem to be working."

"Yeah well that's the way it is right now. Hey, thanks again for including me in Carl's celebration last night," she said, changing the subject.

El decided not to push it. "Yeah that was really fun. He and Garrett are so nice."

"And so is that Bernie." Leticia grinned and raised her eyebrows. "So what's the story with him?"

"I don't know. We're baking a cake next Saturday morning."

"Oh is baking a cake now code for fun in the sack?"

"Nooooo," said El, laughing at her friend. "I just want to bake with him." She paused. "It is a little weird though, no one's ever invited me over to bake with them...well other than that one guy in college who asked me to 'get baked' with him."

Leticia and El both laughed and then Leticia took a sip of her wine. El cut up the chicken. "You never know what a little baking can lead to," Leticia said.

El laughed again. "Yeah. Okay. Actually, I'm really interested in meeting his cats. They are soooo cute."

Leticia laughed, "Girl, focus. Guys first. You don't want to sound like a crazy cat lady. He's kinda cute, too. I mean, not my type, but he's cute in an I can fix your computer kind of way."

"I'll let you know. But first dinner." She stirred the chicken and veggies as they sizzled in the wok while Leticia talked about her current case.

While they were eating, Leticia mentioned Bernie again. "Come on, you've got to admit that's a real meet-cute story."

"Meet-cute?"

"You know, like in those sappy movies you like to watch."

"Excuse me, you seem to enjoy them, too."

"I tolerate them because you like them," countered Leticia.

El stared at her.

"Okay," said Leticia waving her hand. "Maybe I do enjoy them. A little."

El pointed her fork at her friend. "Admit it, you like rom coms."

Leticia groaned, "You can't make me admit it."

"You're so cynical," El teased her friend.

"Seriously, don't go all Hallmark channel on me. There are only two or three story lines and they just play it over and over again."

"Do tell."

Leticia held up one finger, "Okay first there is the past romance reboot where she meets an old boyfriend unexpectedly and they get back together." She held up a second finger. "Then there is the bad meeting but it gets better where she meets someone and they don't like each other at first but then they realize it's a misunderstanding and they get together." She held up a third finger. "Then there's the meet-cute where they meet in an adorable way and they spend the whole movie trying to get together. Oh wait, there's a fourth." She put up another finger. "There's also the woman who's been alone for a long time and who is happy with that but finally meets a partner." She paused. "Though normally that gets mashed together with one of the other ones."

"And how do you know all this wisdom if you're not watching them?"

"Please, four sisters and a mother addicted to them. You know that."

"And maybe you watch them sometimes," teased El.

"Maybe, but I prefer real life."

"Okay, which one would you want?"

"Uh uh. Not me. The question is which story do you want? Do you want the meet up with an old boyfriend story?"

"Nooo," shouted El.

"I don't just mean Derek," said Leticia, "What about one of the other ones?"

El made a face and thought. "Nope, I don't think so."

"Okay, how about the bad meeting that gets better?"

"That always seems like a lot of work. I'm not crazy about that one."

"Yeah, I think you're more of the meet-cute type."

"Or the self-sufficient woman?"

Leticia smiled. "You could do that one. That's my personal favorite."

El smiled and said, "Not surprised." She thought about her Master's in Relationships and said, "What can we learn from these movies?"

"That they're all directed by men?"

They both laughed. "Maybe," said El. "I was thinking more that there are a lot of different stories in the world. There's not just one way to find a special relationship."

Leticia wiped up a bit of sauce she had spilled on the table. "Okay, how about it's up to us to choose the story we want?"

El put down her fork. "I like that. Not only can I choose the story. I can write the story I want."

"Now you're talking," said Leticia holding up her wine and toasting with El. "To writing our own stories."

Leticia left soon after dinner saying that she had to spend that night and the next day prepping for her week. El thought about telling her friend that she needed to stop spending all her time working, but El noted how tired she looked so she gave her a hug and told her to take care of herself.

After Leticia left, El felt lonely. She briefly considered watching a romantic comedy but she wasn't in the mood. She didn't want to watch someone else's romantic life; she wanted to have one.

It sounded easy to do something when she was talking to Leticia, but how was she going to take charge and write her own story? She felt itchy and decided she needed to take action. The Michael Buble song echoed in her head, "You'll come out of nowhere and into my life/ I just haven't met you yet."

She pulled out her phone and downloaded a dating app that friends had recommended. Part of her knew that opening a dating app on a Saturday night was probably a terrible idea, but she went ahead with it. She answered the basic matching questions and uploaded a picture that Teresa had taken of her several weeks before when she had first started thinking about this. She didn't like the pictures that looked like someone had taken selfies by using a bathroom mirror.

Scrolling through the pictures of potential matches was scary and exciting at the same time. At first, El carefully looked at each picture and considered what the person might be like and how they would get along. She felt bad for superficially swiping left on Dean just because he had a moustache and Curtis because he had on an Oakland Raiders cap and shirt. It was strange to think about saying no to people for such shallow reasons. Then she started swiping past them faster, no to Damian—all his pictures were outdoors and he looked too athletic. No to Xavier as his idea of a fun night was going out to a bar, and no to Steve as his pictures showed him on a monstrous Harley.

She went through the profiles she had saved and decided to send a few messages. It felt awkward, but for all of them, she mentioned something about their profile or a picture and asked about it. She spent the most time on messages to Franklin and Ray who seemed to be the most interesting. She changed the message she wrote to Franklin five times and finally hit send before she could change it again.

She closed the app and promised herself that she wouldn't look at it right away. She cleaned up the dinner dishes and wondered what she could do to write her own romance story. Then El started wondering about other people's stories. How did they meet someone special? That gave her an idea. She grabbed her laptop and wrote a note:

Hi,

How are you? I'm doing some research on relationships and I'd love to know the story about how you met X. Thanks so much!

She sent personalized versions of the message to some of her friends on Facebook. She briefly thought about sending a version to members of her family but she wasn't ready for that. She also briefly considered just posting it to everyone she knew and decided she definitely wasn't ready for that either.

She stared at her phone and wondered if she should check her messages. Maybe one little peek wouldn't hurt. She was disappointed that there were no responses from her matches. She told herself that was ridiculous because it hadn't been that long. She sighed and decided that she was definitely not in the mood for a romantic comedy so she scrolled through her movie list and picked something with lots of action and adrenaline but few emotions.

Mr. Fluffy joined her on the couch and kneaded her leg until she pushed him off onto a pillow. The movie was fun and fast and required almost no brain power, which was just what she wanted. She had ignored her phone for most of the movie except for responding to a few texts including one from Jack checking on her.

When the movie was over, she checked the dating app and saw a message from a guy named Lee. El had appreciated the slightly sarcastic tone of his profile and his response didn't disappoint. It was 11:18 and she decided to respond early the next morning.

She woke up Sunday morning wondering if she should check the dating app or look for her friends' responses to her question first. Even though she was dying to see if she got responses from potential dates, she decided to see what her friends said first.

Chapter 6

Still in her pajamas, El poured a cup of black coffee, sat on the sofa, and opened her laptop. The first e-mail she encountered was from her high school friend Sarah, a primary care doctor. She explained that she and Elijah met when her med school asked her to lead a tour for potential applicants and talk to them about her experience. He was two years older than she and had had a short career in a pharmaceutical research lab before deciding to go into medicine. He was now doing his residency and Sarah had joined her mom's family medicine practice; Sarah and Elijah's wedding would be next year. She asked El to reserve the date.

El sighed. Sarah's story reminded her a bit like Michelle and Barack Obama's. In *Becoming*, which El had read, the former First Lady explained how she met Barack when he had been hired to be in an intern at the law firm where she worked and she had been assigned as his official summer mentor. El doubted she'd succumb to an office romance, not because she or her company opposed such a thing, but more because most of the men were older and married.

El's friend Brittany, whom El had met in preschool and stayed connected with through social media after Brittany's family moved across the country while they were in high school, wrote that she got hit on all of the time by the guys she had to arrest (Brittany was a Baltimore police officer), but it wasn't until some cute prosecutor asked if he could buy her a cup of coffee after a trial that she had been "arrested by love." Ugh, El thought at the pun. But she was glad to hear Britt was happy.

Four more friends—two males and two females—said they found love online, one through Bumble, one on Plenty of Fish, one, surprisingly on Tinder, and one playing games through Steam. Oh and two of her friends had hooked up with their partners during college and stayed together through job relocations and the unexpected death of one of their parents. In fact, Sam had written that the way Beatriz had helped during her family's crisis really solidified their relationship and that "life is too short not to be with who we love".

El agreed. Now I just need to find him, she thought.

Her coffee cup was empty so El decided to take a break from her friends' stories. But before she headed into the shower she Googled "where to find love." The first search engine entry was an article on *The Today Show's* website titled "12 Basic Rules to Find Love," and included advice like "Go where people like the same things you like," "look up from your phone," and "don't seek romance, seek partnership." El wondered if the article writer was a man or a woman, since they used the initial A, and the advice didn't seem to be geared to either gender.

The one piece of advice that made El laugh aloud was that happy people attract people so you should act like someone you wanted to meet. That's all good and well, thought El, but where do you go to meet people and to show them you are happy?

A jarring meow sounded from the kitchen, followed by the sound of a paw hitting the empty metal bowl. "Jeez, cat," El said. She set her cup on the counter and poured kibble into the cat's bowl. Mr. Fluffy inhaled the food. "The least you could do is say thank you," El said, ruffling the fur on his head.

When his bowl was empty again, he swatted El with his paw. And then he sat and stared at her, before rolling his eyes down to his empty bowl then back up at her.

El laughed. "You need an attitude adjustment. Remember, *Today* says happiness attracts. Bossiness is unbecoming."

Mr. Fluffy meowed at that and swatted her again.

"Okay, okay. You've made your point." El dumped another dozen bits of kibble into his bowl. "But that's all you get for breakfast." She grabbed a yogurt, kale, an apple, and some berries from the fridge. She cored the apple and then threw everything into the blender and pureed until it was smooth. She poured it into a tall glass and drank her breakfast. After rinsing the glass, she went into the shower. If *Today* said to meet people where you like to go, El figured she'd give it a try.

A 90-minute reggae yoga class started at 11 a.m. and sounded like a fun way to meet new people. El donned her brightest parrot-print leggings and a black tank top. She swiped her eyelashes with the mascara wand and added tinted gloss to her lips and then she put her hair in a ponytail like Pebbles from *The Flintstones*. El filled her water bottle, grabbed her keys, said "good-bye" to Mr. Fluffy, and went out the door.

Bob Marley's "Could You Be Loved" was playing as she grabbed a mat and found floor space next to one of the half a dozen males in the room. His sandy hair was sticking every which way. El couldn't decide if its look was a style, an after thought, or neglect. The guy was mid-forward fold and way more flexible than El, whose chronic choice of heels left her calves bunched and her hamstrings tight.

She plopped onto her mat and entered prayer pose, offering a petition to the yoga gods or goddesses to guide her quest. Suddenly the music stopped, silence ensued, and El popped her head up to see what had happened. A dreadlocked 30-something woman, batik open robe flowing over a black tank unitard stood at the front of the room and said, "Welcome to reggae yoga, where we will dance, flow, and pose our way to peace. We will begin in *tadasana* or mountain pose, hands at heart center."

Bob Marley's "One Love" filled the room, as El and the others put their feet together and stood up tall and straight like the Sierras.

As the music and class continued, El felt uncoordinated as she did her best to follow the rhythmic dance-like yoga moves. She was glad that she hadn't sat in the front row. She took a deep breath and decided to let it go and do what she could. She noticed that the man next to her seemed to be easily keeping up, fluidly moving with the grace of a professional dancer.

The instructor announced a brief break while she changed the music. El was glad for the pause. She turned to the man next to her and said, "What a great work out."

He smiled and said, "Yes, she's amazing."

"Do you come here often?" asked El. She inwardly cringed as the words came out. That was lame, she thought. I'm going to have to come up with something better.

"Mmm hmm," he said and told her how he found the class seven months ago and had been coming as often as he could when he wasn't travelling for work. She started to ask him what he did, but the music started again.

As they turned to face the front of the room, El noticed the wedding ring on his left hand. Oh well, she thought, I was hoping to practice talking to single guys, but maybe I need practice talking to any guys that I don't work with.

El felt satisfied but tired by the end of the class. She chatted with the guy next to her for a few more minutes as she drank from her water bottle.

On the sidewalk in front of the studio, she checked the dating app and saw a message from Lee who was responding to the comments she had sent earlier that morning. She smiled and scrolled through some of the suggested questions offered by the app. She picked What's your favorite food?, Where do you like to go on vacation?, and If you could pick a superpower, what would it be?

There were also responses from three guys that she hadn't contacted. One of them, Jerry, gave his e-mail address and said it would be easier to connect that way. She remembered what one of her friends had told her about online dating. "Stay on the site. There are plenty of weirdos and scammers out there. Do not give out your e-mail or number. You don't even know if these people are real or not." She thought her friend was overly dramatic, but she decided to send a response saying that she'd rather just message through the app.

She checked the app again after she walked home and saw the response from Jerry saying that his account was running out and he was leaving the site, but he really wanted to connect with her because she was so pretty. She ignored it and read Lee's answers. He picked pizza, the beach if she would join him, and he wanted the ability to read animals' minds though he was pretty sure that his dog would just say, "let's play, let's play, let's play now." She laughed and answered the questions he sent to her.

Jack sent a text inviting her over for dinner. She quickly texted "yes" and "red, white, or rosé?"and she wondered what wonderful recipes he would make. During the afternoon, she paid bills and checked messages from friends while flirting with Lee and messaging two other guys. This was more fun than I expected, she thought. By the time she left to go to Jack's condo, she was in a great mood.

Jack opened the door, and El was surprised he was wearing a ripped T-shirt and pants covered in dried paint. He also looked exhausted.

"Thanks for dressing up for me," joked El, as he gave her a hug.

"Hey, it's laundry day and I've been making dinner. Give me a break," he said.

In the kitchen, he handed her a bottle of stout, and told her to sit on the bar stool while he added his special sauce to a delicious smelling pot of pulled pork before shoving it back into the oven and before turning his attention to slicing vegetables for the salad. El decanted the wine she had brought as she told him about Carl's party.

When she got to the part about Bernie, Jack interrupted, "Is it a date?"

"No idea. Not sure it matters." El drained the rest of the beer.

"Of course it matters. He may be using baking as a ploy to get some so you need a plan on how to handle that." Jack was staring at her; his knife was paused above a cucumber.

"You make it sound nefarious, like it can't just be two people who love cake getting together to make one." She dropped her bottle into Jack's recycling container.

"It's rarely that simple." Jack plated food for both of them, and placed them on two placemats at his kitchen bar. "I figured we'd eat in here, if that's okay with you."

"Absolutely." El poured them each a glass of wine. "To fine food and family."

They clinked glasses together while looking each other in the eyes. El's French friend told her in college that not looking someone in the eyes during a toast was wishing them seven years of bad sex, so El and Jack laughingly—if not a bit superstitiously—for years had embraced the tradition.

During dinner El told Jack about meeting Lee online and the funny things he had said. Jack stopped eating and crossed his arms.

"I didn't realize you had started doing that."

"You gave me the suggestions. And not everyone can meet someone at work like you," she joked and referred to Caitlin, a woman Jack had met three months earlier at one of his food trucks, and whom he called his "best customer." They weren't a couple exactly, but El knew that they had hooked up numerous times. Caitlin and El had met once, and El had been surprised that Caitlin was short, with a round face and shoulder length straight black hair. She was quiet and bookish, where Jack was loud and too active to read books beyond cookbooks. El wasn't sure she saw a future for them.

"Very funny," Jack said. "Yeah, but you have to be careful with guys online."

"I'll be fine."

"I just want you to be safe. Promise me…"

She put her hands up. "I promise I'll be careful. I will only meet someone in a public place."

"Take Leticia with you if you do. She can handle it." He forked a big bite of pork into his mouth and made an audible "Mmm."

She shook her head. "I'm not going to bring anyone else with me. That would be lame. And I agree that this pork is excellent."

"Then name the time and place and I'll sit somewhere nearby."

"Ughhh." She sighed.

Jack drank wine and switched gears, "Hey, what about Owen? I just heard from him. His girlfriend broke up with him."

"Owen, your friend from high school? Ewww. Please. Getting set up by my brother sounds so pathetic."

"No it's not. And Owen's a good guy. You haven't seen him lately."

"I just remember a mouth full of braces and lots of stupid jokes."

"I thought that was you," he responded.

"Haha—no that was you, Jacko."

"Don't make me tell Mom," Jack joked.

"Funny." El got off her stool and placed her napkin next to her plate. "Be right back." She took her purse with her into Jack's bathroom so she could change her tampon, but she stopped short seeing the black lace demi-cup bra and matching thong hanging over his shower curtain. El checked the label: La Perla.

She grabbed them and marched down the hall holding them towards him. "You cross dressing or did Caitlin forget her things?"

Jack's eyes were wide. He grabbed them out of her hand. "No and no," he said as he took them back up the hallway to his room.

"Really now?" El stared after him.

"Mind your own business, Rella."

"You have the gall to tell me not to meet guys online and yet you have some random's very expensive bra and thong on display in your bathroom? What'd she do? Run out in the middle of the night without her things?" El's hands were balled on her hips. She wasn't as angry as she sounded, but she didn't like his double standard.

Jack returned to the kitchen and took a swig of wine. Calmly, he said, "They belong to a friend. She left them here and rather than return them unwashed, I used some dish soap and rinsed them in the sink."

El eyed him and totally believed him. He was exactly that kind of guy, conscientious and caring. "Aww, that's sweet," she said. And silently she wished she could find a guy that thoughtful. She sat back down to finish her food.

"Back to your love life," he said, "One of my food truck buddies, Tyler, seems like a nice guy. He makes great chicken and waffles."

"I think just one food truck king is enough in my life, Jack. I'm fine."

Jack ignored her. "Or Dave, he just moved back to the area. I haven't seen him yet, but I've heard he's back." He paused, "Maybe it's time for me to work on my matchmaking skills. I can do more than food, you know."

"I know you're a man of many talents, but being Yenta isn't necessary."

Jack immediately launched into "Matchmaker, matchmaker, make me a match..." before he rose to put his dish in the sink. *Fiddler* had been their mother's favorite musical before she succumbed to *Hamilton* fever. "I made cobbler for dessert. Please scoop the ice cream." Jack handed her two bowls.

"Peachy," El joked.

"Ha. Very funny," Jack said, as he plopped spoonsful of golden fruit and moist topping next to the vanilla mounds El had scooped.

They were silent as they meditated on the mix of cinnamon, ginger, fruit, and melt in their mouths sweetness. When their bowls were empty, El sighed and said, "I think we've reached enlightenment."

"There's a reason the Grail was a chalice or dish," Jack agreed.

El helped him load the dishwasher and clean up the kitchen. Upon his prodding, she promised she'd consider Owen and Dave as long as he promised not to say a word to either of them. And with that, they hugged, El thanked him, and she said she'd see him again soon.

When El got home she messaged Lee to answer some more questions he sent and he said he had an early day on Monday so he was heading to bed. She said good night. She saw another message from Jerry asking again for her e-mail, but she ignored it. And she got a text from Jack saying, "I mean it, Rella, don't meet a stranger by yourself." Instead of responding or stressing, she grabbed Mr. Fluffy and brought him into bed with her. "You think you're all the man I need, right, cat?"

Mr. Fluffy rubbed his head against her shoulder in response and then curled around her head on the pillow.

When her alarm went off the next morning, she grabbed the phone and opened the app. There was no message from Lee but there was one from Jerry. It was just two words: "bye bitch." Not exactly the start to her morning that she had hoped for. She quickly scrolled through some new potential matches but didn't see anyone that she wanted to contact.

As she dressed, she debated whether to send a good morning message to Lee. She decided against it, put on the Girl Power playlist, starting with Beyonce's "Single Ladies," and jumped into the shower. She needed to get moving. Her first meeting was at 8 a.m. with a customer in Europe.

Chapter 7

Over an uninspired lunch of a turkey sandwich and an apple, El worked on her master's degree. First, she opened Amazon and searched for books on dating and relationships, but she was dismayed to find sixteen pages of titles, or 50,000 books on the subject. She'd never get through them all. In order to narrow down the search, she clicked for ones that had at least four-star cumulative reviews. That cut the number of titles down to 20,000, which El thought would be even more than she'd read for a doctorate. She shook her head.

A bunch of titles claimed to tell the "brutal truth" about dating, and El was dismayed to see that very few books on the first page of Amazon's list of titles were written by women. At least the book on "conscious lesbian love" was written by a woman, El joked to herself.

She jumped to Ted.com, hoping to have more luck and found seventy-seven results by searching "online dating." She found a TEDSalon video from New York featuring Amy Webb that was titled "How I Hacked Online Dating." El watched the video, intrigued, and then three-quarters of the way through, she took notes. Webb claimed that the most successful people online dating have ninety-seven words in their profiles, use nonspecific and optimistic language, such as describing themselves as fun, and that they wait an average of twenty-three hours between communications with guys who message them.

El instantly thought of her messages with Lee and realized she had sent too many too fast, and that could be putting out the energy she was needy. As she went to open her profile on the phone app, a text popped up: "Hey, El, it's Bernie. Hope your week is off to a good start. I'm picking up the cake ingredients. You okay if we add Baileys or crème de menthe to the cake?"

She smiled at her phone, started to type a response, stopped, wondered if she should follow Amy Webb's advice and wait, but then decided if he was actually in the store expecting a response, that wasn't a good idea. "Hi. Good for a Monday. Either is fine." She pushed send.

"Awesome," he answered immediately, and then texted his address and said Remington and Qwerty looked forward to meeting her on Saturday.

She was going to ask if she should bring anything, but decided that would be a good way to continue the conversation on another day. Instead, she opened her Facebook app to check for recent photos of Owen and Dave. Owen was certainly more attractive and more filled out than she remembered. Dave, on the other hand, didn't look so great. El wasn't sure if it was the lighting or the angle in two of the photos but he either had the shadow of stubble or a second chin.

She texted Jack: "Why did Owen's girlfriend break up with him?"

"She said it wasn't working. Truth is she hooked up with some old dude with more money than Owen."

"Ouch."

"Yep."

"He works in finance?"

"For a VC company. Why?"

"Just wondering."

"Sure, Rella. And what do you think of his photos?"

El laughed. Leave it to her brother to know she looked. "Looks better than when we were kids."

"Don't we all."

"I gotta get back to work."

"Okay, but you want me to set up a drink? You, the girls, Jordan, me, and Owen?"

"Maybe," El conceded.

"K. Later."

El threw away her apple core and the bag from her sandwich, got up from her desk, stretched, and headed to the ladies room. She had meetings all afternoon with her team and Kate to talk about a new assignment, so she needed to be refreshed and ready.

"Gin and Juice" by Snoop Dogg popped into her head as she walked into the conference room. "Mind on my money and money on my mind," though she wasn't sure if it was triggered by the meeting about to commence or Owen. But a chill ran down her spine when she realized it could have just as easily referenced Derek. Old habits were hard to break. She inhaled deeply, exhaled through her mouth, and took a few more breaths outside the conference room door before entering, and greeting her team and thanking them for clearing their calendars for the afternoon for this new opportunity. Kate entered the room after El and immediately called the meeting to order.

Four and a half hours later, El entered her apartment where Mr. Fluffy greeted her at the door by weaving between her legs and then sinking one paw of claws into the top of her foot. "Yow," El said, inadvertently jerking her foot and the cat with it.

Mr. Fluffy stormed off into the kitchen to bat his empty food bowl. El rolled her eyes. "You're so freaking demanding, cat. Wait until I'm out of my work clothes." El untucked and unbuttoned her blouse while walking towards her bedroom. She kicked her heels into her closet. She added her suit and the blouse to the pile to go to the dry cleaners. She pulled on a Stanford T-shirt (leftover from Derek and jeans and padded barefoot into the kitchen, where the cat held his head high like a general expecting a salute. She dropped a cup of kibble behind him into his bowl so he abruptly did an about-face and ate with gusto.

El poured herself a glass of water from the Brita on the sink and contemplated the contents of her fridge and freezer. Unlike her brother, she wasn't much of a chef. She spied a chunk of lasagna in the freezer that her mom had sent home with her two weeks ago from a family dinner. El pulled it out and wondered how many minutes it needed to thaw and cook in the microwave. While it did its thing, she pulled a bagged salad kit from the fridge and mixed the baby greens, dried cranberries, pecans, and dressing all together in a bowl.

She checked the dating app for messages and found none. While she waited for the microwave's beep, she read through her profile. It was long (more than 300 words and specific, citing favorite movies and books and even her favorite inspirational quote. She grabbed a pen and paper and scribbled ideas for what it could say instead.

She tried to look at her profile from a different perspective. She wondered what it would look like to her ideal guy. Then she thought about something else that Amy Webb suggested in the video and she started to write a list of what she was looking for in a man. He had to be nice and funny and smart. And he had to like animals, especially cats. She paused as she thought about some other things that she had noticed when she was looking through dating profiles. She didn't want someone who had a motorcycle or someone who focused just on exercise. Some exercise was good but not a health nut. And she didn't want another workaholic like Derek. She didn't want someone who smoked.

She took a break to eat her meal and to wash her dishes. Then she sat on the sofa and continued writing. When she stopped to review the list, she realized it was more about what she didn't want than what she did want. She shook her head and thought it was easier to picture what wouldn't work than imagine what she wanted. There were so many possibilities. She put the list aside and decided to come back to it later.

The video also suggested adding a quote and she thought that she should replace the one she had with something a little more fun. She brought her laptop to the sofa and Mr. Fluffy followed her and curled on the cushion next to her leg. El easily found a site with quotes to use for online dating profiles, and thought she really could find anything online. Why not a guy?

She loved a quote she found by Steve Martin, "A day without sunshine is like, you know, night." But she thought that might be too silly. She laughed out loud when she read Kurt Vonnegut's quote, "Those who believe in telekinetics, raise my hand" but she wasn't sure what kind of guy that would attract. She finally decided on a quote from Roald Dahl, "Those who don't believe in magic will never find it."

El decided to put a quote she found from Lewis Carroll up on her mirror. "In the end, we only regret the chances we didn't take." So she wrote it in black Sharpie on a notecard, but as she did, she wondered how ready she was to take chances. Instantly, she realized she wouldn't know her comfort level by thinking, only by doing.

She looked at her profile again and added some optimistic language so she could be seen as more approachable. But she also appreciated the other insight she got from the video that you should be as picky as you want. She wrote and rewrote and fussed over the profile. She looked at the clock and realized that it was almost 11 and made the last change and posted the new version.

She looked through some new matches the next day but was disappointed that there wasn't a message from Lee. She wondered what she could have said that might have upset him. Was there something in her updated profile? Or maybe he got upset because he had seen that she had changed her profile showing that she was interested in meeting other men.

She couldn't understand it. When he first contacted her, he sent her a lot of texts but then he disappeared. Maybe he was on a trip. Maybe he decided she wasn't his type. Or maybe he didn't like cats. She sighed. She hated that so much of this was a guessing game. Maybe she needed to get a thicker skin if she was going to keep dating online.

The rest of the week flew by. She wanted to get more information from Carl about Bernie but wasn't sure what to say. She turned over in her mind what to ask him. She finally brought it up on Thursday. "Carl, thanks for introducing me to Bernie. He invited me over to his place to bake on Saturday."

"Oh that's great. You'll really like him."

In her head she said, is he gay or straight? Is he interested in a relationship? Why did he invite me over for baking? Instead she said aloud, "Yeah, he seems very nice and I can't wait to meet his cats. Is he an old friend of yours?"

"Actually, he and Stu were Garret's friends. Fun guys."

Hmmm, not really helpful, thought El as Carl's phone beeped and he said, "I need to take this. I'll catch you later."

And then Friday was so busy she didn't have a chance to catch up with Carl. She found herself at Bernie's apartment on Saturday morning telling herself that life was an adventure and she needed to stop planning and just see what would happen. She took a deep breath and rang the bell.

Bernie answered the door with a big grin. "So glad you could make it," He opened the door wide to let her in. His brown hair was very short on the top and shaved on the sides. He ran his fingers through it and smiled as he said, "Just got it cut. It's a little shorter than I expected."

El smiled and told him it looked great. He laughed and showed her the apartment. It was small but charming. The combined living and dining room had two mini couches and a kitchen table with two chairs. The framed posters depicted various bands, some she knew and some she didn't. A guitar was mounted over the electric fireplace. A large cat tower stood in the corner.

"Are you a guitarist?" asked El.

"No, but Stu and I love music." He gestured to the large pass through to the kitchen and said, "And here is where we'll create our masterpiece." She commented on how great the apartment looked and then asked about the cats.

"Asleep somewhere I expect. Let's try my room first. Stu's out," he said pointing down the hall, "and the cats like my room better." Separate bedrooms, thought El. Okay that may answer one question.

She followed him into his room which had clothes piled on the bed and papers and books piled on the desk and chairs. He pointed to the bed and said, "Apparently it's the maid's day off."

"Oh that reminds me. Your shirt. What doI owe you for dry-cleaning your shirt?"

"I think you just owe me a great cake."

"Really? I'll be happy to pay."

He smiled and said, "Oh you'll pay all right. You'll pay in flour and sugar." They both laughed.

"Hmm not in here," he said. El followed him back into the living room where a bluish-grey cat with small ears folded forward walked towards Bernie meowing. Bernie scooped him up and said, "This is Remington."

"Oh, he's gorgeous," said El, admiring his orange eyes. The cat squirmed and Bernie put him down.

"And there's his brother," Bernie said, pointing to another cat with grey and black tiger stripes who was ignoring them and licking his outstretched back leg.

"Qwerty?"

"That's him."

"He's beautiful, too. Can I take pictures of them? My friends would love to see them. Their ears are so cute."

As she took the pictures, she asked, "What made you pick Scottish folds? I've heard they have genetic problems." Bernie told the story of how he had gotten them as kittens when a friend's girlfriend realized that she was allergic to cats. "Yeah, the girlfriend didn't last but my friend decided to move and I got to keep the little guys. And yes, I'd read some things about the genetic issues and to be honest, it isn't a breed I'd buy, but I got them for free and I love them now."

"And he named them Remington and Qwerty?"

"Nah, that was me. He named them Ben and Jerry, but I thought that would make me think of ice cream so I renamed them when I got them." He laughed. "It doesn't matter, they don't come when you call them anyway."

"I think the names are adorable, too. But why?"

Bernie looked off to the side and said, "As you know, I get paid to design, but I like to write, and Remington and Qwerty help me by sitting with me. Plus you know, Remington made typewriters and Qwerty is a keyboard so it seemed fitting." He turned back to her. "They're great at inspiring napping scenes."

"Wow. What kind of writing? Adventure? Horror? Mystery?"

"Sci-fi. I'm working on it but it's taking me awhile. Enough about me, the only book I want to talk about is a cookbook. Let's bake." He gestured towards the kitchen.

As they measured and mixed ingredients, Bernie kept El entertained with stories about Carl and Garrett and people he worked with, but she noticed that he didn't talk about himself.

As they were waiting for the oven to heat, El pointed to some magnets on the refrigerator with city names and he said he used to pick up magnets in airports when he was travelling for work. He told her a funny story about getting stuck in a snowstorm in Chicago.

She pointed to a Disneyland magnet with Tinkerbell. "Have you been to Disney lately?"

Bernie briefly frowned and looked down. He said, "Not lately. That was from last year when I went with my ex-girlfriend."

El wasn't sure what to say.

He looked up with a small smile. "The trip was fun. But sometimes things don't work out, you know."

El nodded. She felt bad for him and started to talk about how she and Derek had broken up months before. Suddenly the oven timer went off and she said, "I guess that's all the time we have." They both laughed. El said, "I'm so sorry. I didn't mean to tell you all about my ex-boyfriend. Not a fun subject."

Bernie smiled and said, "No, my fault. I didn't mean to bring up my ex. It just happened a few weeks ago and I'm…" He paused.

El leaned in. "Do you want to talk about it?"

"No. Maybe. Wait. Let's get the cake started." He put it in the oven and set the timer.

They sat at the table and he told her about his girlfriend, Annie, who had decided two weeks ago that she needed space. El listened and added her own stories about Derek.

It seemed like only a few minutes later when the buzzer went off. Bernie jumped up and pulled the cake out after testing it. He gestured to El to get up and said, "Okay, enough about that. Let's finish up the frosting." He told a funny story about how Stu had used the wrong ingredients in a recipe and ended up with a mess. El realized that the conversation was over and helped him to make the frosting.

As the cake cooled, they went into the living room and Bernie explained that he had designed some of the band posters on the wall and that the signed guitar had been a thank-you gift. Qwerty was on the couch and stretched as he let El pet him. Remington jumped up next to her and Bernie said, "I think he's jealous." El scratched Remington on the chin as he purred. They were so cute with their tiny ears and El briefly wondered if Mr. Fluffy would like a friend.

Bernie frosted the cake and cut a slice for each of them. "Heavenly," he said as he tasted it. El agreed and thanked him for inviting her to his place. He said he only did it to show off his cats. He cut the cake in half and put half on a plate and covered it with foil and handed it to her.

"Thanks for coming. That was really fun. Let's get together soon for some more cooking," Bernie said, as he walked El to the door. She thanked him and said that would be great.

He tipped his head to the side and said, "Uh, thanks for listening." He surprised her by giving her a quick hug.

When she got home, she texted Jack. "Can guys just be friends with women?"

His response was, "Seinfeld doesn't think so. Y?"

"I think Bernie wants to be friends."

"Usually doesn't work," he texted back.

"You're friends with my friends," she texted.

"Different. How was the cake?"

"Delicious. I took half home. I might share."

"Deal."

"I said might," and she added a happy face.

She checked her messages and saw nothing from Lee. There was a nice message from Dan who complimented her on her photos and said how pretty she was. She checked his main photo and saw a handsome guy with dark hair and bright blue eyes standing next to a sports car. She read through his profile and saw he was a manager and liked to travel to romantic destinations and spend summers at his vacation house. He looked out of her league, but she couldn't stop thinking about those blue eyes. She didn't want to look too eager so she decided she'd wait the twenty-three hours. She set a timer on her phone.

Chapter 8

Later that afternoon, after El changed into a sundress and sandals, she met Teresa and Leticia at a Noe Valley dress shop. Teresa insisted her joint maids-of-honor help her find the perfect wedding dress. El and Leticia, attired in navy and black snake skin print sleeveless jersey dress, sat on a plush white faux fur sofa and sipped pink champagne while Teresa was in the fitting room trying on the first of the Boho dresses she insisted were her style. Leticia had tried to argue as Teresa plucked gowns from the racks. "I know you like Boho in everyday life, but this is your wedding. You don't have to go fancy or frilly. But trust me when I say a bit fitted is better."

Teresa hated her hips, and didn't want anything that she felt might accentuate them. The dress she was trying on first had a ruched breast area, with skinny gold braiding at the neckline and an empire waist. El thought it was too Grecian and not enough goddess.

Teresa emerged from the dressing room, with Samantha the sales lady and dressing room helper trailing behind her. "I hate it," Teresa said, frowning.

"Thank God," Leticia blurted.

El struggled to find something positive to counter Leticia's bluntness. "Makes your boobs look nice."

"Yes, but the rest of me looks like crap," Teresa countered.

"It is a bit…uh…full from the breasts down." El gulped some champagne and then sneezed as the bubbles tickled her nose.

"Bless you," Teresa called over her shoulder as she re-entered the fitting room.

Samantha topped off their glasses of champagne and then pulled other styles of gowns from the racks for Teresa to try.

While they waited for Teresa to model the next dress, Leticia asked, "So this morning's baking extravaganza, was it a date?" For the first time in weeks, Leticia looked well-rested, energetic, and happy.

"No. He and his girlfriend recently broke up. I think he just needed a friend."

"So he's not gay."

"No. But he lives with that Stu guy. Separate bedrooms."

"Guy with the hat, right?"

"Yes. That's the one. "

Teresa emerged from the fitting room in a sleeveless white lace gown with beige underlay and a plunging neckline embroidered in the same beige. The top of the dress was semi-fitted to her waist while the skirt of the dress hung almost straight before pooling around her on the floor.

"Wow," El gasped. "You look beautiful."

"Much better," Leticia said, "but it's only the second one. Put it on the maybe rack and let's see what else you've got in there."

Teresa twirled around one time. "I feel more like a princess in this one."

"Awww," El said, raising her glass. "To feeling like a princess."

Leticia raised her glass and said, "Better to feel like a queen. The princess doesn't have enough power."

"True enough." Teresa lifted her glass and took a sip, careful not to get any droplets on the dress. She put her glass next to El's and Leticia's on the coffee table and went to try on dress number three.

She emerged wearing full lace sleeves, a fitted bodice with a silk ribbon criss-crossing the front, and a very full floor-length skirt. "I look like Queen Guinevere," Teresa declared, frowning.

"Not the queen I meant," Leticia said. "That's awful."

"Totally not you," El said. "Maybe not anyone…since, like, there are no more knights nor round tables, beyond pizza." El thought the best part of wedding dress shopping was definitely the free champagne. Seeing some of these gowns was painful, and not just because she hadn't found love yet. Which reminded her…She pulled out her phone and checked the dating app for messages, just as Leticia's phone chimed. El had no messages.

Leticia's phone was in her purse and she smiled before even taking it out and looking at the screen.

"Jackson?" El asked.

"Nah, my sister," Leticia said.

El drained her glass. "Really? All these years and I've never once, Leticia, seen you smile at a text from your sister, especially before you have even read said text. I'm calling bullshit."

From inside the fitting room, Teresa called, "I'm with El. If it was your sister, what did she say?"

"Don't know. Haven't looked." Leticia said, draining her own glass and pouring another round for all three of them.

"Well look and please tell," Teresa said, exiting the curtain and stunning them into a second of silence. She had wound her long braid around her head so she could adequately show off the backless dress. The bodice was silk and lace with thinner shoulder straps and a V-neck, showing off a hint of cleavage. The skirt was almost fitted, with a slight mermaid flare around the ankle. When she turned, they could see her smooth skin all the way beyond her natural waist. The skirt started just above Teresa's booty.

Leticia whistled. "Sexy. Now that's what I'm talking about."

"Stunning," El said. "Now that is a dress."

"Are you sure it's not too much?" Teresa said, twirling and craning her head over her shoulder to look at her back in the three-way mirrors. "I mean Jordan's grandmother is coming and she's ninety-seven."

"How do you feel in that dress, compared to the others?" El said, forgetting all about Leticia and the text.

"Like the center of attention," Teresa said. "But I'm not sure if it feels good, like look at me, I'm the bride, or look at me because I'm showing off too much skin. Is it a slutty bride dress?" She furrowed her brow as she stared at herself in the mirrors.

"Definitely not," Leticia said. "It's a power dress. Very I am female, hear me roar."

"And that's a good thing?" Teresa

asked. "Most definitely," Leticia said.

Samantha chimed in, "That dress is one many of our clients wish worked for them, but it needs incredible curves to pull it off. It looks amazing on you, and the sample fits perfectly."

"Are you sure my hips don't look huge?" Teresa said, turning and considering her butt from a number of angles.

"It looks just like J-Lo's," El said.

"El's right. And it's certainly a dress J-Lo would wear. You're the bride. You want the attention. And that is an attention-grabbing dress."

"You're sure it's not too much?" Teresa still eyed the mirror.

"Absolutely not," El said. "And it fits you like a glove and needs no alterations. Sounds like a sign that it's yours."

"Maybe," Teresa was hesitant. "But we still have three other stores to go to."

Leticia and El exchanged looks. They had been in this store for an hour and were on their third glasses of champagne. They weren't going to survive more hours and more stores.

"Samantha, would you be willing to put this dress aside for her while we go get some food?" Leticia asked. "We'll be back before you close."

"Absolutely," Samantha said. "I can help you out of the dress." She motioned Teresa back into the fitting room.

Leticia leaned towards El and whispered, "We have a consensus, right? This is her dress?"

El considered that there could be other dresses at other price points, but she had no desire to explore the depth and breadth of wedding gowns on offer throughout the city. Especially since she knew Teresa expected them to bridesmaid dress shop the next day. "Yes. I agree," El said. "Can we celebrate with Mexican food, and then go home and find bridesmaid dresses online?"

Leticia laughed. "Sounds like a plan. But you know she won't go for that."

"Oh the sacrifices we make for friends," El mumbled. Then she raised the last two swallows in her glass towards Leticia. "To the love of friends," she said. They bumped glasses, drank, and a bit unsteadily got to their feet.

On the way to lunch, they popped into a second store, a little bigger than the first but the dresses all looked the same to El. She helped herself to a bottle of water and washed down some aspirin as Teresa went to try on another dress. El could feel herself getting cranky. She paused for a moment and thought just because she was tired and hungry, there was no reason to ruin Teresa's fun. As she was thinking about how to get through this, her phone rang. It was her mom. This was a great excuse to get some air. "I'm going to take this outside," she said to Leticia.

"Hi El, are you okay?"

"Hi Mom. Yes, why?"

"Well I haven't heard from you lately, honey, and your brother told me that you were thinking about dating again. Don't you think it's a little soon for that? Your dad and I are worried about you."

She was going to thank Jack for that. "Mom, we broke up months ago. I think it's fine."

"Yes, but meeting men online. Aren't there any nice men at work?"

El closed her eyes and tried not to sound annoyed.

"Mom, I'm not going to date anyone at work. That would be a terrible idea. I'm fine really."

"Well okay, honey, you know what you're doing," she said in a voice that clearly showed that she didn't think El did. "Jack did mention that Owen might be a good person for you. Do you remember Owen? He was such a nice boy."

Thanks again, Jack, thought El. "Yes, Mom, he was nice. We'll see what happens."

"Okay. Well your father and I would love to see you soon. It's been way too long. When can you come for dinner?"

El put her hand on her forehead. Her headache was getting worse. "That would be great, Mom. Let me check and get back to you. Hey, I've got to go. I'm out with Teresa and Leticia looking at wedding gowns."

"Oh now that sounds like fun. Say hi to the girls for me. One of these days we'll go shopping for wedding dresses. But there's no rush. I just want you to be happy. Your brother is happy and he's not dating anyone."

"Yes, Mom. Thank you. No rush. Okay, I love you. I'll talk to you soon."

"I love you, too. You'll let me know about dinner?"

"Yes, Mom. Let me check my schedule and get back to you. Love to Dad. I'll talk to you soon."

She shook her head. She never knew what to expect from her mom.

She checked her messages and there was a smile from Dan and two other messages from men that she didn't find very interesting.

There was also a message from PJ asking how the Master's Degree was going. She quickly sent a response that she'd like to talk to her. They set up a time to talk Sunday morning.

She decided that she'd been outside long enough. She breathed in and out and put a smile on her face and walked back in.

Teresa tried on five more dresses but even she seemed to be getting a little tired. She finally said it was time to go and El and Leticia tried not to cheer too much.

They ended up at their favorite Mexican restaurant and quickly ordered the fully loaded vegan nachos. With margaritas in hand, they toasted Teresa.

"To the bride," said Leticia.

"To the bride," agreed El.

Teresa laughed and thanked her friends. "I really appreciate it. I wish my mom could have come but she's still not feeling well. I promised that I'd send her pictures of the ones I really liked." Teresa's mother had recently had a lumpectomy and she was taking chemo, which made her very tired.

El thought about her mom and realized how lucky she was that she was healthy.

Teresa frowned and continued, "I wanted her to come with us but she told me not to wait..." She paused.

Leticia put her hand on her friend's arm. "And we're glad you didn't. Let's look at the pics I took to see which ones you want to send to her." As they scrolled through, El and Leticia again told Teresa how amazing she looked in the dress they were calling the mermaid dress. Leticia had taken more pictures of that one than any other. After Teresa sent the pictures to her mom, she agreed that she would call Samantha after dinner and find out if they could hold the dress for a few days so she could bring her mom to see it.

Teresa was telling them about the wedding planning when the nachos arrived. They briefly stopped talking as they each grabbed a chip. "Mmmm, heaven," said El.

Their dinners arrived soon after and Leticia told her friends about some cases she was working on. It seemed like she barely had time to sleep and then go back to the office. She said it would be over soon and then turned to El. "So, spill it, what's going on with the online dating?"

El told them what she had learned so far and started talking about the guys she had been messaging. Leticia interrupted her. "Pictures, come on, let's see."

El started with some pictures of Lee and talked about some of the sweet things he said. "But then he just stopped messaging me. And I don't know what to do."

"Move on," said Leticia. Teresa giggled and nodded her head. She said, "Yeah, if he stops messaging you, just forget about it."

El then showed pictures of some other guys and talked about the different things they had said. Then she showed them Dan's picture. Leticia took the phone and said, "Mmmm he is cute."

Teresa agreed. "Not Jordan cute of course, but very cute." They laughed.

El read what he had written. "Awww," said Teresa, "that is really sweet."

"I haven't written back yet," said El.

"What are you waiting for?"

She explained the twenty-three-hour rule. Leticia shook her head and said, "I wouldn't wait. I would've contacted him right away."

"Really?" teased El. "I thought you liked to play it cool."

"Not for someone that hot. I'd go for it."

"I don't see you online dating."

"No time. Not interested. We're talking about you."

El smiled and said she would message the next morning and would let them know what happened.

El woke up the next morning and briefly wondered why her alarm was going off on a Sunday. Then she remembered her appointment with PJ. She took a quick shower and had some cereal.

As she waited for PJ's call, she thought about how PJ and her contacts had given her the answers she needed to be more confident at work. Work was going fine and now she wondered if PJ could share some advice that would help her with relationships.

Soon PJ's smiling face popped up on her phone. Her dark curly hair framed her face and she wore an orange T-shirt. She held a coffee cup in one hand and waved at El with the other.

After they greeted each other, PJ asked how the Master's Degree was going. El sighed and started talking about what she had learned about online dating.

PJ interrupted her. "Hold on, before you get into the online dating stuff, what did you do before that?"

El told her about some of the other things she'd done and PJ interrupted her again.

"El, I'm a little concerned that you're jumping into the advanced level courses and you're missing some prerequisites."

"What?" This was not what she had expected.

"When I put together my Master's Degree program, I looked at what my end goals were and worked back from there. I broke it up into basic, intermediate, and advanced material. I made sure I understood the basics. It seems like you're already trying to figure out dating and I think you might have skipped over some things that need to be done first."

"Like what?"

PJ sipped her coffee. "Okay, on the more basic level, before you start to think about another relationship, you must first close out the previous relationship. Make sure that you're really done with Derek. I know it's been months but have you truly said good bye to that relationship? Do you still have things in your apartment that were his? Things that remind you of him?"

El thought guiltily about wearing Derek's old shirt to bed every night. "Well, yeah, there are some things but it's not really that much."

"Uhuh," said PJ, tipping her head to the side. "Seriously, you need to get rid of his stuff. If you don't, that's going to get in your way of the next relationship. One friend of mine had a little ceremony where she put everything that reminded her of her ex on the table and thanked them and said it was time for them to make someone else happy. Then she donated it all to a thrift store that generates money for animals. Another friend took all the cards and notes that her boyfriend had given her and burned them. I'm not saying you have to burn things, but you need to get rid of them."

"But it's not that much," said El.

"Yes, but even a little bit can hold you back."

El sighed, "Yeah I guess that makes sense. Okay, that's one prerequisite that I can work on. What else?"

PJ smiled, "I think this is very important. Before you work on meeting someone for you to love, you need to love yourself."

El smiled. "Okay, okay, I know that's important. But this is a relationship Master's Degree."

"I'm serious. If you aren't happy with yourself, you'll just keep attracting the wrong relationships."

"Hmm, I hadn't thought about it like that. What do you suggest?"

"I'd probably start with one of my favorite books called *You Are A Badass*."

El laughed and wrote it down. "Okay, I like it. I could get that."

"It's got a lot of great information. It doesn't focus on romance but I think it gives some useful overall information about how to live your life better. And to me, when you understand yourself better and you're happier in life, it's a lot easier to have a healthy relationship with others."

El looked off to the side. "I never thought about it like that. I've been so focused on wondering how to meet guys that I haven't been focusing on me." She looked back at PJ and nodded. "Thanks, I will get it and read it."

PJ smiled. "Sounds great. Will you let me know what you think about it?"

"Absolutely. What else?"

"Just those two things. I suggest that you spend some time understanding yourself because I think that will make the next steps easier. I can recommend some other books and I might get a friend of mine to give her perspective."

El thought about some of PJ's other contacts that had been very helpful with her career issues. "That would be so great. I'd really appreciate it."

They spoke for a little while longer and El promised to start reading the book.

When they got off the call, El re-read Dan's message from the day before and sent a response. She had promised PJ that she would focus on learning to love herself, but it was nice to think about meeting someone special.

Chapter 9

Later that morning after El drank more coffee, a big glass of water, and did thirty minutes of YouTube yoga, she opened her laptop. She did a Google search on books about loving yourself. When she saw *I Need Your Love—Is That True? How to Stop Seeking, Love, Approval and Appreciation and Start Finding Them Instead* by Byron Katie, she stopped and virtually opened the front cover to see what was inside.

The table of contents contained these words: "Love is wonderful—except when we are searching for it, trying to hold on to it, or missing it. Hours of every day are taken up with difficult, painful thoughts about our relationships." El stopped and thought about how often her mind wandered to have the guys online messaged me yet? No matter what else she was doing, this thought and the expectancy, hope, almost obsession that it was becoming made her feel like a child who was counting down the hours until Santa's arrival. And then when she got no response or was trolled, she felt like Santa had delivered reindeer poop instead of the most coveted toy.

She flipped through more of the book. Chapter two said, "Until you understand your thoughts, you aren't relating to people or to yourself; you're relating to concepts that you haven't questioned." Later chapters delved into the myth that people think that love is having their needs met, and how to deal with flaws in people, and the way you need to come to your own aid to find freedom in love. The more El read, the more she knew she needed this book. And she briefly considered if it would be a good shower gift for Teresa. I Need Your Love had many exercises that could give Teresa and Jordan an even stronger foundation for their marriage. But El wasn't sure if her friend would appreciate it or see it as criticism of their whirlwind romance.

She looked at what other books existed in the same category. One was a book with a guy holding a gun to his temple and was called Love Yourself Like Your Life Depends On It by Kamal Ravikant. The gun image unsettled El and even though the reviews were good, she couldn't bring herself to buy it. But a book with a bright yellow cover titled Choosing Me Before We beckoned to her in a way the Byron Katie book did. The book claimed to have insights on love, relationships, and dating and promised to "replace old habits that sabotage your success with new ways of thinking that promote self-respect and well-being." El stopped at that phrase. She wasn't sure she needed more self–respect.

But then Derek's put downs of her apartment, her salary, and herself started on a loop inside her head. Rarely, if ever, had she stuck up for herself. Only at the end…two years into the relationship…did she finally get angry enough to counter his thinking and comments. Maybe she did need more self-respect. She knew Leticia would have never put up with all of the put-downs.

Is that what self-respect is? El looked it up in the online Oxford dictionary. Self-respect was defined as "pride and confidence in oneself; a feeling that one is behaving with honor and dignity." She thought of some of the people she knew at work and back in her university days. Many of them acted with a sense of pride and a lot of confidence, or at least they faked confidence, but she wasn't sure their decisions or behavior was honorable. She stared at the definition pondering it.

And suddenly her phone chirped, jarring her from her thoughts. The text was from Teresa and said to meet her at the Saks in Union Square. "I saw a dress online that I'm hoping they have for you and L," Teresa texted.

"K," El texted. "Oh joy," El said aloud. Mr. Fluffy picked up his head from the other end of the sofa and eyed her sarcasm.

"Sorry to disturb you, your highness," El said as he passed him on the way to the kitchen. She drank another glass of water, ate an apple smothered in peanut butter, washed off the knife she used, filled the cat's bowl with kibble and refreshed his water, and then headed into the bathroom to take a shower.

After she toweled off, styled her hair, donned a pine green casual dress, and swiped her eyelashes with some mascara, she glanced at her phone. Leticia had texted, "Ready to do this? Let's find something quickly."

"Agreed," El responded. "See you in twenty."

Then El found herself checking the dating app for messages before she realized what she was doing. Habits are hard to break, she thought. The only thing in the inbox was a message from some guy hating on cats. Reindeer poop, she thought first, and then that some people have way too much time on their hands and must like to be mean.

Maybe PJ was right and she wasn't ready for dating in the online world. She'd get the books tomorrow. In the meantime, El decided it was best to deactivate her profile.

Twenty minutes later, El craned her neck to look for her friends as she rode the escalator in the middle of Saks up to the dress department. Leticia, who was at the railing above and wore an all-black sheath dress, waved and smiled.

El hugged her best friends and then they moved to a rack with a rainbow of dresses. Teresa said, "I'm looking for one in particular. It's blue lace with a nude underlay." Leticia eyed El and grimaced.

"Teresa, we've been friends forever, right?" Leticia said.

"Yes."

"Nude underlay is never nude on me. It'll be dark on Red and look ghostly on me." Leticia held her darker forearm to El's super pale, freckly one.

"Ugh. Sorry. I wasn't thinking. The dress was so gorgeous on the model on the website." Teresa explained. She flipped through dresses in crimson, hot pink, magenta, canary yellow, and burnt orange.

El was looking through the emerald, evergreen, navy, cobalt, and turquoise dresses. She knew these colors looked great on both her and Leticia. Teresa and Jordan hadn't chosen wedding colors yet beyond black and white. Leticia was going through the charcoal and black dresses. Leticia and El had already privately discussed that they wanted dresses that were fitted as opposed to poofy or boho so El stuck to that style and created a small collection of "maybes" in her size. She carried them to a fitting room.

The first dress she modeled for her BFFs was a sleeveless navy sheath dress, not dissimilar to the dress Leticia had worn into Saks. El thought its silk hugged her in all the right places.

But the first words out of Teresa's mouth were, "Too plain. The style is good. But would be better in a floral or a print or with some lace or something."

Leticia commented, "Well, we certainly wouldn't upstage the bride in that."

"True," Teresa said, as El slid back into the fitting room. She reappeared moments later in a V-neck cobalt blue chiffon floor-length gown that had a slit to mid thigh. The bodice crossed one side over the other to form the V and the waist had a wide gathering of horizontal fabric in the same color that formed a band, accentuating El's slender middle.

"Oh my God," Leticia said. "That dress is hot. You look so hot. That's the one."

Teresa said, "It does look amazing, but it is only the second dress."

El spun around to see the skirt arc in the three-way mirrors. She stuck her leg out of the high slit. She felt amazing, like in this dress she could get any man she wanted.

Teresa repeated, "It's only the second dress. Try on more." And she feverishly flipped through another rack.

Leticia had grabbed the blue gown in her size and came into El's fitting room. She stripped immediately, stepped into the dress, and asked El to zip her.

They stood side by side looking into the mirror. "Twins from separate mothers," Leticia joked. "With silver or nude heels and sparkly drop earrings, it's a knock 'em to their knees look."

El put her arm around Leticia and whispered, "Now we need to persuade the bride. I'm done here. I'm trying on nothing else." And just as those words were spoken, the word "self-respect" popped into El's head.

She took a deep breath and exited the fitting room, with Leticia on her heels. When she reached Teresa, who had a pile of dresses draped over her one arm, El stopped and cleared her throat. "Look at me, T, and look at Leticia. This dress fits us. The color is excellent. I've never felt more beautiful or powerful than I do right now. This is our dress.

I'll help you hang the ones on your arm. We're getting this one."

Teresa opened her mouth and then shut it, reminding El of her childhood goldfish that she and Jack had named Stinky. She held the dress arm aloft towards El and she and Leticia helped restock the dress racks.

When they finished, El and Leticia went back into the fitting room to change back into their own clothes. Leticia whispered, "Assertive. Impressive. And thank you. Lunch is on me since you made this painless."

El smiled, even more at herself than to Leticia. "You taking us somewhere nice?"

"Anywhere you want to go," Leticia said.

El suggested a French restaurant that had extensive gluten-free and vegetarian options.

After they paid for the gowns and they were wrapped up, Leticia told Teresa their thoughts for shoes and accessories and that lunch was on her. "Such a productive weekend. Look how much you've accomplished in your wedding planning, Teresa. Let's celebrate."

Teresa smiled. "I couldn't have done it without you. Thank you."

As they walked to the restaurant, Leticia's phone started playing En Vogue and Salt 'N' Pepa's "Whatta Man." She grinned but didn't engage with her phone.

El said, "What the hell?"

Teresa said, "When did you start creating ringtones? That's so a decade ago."

Leticia laughed. "It was a joke."

"Between you and Jackson?"

"Nah, just a guy I know. A friend."

El stopped on the sidewalk, causing people to jostle them, make WTF comments, and go around them. "A friend? I thought that wasn't possible."

"Depends," Leticia said. "Let's move. We're pissing people off. Sidewalks are for walking not standing."

She took ten more steps and they were at the restaurant's red door.

"So who is it?" Teresa asked.

"Just a friend. Some guy. We were joking around with our phones one night."

The hostess asked how many in their party, and then seated them. Leticia immediately buried her nose in the menu, like it was the end of the discussion.

Teresa and El eyed each other over the tops of their menus. El mouthed "weird" to Teresa. Over the years they had shared almost everything. Best friends didn't keep secrets.

El wondered what was going on and suddenly she thought about Leticia's boss Antonio. He was smart, funny, and hot. Leticia had joked that if he was single and she wasn't working for him, she'd hit that. No, that was ridiculous, El thought. But she was working an awful lot... Late nights... And she didn't want to talk about it... But, she wouldn't do that. El stared at the menu. No, she thought, Leticia wouldn't.

She was interrupted by a text from Bernie, "Thanks again for yesterday. The cake is even better the second day. I'm going to see the Darryl Stone band on Thursday night and I have an extra ticket. Would you like to go?"

She read it to her friends and they discussed whether it was a date or not. Teresa seemed to think it was a date, but El wasn't convinced and said he might just be trying to get rid of an extra ticket. She wasn't familiar with the band and decided to check them out later.

After lunch, El considered what to do next. She could give into the Catholic guilt and call her mom and join her parents for Sunday night dinner. Or she could keep working on her degree. It wasn't a difficult choice.

El called her bookstore, The Ink Spot, and asked if they had the two books she wanted. They did and said they would hold the books for her. She said she'd be there soon, dragging her bridesmaid dress behind her, she thought.

El smiled when she got to the door of The Ink Spot. She held it open for a mom and three kids clutching their new books. The smell of coffee from the café made her sigh happily as she walked in and she could feel the tension of the day disappear as she looked at customers reading in the comfy chairs nestled between the aisles.

She walked to the front counter and waited as the family at the register asked questions. From her left she heard, "I can help you over here," as a man walked to the other register and waved her over. She stepped up to the counter and asked for the books they were holding for her. He couldn't find them and told her he'd check in the office and would be right back. He quickly returned with the books and put them on the counter.

"Here they are. Thank you so much for calling and letting us get them for you. They look like great books. Gifts for someone? Or a little light reading for you?" He smiled.

"Actually, they're for a project."

"A project, that sounds interesting. What kind of a project?" His bright blue eyes looked interested.

El hesitated as he rang up the order and she gave him her Think Ink frequent book buyer card. By this time, the family at the other register was finished and the cashier was busy moving books to a discount table.

"Actually, I'm doing some research on relationships. I asked my friends for suggestions and one recommended the Badass book and I found the other on my own."

He tipped his head to the side. "Really? What are you going to do with this research? Are you a professor?"

El laughed. "No, no, the research is only for me and maybe my friends. I just want to understand people better. I love books and I think everyone can learn more about themselves and how to get along better with others."

He looked at her as he adjusted his round black glasses. El felt she had said too much.

"Actually, I think that's a great idea. A really great idea." He paused. "And that makes me think about a possible store event. I'm Todd, the new store manager and since you're such a good customer of ours, I'd like to get your opinion on something."

"Sure, I'd be happy to. I love this place."

They finished the transaction and Todd said, "How about I buy you a cup of coffee so I can get your opinion?" He pointed to the Ink Link café.

"Make it a tea, and you've got a deal."

As Todd ordered the drinks, El noticed that he was probably just a few years older than her. He was slender with short light brown hair. His face was pale with a red nose and cheeks. He wore a blue button up shirt with khakis and dark brown boat shoes with white soles.

He joined her at the table and told her about his idea to start some new book club events for customers. They had done them in the past and he wanted to re-energize the idea. They'd announce the book choice to customers, give them a discount, and schedule a time to discuss it. They were going to try different genres to see what customers liked best. He said that he knew she was a long-time customer from her Think Ink book buying card, so he wanted her opinion about it. El told him she thought it was a great idea. "I love to talk about books. I think that would be really fun."

He grinned. "That's what I was hoping you'd say. How would you like to run a book club meeting about the *You Are A Badass* book?"

El had the tea halfway to her lips and stopped. "What do you mean?"

"I think that would be a fun book for our customers and I think you'd be great to talk about what you think about it."

"Uh. But I've never done that. I wouldn't know what to do." And as soon as the words left her mouth she remembered the business advice she'd been given about how men and women view opportunities differently. Men jump into new situations believing they will figure it out as they go; whereas, women think they have to have it all figured out ahead of time.

"I can help you. I'll put together some guidelines and some general questions. You know, what did you like most? What was most surprising? What didn't you like? It doesn't have to be perfect. It'll be fun."

"Why don't you have one of the booksellers here do it?"

"That's just the point," he said leaning toward her. "I don't want it to be one of us; it should be a customer, someone who loves books, someone like you."

El looked at Todd's eager face. She could say no. Or she could practice confidence by trying something new. After all, it was a book, how hard could this be? "Okay, let's give it a try."

"Excellent! I can't wait to tell my boss." said Todd. Suddenly he looked concerned. "Oh wait, you didn't get a discount on this one. We'll give you a discount on a future book, don't worry."

El laughed and said, "Really, not a problem."

They spent a few minutes discussing logistics. They picked a date a few weeks later and Todd said that they'd send out a message to their customer list announcing the book club and the discount.

When El got home, she hung up the gown in the back of her closet and then she looked up the Darryl Stone band and watched a video. She didn't know any of their songs but liked the way they sounded. She texted Bernie, "Sounds like fun. Thanks. How much is the ticket?"

He texted right back. "My treat. I already paid for it. Do you want to go?"

"Yes, sounds like fun. Thanks!"

He texted the name of the club and suggested they meet before the show at a nearby fast casual restaurant known for its sandwiches and salads.

"Since you got the ticket, how about I buy dinner?"

He agreed and they decided to meet at the restaurant at 6 p.m. El smiled. She still wasn't sure if it was a date or not but it sounded like fun and she hadn't been to a show in ages. Derek thought they were a waste of money. She stopped herself. I need to stop thinking about what Derek would or wouldn't do. It doesn't matter anymore. I need to get him out of my head, she thought.

She grabbed the *You Are A Badass* book and sat on the couch next to the cat. El wanted to jump right to the section, "How To Embrace Your Inner Badness." She was also intrigued by "How To Kick Some Ass." Instead, she started with the first section, "How You Got This Way." It described how we're controlled by our subconscious beliefs and how we need to recognize negative beliefs and replace them with fresh ones.

She closed the book briefly. "Well, Mr. Fluffy. I think I have some work to do." She opened her laptop and typed "http://www.JenSincero. com" to see what kinds of things the author had on her website. Maybe she has questions for book clubs, El thought.

She couldn't find any, but when she checked under resources, Jen Sincero had a bunch of recommended books by category, including books on relationships, one of which was written by a dude who pretended he was a woman writing a letter to her lover. Weird, El thought. I'll pass.

El decided to give up on the Badass book for the evening and typed "How to Learn to Love Yourself" into her search engine. More than 700 million hits came from that, everything from TedTalks, to psychology and wellness-themed sites, to mainstream media articles. One guy's website said, "Loving yourself is so f...ing hard. Here's how to do it." Another site included a list of "forgive yourself for your mistakes, travel once per year, have fun by yourself, start a journal, learn to say no to others." While El sort of agreed with the advice, she didn't think that is what PJ had in mind when she said she should start with her relationship to herself.

El didn't really want to travel solo nor did she have any desire to journal.

What struck El about her search was the number of online courses devoted to the topic. From Louise Hay and Robert Holden's 21-day Loving Yourself program to others focused on happiness or self-esteem to more than 700 million other options, some free and some with hefty price tags. El realized that people and their relationships, with themselves or with others, was big business.

And thinking of business, El decided to review her schedule for tomorrow, and to put together an outfit. She and her team were presenting to a new client for the first time so she wanted to look her best and be well rested.

Chapter 10

As El washed her hair early the next morning she found herself humming "Whatta Man," which made her pause mid-lather. Who was Leticia's mystery man? And why was she being so secretive? The word sneaky popped into El's head.

Leticia was always so forthright about whomever she was sleeping with. El couldn't figure it out. Could he be married? Nah. El dismissed that idea as soon as she thought it. The one time L hooked up with a married guy, she had been honest about it. And she had been furious. Since he hadn't told her he was married until after the fact.

Games like that Leticia didn't play.

So if he wasn't married, and it wasn't Jackson, just who was she seeing? El rinsed her hair and wracked her brain. It could be Leticia's boss, but El was mostly certain she'd tell them if she had started banging her boss. It seemed unlikely anyway. Leticia had a strict personal policy against mixing business and pleasure. She wouldn't even date or sleep with other lawyers, just in case their paths crossed professionally.

After El dried off, she texted Leticia, "Reggae yoga at 7 p.m.?"

No immediate response, so El did her makeup and hair, and then dressed in an evergreen faux-wrap dress, added jade earrings to her lobes, and donned her feet in black strappy heels.

She put kibble and fresh water in Mr. Fluffy's bowls. He was still curled on her pillow ignoring that it was morning and that she was leaving. She grabbed a pre-made smoothie from the fridge and threw an already made salad and an apple in her tote bag, and was out the door with fifteen minutes to spare.

She still had no word from Leticia, but "Whatta Man" was again on repeat in her head. So she found the first song on her phone's playlist and listened to it on her commute. Other music was the only way to abolish a stuck song, El had read somewhere years ago.

When she made it to her desk and still hadn't heard from Leticia, she texted her again. "You okay?"

El stared at the phone willing Leticia to respond.

Her iMessage flashed, but it was Bernie. "Happy Monday."

El smiled at the phone and then typed "Thank you. Have an incredible day."

She checked e-mail using her work computer while she drank her smoothie and the day's second cup of coffee.

Ten minutes later, she finally got a text from Leticia. "Was in a meeting."

El thought, at this hour? Really? "With Pastor Pillow and Sister Sheets?" El joked.

"Funny. And no."

"No to yoga or no to PP and SS? :)"

"No to both. Have to work late. More later. xoxo."

Hmmm, El narrowed her eyes at iMessage. Something was off. Leticia was busier now than before she made partner.

A buzz sound from El's desk phone interrupted her thoughts. It was the front desk calling with the news that the clients had arrived and were being escorted to the conference room on the sixth floor. She reapplied her lipstick, stood and straightened the skirt on her dress, and grabbed her notes. Work now, friends later, she thought. Show time.

The meeting with the clients had gone better than expected and the sales director pulled El aside after and thanked her for her help. El felt elated as she walked back to her desk. Carl waved at her and said, "Do you have a few minutes?"

"Now? Yes." This would be a good time to ask him more about Bernie, she thought.

They walked into a small conference room and sat down.

"What's up?" said El with a smile.

"Wellllll," he paused briefly and ran his fingers through his hair. "I wanted to let you know what's going on before anyone else." He paused again. "I turned in my resignation today."

El sat back in her chair and just looked at him. She was not expecting this at all. "What are you talking about?"

"I resigned. I got an offer last week from an old boss of mine and it was so sweet I couldn't resist."

El stared at him and he continued, "He had moved on to a new company and they're ramping up so he thought about me. I wasn't planning to move but the offer was so good…" His voice trailed off.

"But you can't leave," protested El. "We're just starting to get great results here. Don't you want to see them through?"

"El, come on, of course I do. But this job is an awesome opportunity." He described some of his new perks.

"I'm sorry, I'm sorry. I'm happy for you," said El leaning forward. "It's just such a surprise. I mean we built this team together. I don't know what I'm going to do. After all, we have all the new customer information and the database situation…"

Carl smiled. "You'll be fine."

She frowned.

"Seriously," he said. He shook his head. "Why do you always go to the negative?" He waved his finger at her. "This creates some real opportunities for you."

"What?"

"Okay, look, now you're in charge of the team and you can go to Kate and let her know what changes you want to make."

"But I can't do it on my own," moaned El.

"No, but you can tell Kate what kind of person you want to hire to replace me. Maybe you can get a promotion out of it and have the new person report to you. This could be your ticket to being a senior manager."

El looked at Carl. He was right. She immediately thought about all the negatives and not the positives. Even though she would be really sorry to see him go, this did open up some opportunities for her. And now she'd have an advocate in another company and they could continue to help each other.

They talked some more and Carl told her that only Kate knew at this point and he'd be there for another two weeks and would then take a week off before starting his new job.

That night at reggae yoga, El wondered why she immediately went to the negative. Not just at work, but with everything. She greeted the guy she had talked to last time and tried her best to keep up with the pulsating music and fast moving pace of the poses.

When she got home, she thought about her relationship with Derek and how she was still feeling bad about it. She pulled out a piece of paper and wrote down all the positives of being single.

- *She could eat ice cream in bed and nobody complained.*
- *She could spend money on what she wanted without explaining it to anyone.*
- *It gave her the chance to work with PJ again and read some great books.*
- *She didn't need to wear makeup on the weekends.*

She wrote and wrote and forced herself to come up with as many as possible. She finally got to seventeen reasons and decided it was enough. She said to herself and to Mr. Fluffy who sat next to her, "I need to focus more on the positive."

She made herself a cup of chamomile tea and opened the new book, *I Need Your Love—Is That True?* She hadn't finished the *Badass* book but she needed something different.

El started reading and felt like the author was speaking directly to her. There were several questions to ask yourself to help you see relationships from a different perspective. She worked on an exercise where she had to think about something that was bothering her. The thought that popped into her head right away was "I'm never going to find someone special for me." Just focusing on that was painful, but she knew that's what was really hurting her.

When she asked herself the first question, "Is it true?" she thought that it probably wasn't.

The next question was: how do you feel when you believe this thought? It's horrible, El thought. She grimaced as she relived how sad it made her and how anxious she was when she thought about dating someone again. It made her feel like she was constantly worried about whether this guy was the one or not.

Then she asked herself the following question, what would life be like without that thought? El sighed. It would be great. She could relax. She could really enjoy helping Teresa plan her wedding. She wouldn't feel so stressed around guys.

El paused. She thought more about what life would be like if she got rid of her "I'll never find anyone" mindset. She felt her shoulders relax and realized how tense she had been feeling. She looked at her tea. She had been so engrossed by the book that it was still untouched.

The final question was actually a challenge. The book asked the reader to think about other versions of the thought that could be true. She pondered, I am going to find someone special for me. Then she thought, I don't need to find someone special for me. I am special with or without someone. She continued thinking of different versions. There are many special guys out there for me. Special guys are looking to find me. She smiled. She was only at the end of chapter two. She closed the book. That was enough for one night.

The rest of the week at work was stressful. Carl told her the next day not to let anyone else know that he had resigned. Kate wanted him to stay and was discussing a possible counter-offer with him.

El was happy when it was finally Thursday and she could have fun with Bernie. He had texted her several times during the week and she was really looking forward to seeing him. When she worried about whether it was a date or not, she asked herself one of the questions from the book: what would it be like without that thought? Instead of stressing about it, she could just have fun. She had gone through more of the book during the week and had read stories about how other people used these questions. It helped her to put things in a different perspective.

Instead of stressing all week about what to wear, she asked herself what she would like to wear if it wasn't a date. Since she was going right after work, she wore a black business suit with a casual green and yellow blouse that looked great without the jacket.

She got to the restaurant fifteen minutes early because she wasn't sure how long it would take her to get there. She'd found that her GPS wasn't always 100 percent accurate about the time estimates so she left a little extra time. While she waited for Bernie, she looked at the menu. She made a conscious choice that she wasn't going to worry about whether he was her special guy or not; that wasn't going to get in her way of having fun.

As she was trying to decide between the caprese salad with chicken or a specialty steak sandwich, Bernie came in and gave her a hug and they were seated. He had on a black button-down shirt, jeans, and solid black wingtips. He ordered a Deschutes Fresh Squeezed IPA and El chose a local merlot.

As they waited for the food to come, Bernie and El talked about Carl. She asked Bernie what he thought would happen. Bernie shrugged. "I don't know. I think it's a good idea to hear what they have to say, but it would be kind of strange to stay at the company after you've resigned. When you're ready to leave, you should move on."

The mozzarella on El's salad was delicious. Bernie took a big bite of his hot steak sandwich. El asked him about the band and how he had first heard of them. He didn't say anything and she thought he was still chewing.

"Funny story," he said. "My ex-girlfriend, Annie, first heard of the band last year. She had me listen to them and then I liked them, too."

"Oh," said El. Not sure what to say.

"Yeah," he continued. "So when I heard they were going to be playing here, I got two tickets thinking she and I would go. Well then, of course, we broke up. And I thought you might like to go." He looked down at the table. "Annie texted me a few days ago and wanted to know what I was going to do with the other ticket. She wanted to go. But I'd already given you the ticket."

El felt terrible. "Oh no, you could have told me and she could have had the ticket."

Bernie looked up at her with a partial smile, "No, I didn't want to go with her." He paused. "She wasn't happy though when she found out that I was going with you. I think she just wanted me to go by myself if she wasn't going."

El just stared at him.

Bernie waved his hand as if brushing the thought away. "Forget it. I didn't want to go with her. I thought it would be fun to go with you. I'm sorry, I probably shouldn't have told you that about Annie."

"No, no," said El, trying to think of the right thing to say. "That's fine. I'd rather know. Let's not worry about that. Let's enjoy ourselves." She laughed and raised her glass, "Here's to a fun evening."

Bernie raised his glass and lightly clinked hers. "Yes, a fun evening.

Thanks." They both took a drink and El silently congratulated herself for staying in the present instead of focusing on Bernie's past or if they have a future together.

Chapter 11

El's alarm went off way too early the next morning. She smacked the snooze twice. The third time the alarm went off, Mr. Fluffy's paw and claw made contact with her throat. "Owww! Damn, cat!" El hopped from bed and surveyed the damage in the bathroom mirror. Three beads of blood glistened on the right side of her neck, and that, coupled with her paleness and the dark shadows under her eyes made it look like El had been drained of her vital fluids by a three fanged vampire.

"You're a sight," she said to her reflection, and then thought, healthy relationships start with loving yourself, so she added, "But I love you anyway." And then El giggled.

Last night when they got to the concert and found their assigned table in the venue, Bernie asked El if she wanted to do a shot with him, in the name of fun. El responded, "Sure," and laughed. They clicked shot glasses of honeyed Jack Daniels together and then drained them. And just as they set the glasses on the table, El heard someone shout Bernie's name.

A lanky six-foot tall man with sandy, thinning hair, attired in jeans and a black T-shirt and black boots, rushed towards them, embracing Bernie and kissing him full on the mouth. El felt her eyes get wide but tried not to display her shock. When they parted, Bernie said, "El, meet Greyson, my ex. Greyson, this is El."

Greyson extended his hand and said, "Well she's certainly prettier than me."

El grinned and chuckled. "Thank you." She didn't know what else to say.

Bernie filled in the silence by saying, "I was with Greyson before Annie," and then he turned back to Greyson, "So, how the hell are you?

Back in the city again?"

"Just got back last week," Greyson said. "Not sure for how long though."

"You look great. Africa must have agreed with you. Let's get a drink this weekend and catch up. Still have the same number?"

"Yes. Text me. I'm free tomorrow or Sunday." To El he said, "Bernie's a great guy. Nice to meet you."

"Nice to meet you, too," El said before Greyson weaved his way back the way he came. El signaled the bartender for a second round. She had no idea what to think.

Bernie said, "Wow. I can't believe he's back. Greyson's a surgeon but he's been traveling with Doctors Without Borders and Team Rubicon, doing good in the world and helping the underserved. He's an amazing man."

"Wow," El said. "That's so great."

"Yeah," Bernie looked a bit wistful. "We ended our relationship because he was leaving."

The second round of shots arrived and El held hers up towards Bernie. "To special people in our lives," she said, thinking that was the most appropriate thing she could say.

Bernie picked up his glass, raised it to her, and then swallowed the contents. When he put his glass on the table, he sat down. El did, too. And just as they did, the band came out and the crowd went wild.

The next two hours were filled with music, another drink followed by a lot of water, and dancing at their seats. El had such a good time, and at the end of the evening, she told that to Bernie and he hugged her and gave her a quick kiss.

"Thank you, El, for accompanying me, and for dinner. Let's get together again soon," he said.

"I'd like that," El said.

Bernie hugged her again and they parted.

She still wasn't sure if it had been a date or friendship. But she couldn't wait to debrief with the girls.

El turned the shower water on as hot as she could stand it and let the water wash away her tiredness. She threw on an evergreen wrap dress because it was easy, simple silver hoops, and black shoes. She refilled

Mr. Fluffy's water and gave him some kibble and then ran out the door, already twenty minutes late.

In the office she poured black coffee and she ate an apple she had left on her desk the day before. The glare of the computer screen hurt her eyes a little even though she didn't feel hungover. As she went through her e-mail, a text appeared from Leticia. It only said one word: "Well?"

"No idea. But apparently he's bi," El texted back.

"WHAT?"

"Met his ex-BF."

"No shit. Did he make a move on you?"

"Hugs and a chaste kiss."

"Sorry," Leticia texted.

"It's okay," El wrote. "Never dated someone bi. Not sure how I feel." "Drinks at the Gecko at 5:30? I'll check with T."

El texted, "Drinks yes. But maybe you and me," before she had time to consider what she was saying. When she did, she realized she wanted space and time without any reminders of marriage or weddings or couplehood. While she loved Teresa, that place wasn't what Teresa inhabited. El needed space with another single.

El grabbed her laptop and headed to her next meeting. She and Carl were reviewing the projects he was working on and what she needed to take over. He had decided not to stay and Kate had announced that his last day would be the next Friday.

Carl had told El that even though the counter-offer was tempting, he had taken some time to think about why he had decided to leave. His current job didn't have some opportunities that he really wanted to explore. Carl said that it was flattering to get asked to stay but like any relationship, it was dangerous to go back without thinking about why you really wanted to leave.

El immediately thought about Derek. What if he had contacted her after they had broken up and said he wanted to get back together? She might have done it in the few months after the breakup when every song she heard and everything she saw seemed to remind her of him. But now… Now it was a little easier to clearly see what her friends had seen: it wasn't a good relationship for her.

As El waited in the conference room sipping her coffee, she wondered if she should say anything to Carl about going to the show with Bernie and meeting Greyson. As she thought about it, Carl rushed into the room, "Sorry, sorry. I have back-to-back meetings and the last one ran late."

El smiled. "Well that's what you get when you quit. Everyone wants to talk to you before you go."

He laughed. "It's worth it. I want to make sure everyone gets what they need. And, of course you know you can always call me." El pulled out her list of things she had questions about and they started working. They'd only gotten through the first three on the list when Carl's alarm reminded him of his next meeting and he rushed out the door.

At the end of the day, El looked at the piles of papers on her desk and felt a little overwhelmed. Kate was out of town and they were scheduled to meet the next week to talk about hiring Carl's replacement and how to handle the work. She was happy to leave it all behind and head to the Gecko.

The patio was already busy and El was glad to find a table. She felt a little bad that they hadn't invited Teresa, but she reasoned that her friend was probably with Jordan for the night. Leticia showed up fifteen minutes late and gave El a big hug. "Ugh traffic."

They glanced at the happy hour menu and ordered margaritas and the beef and chicken loaded nachos, a treat they wouldn't have had with Teresa. El asked what was going on at work and Leticia complained about a case she was working on. El then told her about all the work she had with Carl leaving.

"Okay. Spill it. What happened last night?" said Leticia sipping her drink.

El smiled. "The concert was great. Awesome band. Lots of fun."

Leticia tipped her head to the side. "Really? You know what I mean. Get to the good stuff."

"You mean how great dinner was, or how nice the place was, or what it was like meeting his ex-boyfriend?" El teased.

"Yep, back up. That's it."

El told her about meeting Greyson. "It was weird. I mean it would have been strange meeting Annie, his ex-girlfriend, but I didn't expect this."

"Do you want to date him?" asked Leticia. The nachos arrived, and they paused while they each tried a chip heavy with cheese and meat.

El's phone beeped and she looked down and laughed. "Perfect timing. It's him. He wants to know if I want to go out to dinner and a movie tomorrow night."

"And do you?"

"I don't know how I feel about dating a bi guy, and I don't even know if this is a date or not."

"El, you decide what you want and you tell him or ask him."

"What do you mean? Text him, hey is this a date or not? I can't do that. That'd be too weird."

"Weirder than worrying over and over about it?"

El nodded her head. "Still. I don't know."

"Don't text him," said Leticia draining her glass. "If it's bothering you so much, why don't you just call him and ask if he wants to go as friends or as a date? Or if you just want to be friends, let him know."

"Easy for you to say," mumbled El. She decided to change the subject. "And what about you and your mystery guy. Are you dating or just friends?"

Leticia pursed her lips and waved her hand dismissively. "I told you to drop it. What's so hard about that?" she snapped.

El sat back and stared with her mouth open. She rarely heard her friend sound like that, and certainly never towards her.

Leticia put her hand to her forehead and closed her eyes. She opened them, leaned forward, and spoke in a quiet voice. "I'm sorry. It's this case. It's driving me crazy. Between that and the hours, it's all getting to me." She called over the waitress and ordered another round of drinks and then launched into a story about how difficult her boss was being and how he was questioning her decisions on the case and denying her requests for additional help.

El stayed quiet as she listened and wondered what was causing her normally calm friend to act this way. Leticia switched the topic to the bridesmaids dresses and they talked about the wedding. Once they reached that point of discussion, El told Leticia that she was tired and left early. It hadn't been the fun evening she had been hoping for.

At home, she thought about what Leticia had said. She should decide what she wanted from Bernie instead of waiting for him to let her know. The problem was that she wasn't sure what she wanted. She thought back to the Byron Katie book and asked herself how she would feel if she didn't have this thought questioning if this was a date or not. The answer was clear. I'd feel great. I could just go and have a good time.

She texted Bernie. "Maybe." Smiley face. "What movie?"

"Your choice" came back the immediate response, followed by "Do you eat sushi?"

"Love it," El texted back. Then she opened the movies phone app and scoped out the independent and foreign film houses nearby. El watched a trailer for a documentary about mushrooms and laughed thinking it might be just quirky enough to be fun. She texted, "Fantastic Fungi?"

El's phone rang almost immediately. "Power to the Portabello. I'm wild about wild mushrooms." Bernie's voice boomed through the phone.

El laughed. "Fish and fungi it is then. What time? There's a showing of the film at 7 and another that starts at 9:20."

"I'll make a reservation for 6:30 and we'll shoot for the 9 p.m. show. So, how was your day?"

"Mixed." El didn't want to complain so she asked, "How was your day?"

"Great. A client was thrilled with the new logo I designed for his company, I had a short story accepted for publication, and I caught up with Greyson over drinks after work."

"Oh," El said again. "That's great news about your work." She wanted to ask how it felt spending time with Greyson, but she thought that might be too personal to ask. Instead she said, "I'm sure it was great to catch up."

"Yes, turns out he's involved with another emergency med doc, and it is serious enough that they are asking for assignments together. He showed me photos of them in Tanzania. The guy looks a lot like Henry Cavill. Greyson's a lucky man."

El was unsure if it was awe or jealousy in Bernie's voice. She wished they were on FaceTime so she could see the look in his eyes and his expression. Her mouth seemed to have a mind of its own: "Do you miss being with him?"

"I miss his humor, and I miss the ease. Being with Annie was much more work. But I'm grateful for every relationship I've had and every person I've dated. I learn more about myself and about humanity each time. Personal connections are important to me, El." Bernie paused, but before El could respond, he asked, "Is El short for something?"

El grinned. "My parents named me Cinderella. And despite that I have a brother Jack, we weren't named from fairytales." Nor do I live one, El silently added.

Bernie laughed. "If not from fairytales—"

El cut him off, knowing where they were headed. "My mom is from Philly and was in high school with the guys from the 80's glam band Cinderella. I think the one dude was maybe her first boyfriend or something."

"Wow."

"Exactly. So El is easier. Jack calls me Rella, but he's the only one."

"And Jack had nothing to do with beanstalks or candlesticks?"

"Nope. My grandfather and his father and grandfather were all named John, and Jack is a variation on that. My dad, who is John the fourth, didn't want to saddle his son with a fifth—"

"So instead he christened his son with Jack, which is sold by the fifth," Bernie cut in quick with the joke.

"You got it," El said.

"You have interesting parents."

"That's one way of looking at it." El laughed.

Feeling at ease with Bernie and their bantering, El took a quick breath and asked, "So may I ask you something?"

"Sure."

"Is tomorrow night a date? Or are we just two friends hanging out?"

Bernie chuckled. "Would you like it to be a date?"

"Yes. I think so," El said before thinking about the words.

"You think?"

"I mean yes," El said.

"No pressure," Bernie chuckled again. "I like you, El. We laugh and have fun together. Or at least I do and I think you're having fun, too."

"Oh I am." El said, but then added, " I haven't dated in a while. Long term relationship then six months of trying to figure out what being single is like..." She almost mentioned her research and the degree she was putting together but then decided that was TMI.

"And now?" Bernie coaxed and she could hear amusement in his voice.

"Now, I'm talking to a bi-guy about sushi and mushrooms and..." And El realized she said "bi-guy" and let the sentence trail off unsure of what to do.

"Does it bother you that I date men and women, El?

"No," she said automatically.

"Really?" Bernie sounded skeptical but not angry or sad. Again El wished she could see his face.

"It's new to me. I mean I've had bisexual and gay friends and classmates, but I've not dated anyone who was." El immediately wondered if she had stuck her foot in her mouth. They were going on one date...unless they counted the baking and the concert and she didn't know if Bernie did. Ugh! She felt uncomfortable and a bit out of control. She took a deep breath.

"It's okay, El. Thank you for being honest."

"Are you sure? I didn't mean to call you a bi-guy. It slipped out."

"It's fine. It is what I am. I'm attracted to people. The man or woman part is secondary. I wish we were face to face talking about this. That way I could touch your hair and tell you that when I saw you across the room at Carl's party, strangely, some lines from Stephen King's *It* came to me. 'Your hair is winter fire / January embers / My heart burns there, too.' I felt compelled to meet you."

El's heart raced. Compelled. He said, compelled. "That's so sweet. I'm glad you did. Of course it would have been better if I hadn't..."

"Wine under the bridge," Bernie joked. "But seriously, El. Let's hang out tomorrow. Seriously no pressure. We'll put the fun in fungi and see where this goes."

El laughed. "Sounds like a good plan."

Mr. Fluffy stalked into the room and let loose a big meow.

"That is one pissed off cat," Bernie said. "I'd hate to get on his bad side."

El laughed. "He's demanding more dinner. At this rate, he'll be thirty pounds by Thanksgiving."

"Tell him to save the butterball for the turkey," Bernie said. "And how about if I swing by to get you tomorrow and meet the fierce beast. Mr. Fluffy, I believe you said he was called."

"Sounds good. Thank you, Bernie. Have a good night."

"*A demain*, El."

El smiled at the phone before standing up and dancing her way into the kitchen to take care of the cat's needs. She had a date. A real date. Woohooo.

Chapter 12

El awoke the next morning with Pharrell Williams' "Happy" running through her head. She shimmied her way into the shower and sung along with the music in her mind. Damn, the acoustics were good in her shower. She wished she always sounded that way.

When she got out, she saw a message from Jack asking if she would join him for coffee. He said he was considering adding a local brew to one of his trucks and wanted her opinion. She was not a coffee connoisseur but thought it would be fun and texted a quick "yes" and got the name of the place.

A few minutes later he sent, "Great, Owen will be joining us too."

Idiot! She thought, it's a good thing that family is so important to me. She knew he was trying to help her, but she didn't know if she wanted to reconnect with Owen. After all, she was going out on a date that night. She thought about what Leticia would say and realized that it was the perfect time to meet him. She was in a great mood and wasn't feeling any pressure to like him or not since she had a date later. Why not?

She briefly debated what to wear. When she thought she was just meeting Jack, she was just going to wear a comfy T-shirt and yoga pants. She decided to go with that anyway, but she put on a little more makeup and a new bright pink lipstick she had just picked up.

Corner Coffee was easy to find, and when she walked in, she saw Jack waving at her. The other person at the table turned to her and she momentarily paused. He had definitely grown up. He smiled when he saw her and stood up to greet her. His black hair was cropped close and he had a neatly trimmed goatee. She had not remembered how white his teeth were or how broad his shoulders were in his dark green Ralph Lauren polo shirt. She wished she had worn something else.

"El, it's so nice to see you."

"You, too." And she meant it.

He gestured to the chair next to him. "When Jack said that you were going to join us, I couldn't wait to catch up with you."

El remembered that Jack was there and looked at his slightly amused face.

"Yeah, El, why don't you sit and I'll order one for you. Iced Caramel Macchiato with Soy?"

"Sure." She thought, whatever, let me talk to Owen. She sat down and tried to re-engage her brain. She was having a hard time reconciling the geeky high schooler that she remembered with the man sitting next to her.

She smiled and said, "What are you up to?"

He said, "Well actually, I've been in New York the last few years and just moved back to the area last year for a great opportunity." He talked about how much he had enjoyed being on the East Coast but how happy he was to be back. He described his new job and the company he was working for.

When Jack came back to the table, he started teasing Owen about something he had done back in high school. El watched them joke back and forth. Then Jack got back to business and asked Owen questions about his coffee and talked about some of his new ideas to expand the food trucks. El sipped her coffee when it was ready and answered Jack's questions. Jack took it from her, tasted it, and nodded.

When Jack was finished discussing the coffees, he said, "Rella, tell him about what you're doing now." El talked about work and the problems she was having with Carl leaving. She briefly thought about Bernie and felt bad until she looked at Owen's chocolate brown eyes.

Owen told some funny stories about his co-workers and new boss. The time went by quickly. El enjoyed listening to Owen and Jack joking back and forth. Jack finally asked, "So Owen, did you tell Rella about your new project?"

"Project?" asked Owen, looking at Jack.

"You know, now that you're back in the area, checking out interesting restaurants."

"Oh yeah, I wasn't really thinking about that as a project. I just thought it would be fun to check out lists of restaurants and try some new places." He looked at El, "I found a great brunch place that I've wanted to try. It's supposed to have awesome stuffed French toast and crepes. Would you two like to go tomorrow?"

"Not me, I already have plans, but you should go," said Jack quickly.

El would have been annoyed at her brother as this was clearly a set up...but she was dying to spend more time with Owen.

"That sounds like fun," she said. "When and where should I meet you?"

She couldn't wait to text Leticia and Teresa with the news. This was turning out to be an interesting weekend.

Her friends responded quickly: they wanted details. She texted Teresa back first since she felt bad about going out without her the night before. She mentioned to both of them how much cuter Owen looked than she had remembered.

She sat back on the couch and sighed. Bernie. Owen. Relationships. This was so complicated.

She was about to text Leticia again when she saw a message from PJ setting up a meeting for El to talk to her friend, Kimbry, during the following week. El happily accepted the meeting. PJ messaged, "The topic is authenticity. Before the meeting, you need to find a list of values online and pick your top ten values. Things you won't compromise."

El was excited to meet one of PJ's contacts but surprised by the assignment. She hadn't really spent a lot of time thinking about her values. How difficult could it be? Most values were probably pretty universal, right? She decided this would be a great time for her to review them. That way she wouldn't have to think about Bernie or Owen.

She looked online for values lists and found plenty. She picked one from Carnegie Mellon University and started to review it. She laughed to herself when she saw relationships and love on the list. She agreed with many of the values, things like acceptance, preparedness, professionalism, and teamwork, so El thought paring the list to only ten would be difficult. She decided to pick all the ones that resonated and would then start to reduce the list.

When she saw values like success and wealth, she thought that they were important but not as important to her as some of the other ones. Derek would have picked those first. She paused and thought about how mismatched she and Derek had been. He really believed those were most important. When she tried to focus on wealth the way he did, it felt like she was doing it for him not for her.

She went back to her list and carefully culled out the values that sounded good but that didn't really connect with her. She cut being the best, advocacy, grace, and brilliance from the list. Resilience was great to have but it didn't resonate with her as a core value. Neither did daring. She thought about where she spent her time and energy. It felt strange not to pick success because she did want to be successful but her work was more than that. It was also about having fun doing interesting work that made a difference.

She finally ended up with a list of ten words. Kindness and learning were at the top. Yes, she thought, these are the things that I care about. Friendship and family were also on her list. Even though Jack could be annoying, she appreciated him, and she had learned a lot from him, but at times she hated to admit that about her "little" brother.

Reading through that list of values made El think about what she valued in others. Honesty and humor were probably at the top of her list, for both her friendships and any romantic interests. When she saw originality, open-mindedness, and creativity on the list, she automatically thought of Bernie. Warmth made her think of the way Owen looked at her; his brown eyes made her melt. She sighed, and then felt her heart flutter. Two dates with two different guys in one weekend. Not even in college had she done that. She felt giddy.

She walked into the kitchen to make some tea and saw that Mr. Fluffy's bowl was empty. She filled it before the cat threw a fit. She glanced at the clock and realized she needed to start to get ready. Bernie would arrive in an hour for their date.

She took her cup of tea into the bathroom and plugged in her curling iron. While it heated, she flipped through the tops hanging in her closet. Nothing seemed quite right. She pulled her favorite pair of jeans from a drawer and laid them on the bed. She found a featherweight black cashmere sweater in a different drawer. It had a deep v in the front. El exchanged her T-shirt for the sweater and looked in the mirror. It looked okay but not awesome.

She texted Leticia. "Got a minute? I need date outfit advice."

El's FaceTime rang. "Hey," El said to Leticia's face. She was holding the phone so close to her face that no background was showing. "Where are you?"

"Uh, work."

"On a Saturday?"

"Where's the outfit?" Leticia changed the subject.

"I was thinking this sweater and jeans but it isn't wowing me."

"Pull the phone back or show me you in the mirror."

El put the phone at arm's length so Leticia could see the whole sweater.

"That sweater needs some cleavage. Just a hint. Where's your push up bra?"

"Hang on." El put the phone down so Leticia was looking at the ceiling. She took off the sweater and her bra and changed into her lace demi bra and then put the sweater back on. As she was doing that she heard Leticia's snarky comment: "This is the way it is with some guys. I stare at the ceiling and wait for them to be done."

"Very funny," El said though she wasn't laughing. That's how it felt with Derek too often towards the end of their relationship.

She picked the phone back up and held it out for Leticia to see. Just a bit of breast swell could be seen at the bottom of the v. Leticia whistled. "Pair with butt hugging jeans and boots, and maybe some hoop earrings and curl your hair and you're good to go."

"Thank you." El said. She was scrutinizing the sliver of space she could see behind Leticia's head. It didn't look like her office. The wall was kind of bare. "Hey, can I call you before tomorrow's brunch date?"

"Text first," Leticia said. "I'm supposed to meet a friend later tonight so I might not be free."

"A friend, huh?" El grinned. "Does the friend have a name?"

"I have to go," Leticia said. "Have fun and don't do anything I wouldn't do."

"Ha," El said. "Then I'm wide open."

"Kiss kiss," Leticia said and quickly signed off.

Weird, El thought. Why was Leticia so damn secretive lately, and where was she? El wasn't buying the "I'm at the office" routine.

She went into the bathroom to drink her lukewarm tea and curl her hair. As she did, she used the speakerphone to call Teresa, who answered on the second ring with, "What's up, date girl?"

El chuckled. "Do you know what's going on with Leticia? We just FaceTimed to choose my outfit—"

"I wanna see," Teresa said, and she hung up and FaceTimed immediately.

"I'm not completely done yet," El said. "But here's the sweater."

"Oooo, nice cleavage. A hint of the girls can be so enticing." Teresa grinned.

"Right," El said. And I'll put my jeans and boots and earrings on when I'm done with my hair." She had ringlets hanging on one side of her head now. "But about Leticia. She held the phone so close up she was almost all nose. It was like she didn't want me to see where she was. And when I asked she said, 'work,' but the glimpse I got had no bookshelves and was of a fairly bare wall."

Before Teresa could say anything, a thought occurred to El that she voiced aloud with her eyebrows furrowed. "You don't think she'd be hooking up in a hotel room, do you?"

Teresa grimaced. "Not unless she met an out-of-towner. We know how she feels about married men. And she didn't mention a weekend getaway."

"She said tonight she was meeting up with a friend."

"What's his name? Jackson?"

"She wouldn't say," El said. She twirled another set of hairs around the wand.

"Weird. She has been acting strangely," Teresa said. "At first I thought it was because of me and Jordan and the wedding, like she was either sick of the planning or jealous that I found my soulmate."

El started to say that Leticia wasn't the jealous type but then stopped herself. Leticia was totally driven and envied certain things people had attained or purchased. But like Derek, Leticia's need to accomplish, be recognized, and achieve success fueled the comparisons. Intimacy, love, and permanent romantic partnerships were not Leticia's top values.

"Why would Leticia not tell us who she's seeing? She's never been embarrassed so it can't be that."

"And I doubt he's married," Teresa said. "Could it be someone we know and we'd disapprove of?"

"Maybe," El said. "Though we've never stopped one another from dating anyone, even people we couldn't stand. Remember when L was hooking up with that senior baller during freshman year? He was such a player and the worst, but we told her what we thought and let her do her thing. And were there to pick up the pieces afterwards. It's what we do. Just like you guys did with me and Derek, and we did with you and what's his face." Holy crap, El couldn't believe she was blanking on Teresa's ex's name.

"Good old what's his face. What a dumbass," Teresa shook her head. "Best breakup that ever happened to me because it prepared me for Jordan." Teresa sighed and smiled dreamily.

"Yep." El curled her last clump of hair and then unplugged the iron. "I've gotta finish getting ready. Bernie will be here soon."

"You kids have fun," Teresa waved and laughed.

"That's the plan," El said. "Goodnight." She blew Teresa a kiss and hung up.

El drank the last swallow of her cold tea, brushed her teeth, spritzed just a bit of perfume on her neck below each ear lobe, and then finished getting dressed. She appraised herself in the full-length mirror inside her closet door. She liked the way she looked and the way she felt: sexy, stylish, and happy.

And as she shut the closet door, her buzzer rang. She raced to the living room and said, "Yes?" into the intercom.

"It's Bernie."

"Come on up," El said, while pushing the downstairs door release. She had told him which apartment number earlier. She opened the living room door and turned to Mr. Fluffy and said, "Here it goes. You be nice."

Mr. Fluffy licked the back of one paw like he was bored with her request.

"I mean it," El said.

Bernie, attired in black jeans, a ruby sweater, and short black biker boots, hugged El when he saw her. "You look great," he said. "And you smell great too."

El smiled. "Thank you. You too. I mean, I love the color of your sweater and how soft it is." She ran a hand down his sleeve. "So soft."

"I know," he grinned. "And you're not exactly spiky yourself." He ran his hand on El's sweater at her forearm.

She laughed, and then felt self conscious so she turned towards the living room and said, "This is Mr. Fluffy. Mr. Fluffy meet Bernie."

Bernie crouched to the cat's level and held out his hand. "Aren't you a looker?"

The cat licked the back of his left paw, and then deliberately stalked towards Bernie, who stayed perfectly still. El held her breath, unsure of what Mr. Fluffy would do. When he reached Bernie's outstretched hand, Mr. Fluffy batted it with his paw, but only with his soft paw; no claws were extended.

"Ah, so you high five, I see," Bernie said. He fist bumped the cat's paw, and the cat lunged at him, and El shrieked no. But Bernie's reflexes were quick and the cat's intentions were not what El thought. Mr. Fluffy put a paw on each side of Bernie's neck in a cat-hug and licked him once on the nose. Bernie held the cat's back end to his chest. "What an affectionate, bugger." Bernie said. "I love him."

El's mouth was gaping. Even Jack, the favorite male in Mr. Fluffy's and El's life, had never had a welcome like this. "Maybe he smells Remington and Qwerty," El said, trying to rationalize the response. Hell, Mr. Fluffy never even welcomed her like this…ever.

Bernie put Mr. Fluffy down on the sofa. "He is a beauty."

"Thank you," El said to Bernie. To Mr. Fluffy, she said, "Now you be good, while I go out with Bernie."

As she shut and locked her front door she remarked, "Mr. Fluffy would probably love to eat sushi with us."

"What a business idea: a cat-friendly sushi place. Though all of their profits would probably be stolen by sneaky paws," Bernie said. He put his arm around El's shoulder as they walked down the hallway and entered the elevator. El liked the way his arm felt on her. When they got to his Prius, he opened the passenger door for her.

The restaurant Bernie had chosen had a number of tables for two

100

and the option of a chef's choice prix fixe menu or a la cart. Bernie suggested they do the lower number chef's choice as that still gave them nineteen servings of sushi each. El tried not to gawk at the price, and suggested instead choosing a few things a la cart.

Bernie said, "El, this is one of my favorite places. It's all great, but trust me when I say let's do the chef's choice. It's well worth it and it's my treat. Do you like your sake hot or cold?"

El had never had it hot, but she didn't want to seem ignorant so she said, "I'll have it however it pairs best with the food."

"Good," Bernie said. He chatted a few moments with the waitress over what sake she recommended with today's fish choices and offerings. El looked around at the spartan yet elegant decor. So many natural elements in the room, from the wood tables and chairs to the stone chopstick rests at each place setting, the calligraphy on scrolls of rice paper on the walls, the candlelight. The place was elegant and romantic. And El felt sophisticated just being there.

When the waitress poured the sushi, Bernie raised his cup toward El, "To a fun evening with a beautiful redhead." El grinned and touched her cup to his.

"Thank you," she said, as the first course, tiny bowls of miso soup arrived. The soup was the most fragrant miso El had ever eaten and she loved its almost silky texture.

Bernie closed his eyes as he drank the soup. He looks so peaceful and happy, El thought.

The courses arrived at a leisurely pace and with each one, El thought the food couldn't get any better. She had eaten a lot of sushi in her life, from grocery store California rolls to rectangles of glistening sashimi at local hot spots, but never before had she had a sushi experience like this. The flavors were somehow both delicate and powerful at the same time. The textures were smooth and dense and light all at the same time. Her sense of smell felt heightened and her sense of taste seemed sensual.

She and Bernie talked of work and world events and random things but their conversation kept returning to the round at hand or to the fruity yet dry icy sake that enlivened their tastebuds and refreshed their mouths between courses.

After a bit of yellowtail with jalapeno and a dollop of sauce, El remarked, "I think I'm having a religious experience. You've permanently converted me from supermarket sushi."

Bernie laughed. "Food fresh from the source is sacred and divine. And when simply prepared, it's at its best. I may not know how to cook much but I know food. I love food." He raised his glass again. "To food. This is divine. And so is being with you."

El felt herself blush. She wanted to protest, like she didn't deserve the compliment, but she stopped herself remembering one of PJ's business lessons: Take the compliment. Accept it. Don't discount it. Move on. "I'm having a wonderful time," El said. "Thank you very much." She reached across the table and squeezed his hand.

"I'm glad, El," he said. "And sad that we only have two courses left. Oh, except for dessert. Maybe a bit of green tea ice cream? We'll see what they have tonight."

As they left the restaurant and walked to the movie theater, Bernie put his arm around El and leaned down and kissed the top of her head. "Thank you," he said.

"For what?"El's eyes searched his.

"For being you. For taking me to the movies. For joining my religious movement." Bernie chuckled at his own joke.

"Thank you for sharing one of your favorite places with me," El said, "but don't thank me for the movie yet. It may not be fun with fungi."

"Oh. I think almost anywhere might be fun with you," Bernie said. They had stopped in front of the theater and he was looking at her intensely. El, almost on autopilot, leaned up to meet his lips with hers. She wasn't sure if it was the half-bottle of sake she had drunk or the power of the kiss's passion, but El felt a bit lightheaded. It was a good thing Bernie's arms were around her holding her up.

She felt her body relax and focused on the feeling of his lips against hers. Bernie's hand pressed against her back and pulled her closer. His other hand caressed the nape of her neck.

"Nice," he whispered into her ear as he continued to hold her close. His breath tickled her ear.

"Yes, very nice," she agreed.

"Maybe we should skip the movie," said Bernie. He pulled back so she could see his eyes and teasing smile.

She smiled back, "I think we should still go."

"Oh all right," he said. "If that's what you want." He unwrapped his arms and El momentarily wondered if maybe they should skip the movie. His left hand reached for El's right hand and she felt the warmth of his fingers.

When they sat down, Bernie gently rested his hand on hers. Normally El would have enjoyed the movie—it had the right amount of action and humor—but El found herself thinking back to that kiss. When Bernie lightly rubbed his finger against the back of her hand, she momentarily closed her eyes to remember how his body had felt against hers. It took effort to focus back on the screen.

During the ride home, as they joked about parts of the movie, El wondered what would happen when they got to her place. More importantly, she wondered what did she want to happen?

When the car stopped, she turned to look at him, saw his half-smile, and paused. Before she could say anything, he said, "Can I walk you to your door?"

"That would be very nice. Thank you."

At her door, she turned and felt his arms around her. His lips pressed against hers and he stroked her hair. "Thank you for a wonderful night, Cinderella."

"Nobody calls me that," she protested.

"Well maybe I will," he said, kissing her again.

When she went into the apartment, she fell back on the bed. She wanted to text her friends but decided that it was too late. It would have to wait until morning. Ugh, morning. She thought about having brunch with Owen. Suddenly that didn't seem like such a good idea.

As she got ready for bed, her phone beeped. She grabbed it wondering if it was from one of the girls. It was from Bernie and said, "That kiss was amazing and so are you. Sweet dreams, Cinderella."

She wondered what to say. Finally she sent "sweet dreams" with a kiss emoji.

Chapter 13

When she got up the next morning, she briefly considered calling Owen and cancelling brunch. But then she thought that Jack would be annoyed at her and it wouldn't be very nice. Owen did say that he wanted to try the place, so why not. It wasn't a date. It was simply two old friends getting together to share a meal. Okay, technically he was Jack's friend but she'd spent time with him when they were in high school also, mostly when he was hanging around the house with Jack and they were bothering her.

She texted Leticia and Teresa, "Awesome date with Bernie! Talk later?" Teresa responded right away and said she wanted details. El laughed when she thought about what her friends would say. She looked at the clock and realized that she needed to hurry. She wanted to upgrade from the yoga pants she had worn the day before when she had met Owen. She picked out a bright green T-shirt that set off her hair, along with tan khakis and open-toed heels that showed off her orange toenails. Right before leaving, she got Leticia's response saying she wanted to hear all about it.

Owen was waiting for her inside the restaurant and greeted her with a big smile. "I already put in our name. It'll be a few minutes." His blue, green, and white striped polo shirt emphasized his wide shoulders and El remembered why she had been so eager to say "yes" to brunch.

As they waited, Owen continued the conversation that they had been having yesterday with Jack. For a moment, it felt odd to El because so much had happened to her since then.

They were soon seated at a four-person table and instead of sitting opposite her, Owen sat next to her. She breathed in the slight muskiness of his cologne. "What are you in the mood for today?" he asked, smiling.

"What do you recommend?"

"I've never been here before but I've heard their eggs benedict with brisket is delicious and so are their raspberry chocolate crepes and stuffed French toast."

El looked at the menu. "Mmmm, it all sounds delicious. It's going to be hard to decide." They discussed some options back and forth.

"How about this, I'll get the eggs benedict and you get the french toast and we can share."

"Awesome idea. I'm in," she agreed.

He grinned and El noticed the dimples on his cheeks. She hadn't remembered that from the day before or from high school. He leaned toward her, his forearm almost touching hers.

"How are your parents doing? Your mom was always so nice to me."

El smiled, "She liked you. She said you were always very polite."

Owen laughed. "I don't know about that. But I do know it was great being at your place. It was so much quieter than my house."

El thought about his older brother and sister and two younger twin sisters. "I bet that was a little noisy." They talked about their parents and siblings. Owen shared that his brother was married with a new baby and he loved being an uncle. He was filling El in on what his sisters were doing when the server came and they ordered breakfast with a Bloody Mary for Owen and a mimosa for El.

When the food arrived, El took a bite of the crunchy French toast stuffed with a sweet ricotta filling and declared it to be delicious. She thought that she'd really need to work out extra that week to take care of the previous night's dinner and this meal. She momentarily felt guilty about Bernie and reminded herself that this was just brunch.

Owen took a bite of the eggs benedict, closed his eyes, and said it was heavenly. His satisfied grin made El laugh and she said, "It must be really good for you to say that."

"Here, you try it," he said, putting some on his fork and holding it out for her so she could take a bite. She hesitated and then ate it. She'd never had anyone feed her. She agreed it was wonderful and asked if he wanted some of hers. He nodded and she fed it to him while he looked into her eyes. "Delicious," he said slowly and she felt herself blushing.

She decided to change the subject and asked how he had gotten in touch with Jack. Owen explained that they'd stayed connected but only started messaging a few months earlier when he had moved back to the area. "We got together about a month ago for beers. It was great to hear what he's done with the food trucks."

They continued to talk about Jack as they ate. Owen brought up several stories about high school and asked if she remembered some of the homecoming games and other events. They joked about old times and some of the funny things they had done.

"Remember the semi-formal dances?" he said.

El laughed. "Yeah, I remember that my friend Maureen's dad was the DJ. He was really nice but he always told the same lame jokes."

"But he played great songs." He paused. "Do you remember the semi-formal your senior year?" He looked down at his coffee. "I wanted to go to the dance with you, but I was too nervous to ask you out." He looked up at her, his brown eyes serious. "Pretty silly, huh."

El felt herself start to blush again. "No, that's really sweet. I had no idea."

He leaned closer to her. "Well, I was just a friend of your little brother. I didn't think that would go over very well." He put his hand on her arm. "Do you think it's too late to ask you out?"

The blushing continued and El felt that she must be bright red. "I don't think it's too late."

"There's no dance coming up, so we'll have to think of something else to do."

El grinned. "Sounds good to me."

After brunch, Owen walked her to her car. When they got to the car, he said, "Is this where I get the kiss I could have gotten after the school dance?"

She put her hand out and rested it lightly on his chest. She tilted her head to the side and smiled. "I think you're going to have to wait until after the dance."

He smiled and showed his dimples. "Fair enough," he said. "Until the dance."

She took her hand away, said good-bye, and stepped into the car. She didn't remember the drive to her apartment. She walked in and her phone beeped. It was a message from Bernie. "Hope you're having a great day. When can we get together again?"

El smiled but decided not to answer right away. She sat on the sofa, and Mr. Fluffy immediately joined her. He sniffed her suspiciously before circling once and lying down next to her. El scratched his chin, sighed, and then texted Teresa and Leticia. "Two dates within 18 hours. Need to debrief."

Teresa responded immediately with, "Three pints of Ben & Jerry's are on their way. See you within the hour."

Leticia didn't respond via text. Instead, ten minutes after El had texted, she buzzed El to be let into her building. El and Mr. Fluffy were both waiting in the open doorway when Leticia appeared in the hallway. She was wearing a T-shirt emblazoned with the logo of Jack's most recent food truck enterprise, tied into a knot at her waist, atop higher waisted jeans. El marveled that even in casual clothes, Leticia looked stylish, like a runway model between shows.

Leticia carried a bottle of Veuve Clicquot pink champagne. "You entering the dating pool is something to celebrate," she said to El as she entered the apartment and hugged her. "Greetings, Mr. Fluffy. You may now have some competition for her affection again."

El laughed. She took the proffered bottle of bubbly into the kitchen. "I'll open this when T gets here." She put the bottle into the refrigerator to keep it cold, then she turned to Leticia. "Since when did you turn into a walking billboard for Jack?"

"Since his truck was near my office and I needed a smoothie. He was there that day and gave me a free shirt."

"That was nice of him," El said.

"Besides, the color looks great on me." Leticia batted her eyes playfully, completely out of character, which made El laugh.

"It most certainly does. But you look good in almost anything. It's me with my red hair and pale skin that doesn't have so many options." El frowned.

"Said the woman two guys will be vying over soon." Leticia sat on El's sofa and faced her, "So, how does it feel to be playing the field?"

"It feels great. And scary. And awesome. And nerve-wracking. Both of them wanted to kiss me, well, Bernie and I did…a few times...

very intensely actually."

"And?"

"Then when Owen wanted to kiss me a few hours later, it seemed wrong or too soon or slutty."

Leticia laughed. "A kiss is a kiss. It doesn't have to mean anything. And you can kiss as many people as you want. In whatever time frame you want. No judgment."

"Well, not from you," El acknowledged. "You kiss or do whatever you please with whomever you please, no commitment."

"You can, too," Leticia said. "The only one judging you is yourself, and you can free yourself from that."

"Maybe," El said. "So tell me, who are you seeing, or how many? You always seem so busy anymore and I'm not buying that it's all work."

Leticia smiled in a way that made El think she enjoyed her secret. "It is...mostly."

"And when it isn't?" El maintained eye contact with her best friend. Leticia shrugged.

"You're not sleeping with your boss, are you?"

"Oh hell, no. El, you know me better than that."

"I do. But in all of these years, you've never been as secretive as you have been lately. That has me worried. You and me and T, for eight years we've told each other everything."

"True. But for once, this doesn't concern just me. I promise I'll tell you when we're ready."

"We? You are part of a we?" El was stunned.

Leticia recovered quickly and said, "Not exactly. But what started as casual may not be. But today isn't about me. It's about you. So tell me about those two hot men. I want details, now. And we need wine for this if you're holding off on the champagne until Teresa gets here..." Leticia stood up and walked towards El's kitchen to check for wine just as the buzzer went off announcing Teresa's arrival.

"This isn't over, Leticia." El said as she opened the door and waited for Teresa. She heard the champagne cork pop.

"It is for now, El. I promise, I'll spill everything soon. Trust me."

The "trust me" cut to El's heart. Her best friends had never had to say that before. Of course she trusted Leticia and Teresa. She trusted them as much as she trusted Jack. Hell, she trusted the three of them more than Mr. Fluffy. He was way more unpredictable. The thought made El smile.

She hugged Teresa before she walked through the apartment door. Teresa asked, "Leticia never responded?"

El said, "She's here. Didn't text but showed up. Brought bubbly and just opened it so you're right on time." She took the bag of ice cream from Teresa and pulled out the three pints. "Oooo, Phish Food, my favorite. Thank you, T."

"Of course. I got Leticia Cherry Garcia as I know how much she likes it, and I saw they had that new unicorn flavor so I figured I'd try that." Teresa wore a navy boho dress that had a small floral pattern; her hair was in a single braid down her back. On her feet were Birkenstocks.

El was once again struck by their closeness despite their very different styles. She loved them more than sisters. They were the best. She held her fluted glass aloft and said, "To my very best friends. I couldn't navigate through life or dating without you."

"Ditto," Leticia said.

"Cheers," Teresa said, as she clinked her glass to theirs.

After they settled in the living room and dug into the pints of ice cream, Teresa said, "So start with last night. How was the date? Oh wait, before you tell us, I've never seen Bernie so Google a photo of him. One of Owen, too. I need to see who we are talking about."

El grabbed her laptop and searched for images of each guy. Teresa declared Bernie, "cute in a creative hipster kind of way" and she cooed over Owen's angular jawline and broad shoulders. "Bet you'd feel enclosed in his hug," she said.

"Yes, he's a great hugger." El grinned.

Leticia eyed Owen's photo. "Big, hot, and handsome. Way to go, El."

El laughed. "Thank you. They are both great. And you're right: they are very different. Bernie took me to a sushi restaurant that served some of the best food I've ever eaten. Best sake I've ever had, too. And we mostly watched a documentary about mushrooms...in between kissing." El laughed nervously. "I think he would have been happier to skip the movie and come back here, but I wasn't ready for that."

"And how did you end things for the night? Teresa asked.

"Oh he texted me after I got home, and then again today asking me on another date." El giggled, and shoved a big bite of ice cream into her mouth.

"You must be some kisser," Leticia joked. "What'd you tell him?"

"I haven't answered. I'm playing harder to get." El grinned.

"Or making him want you more," Leticia said.

"It's good to make him wait," Teresa said. "Of course with Jordan and me, it was different. I just knew on that first date that he was the one—"

Leticia rolled her eyes at El and said, "Yeah, yeah. He's the one. But we're talking about El here. And she was just about to move on to Ooooowen who will make her say 'oooooh, baby.'" A devilish grin was on Leticia's face and her eyes sparkled.

El and Teresa laughed. "Owen. Yes, he's definitely something to look at. And those biceps. Wow. And he's sooo nice. He admitted that he wanted to ask me out while we were in high school but was too shy and thought I'd say no because he was Jack's friend. And he's right. I might have. He seemed dorky then and annoying. Just like Jack." El sighed. "But now…"

She ate another bite of Ben & Jerry's chocolate heaven. "Now he's super hot and wants to take me dancing."

"Dancing is not the only thing I'd want to do with him," Leticia said.

"Yeah, me neither," El admitted. "But what do I do? How do I do this? I can't just date both of them."

"Why can't you?" Leticia asked.

"Yes, El, why can't you?" Teresa agreed. "You need to get to know them. No one is asking you to make a decision or choose. They certainly aren't. They see a pretty woman they want to date. They aren't thinking of forever. Don't limit yourself. Have fun."

Leticia stared with her mouth agape at Teresa. "Aren't those usually my lines?"

Teresa laughed. "Maybe. I mean things are different with me and Jordan. But El, you've hardly dated. You aren't even sure what you want in a long-term guy. And what'd you say PJ said, you have to work on you first. You have to know who you are and what you want so you don't end up the second-class citizen in a relationship like you were with Derek."

"Ouch," El said.

"Sorry. You know I love you. I want what's best. And that's to see you in a relationship where you don't lose or suppress yourself. Be the awesome Wonder Woman we know you are," Teresa said.

"Thank you," El said. "I don't want another relationship like that either."

"And you need to give yourself permission to date two guys or two hundred. The number doesn't matter," Leticia said. "Figure out what makes you happy. That's what matters."

"Speaking of happiness," Teresa said. "El, I hope you don't mind, but I signed us up for a fun class."

"Huh?" El said, spoon of ice cream halfway to her mouth.

"Well, I would have signed up Leticia, too, but she never seems to have any time any more." Teresa eyed Leticia, who smiled at her, and said, "True. So what are you and El doing?"

"We're going to learn to pole dance," Teresa said, a smile plastered on her face.

"Oh hell, no," El said.

"Please? I need you to come with me. I can't do this alone. And I planned it as a wedding night surprise for Jordan. Please don't let me down." Teresa pleaded with El.

El sighed. "When is it?"

"Thursday night for an hour and a half. Come to the teaser class with me, and if you absolutely hate it, you don't have to go again. I promise. But I need you there, and it will be fun. Seriously."

El tilted her head. "And what does one wear to pole dancing?" she asked aloud while thinking, good grief, the things we do for our best friends.

"Thank you! You're a peach!" Teresa grinned.

"Apparently, a pole dancing peach."

When her friends left, El thought more about dating Owen and Bernie. Her friends had helped put the situation into perspective but she still felt uneasy. She texted Bernie and said she'd like to get together with him soon.

Chapter 14

It was Carl's last week at work so Monday was busy as El tried to make sure she got as much information from him as possible. Fortunately, that meant she barely had time to think about her dating issues. At the end of the day, she left later than normal and barely had time for a quick salad before her call with PJ's friend, Kimbry.

While she was eating her salad, El reviewed the values work that she had done in preparation. She had compared each of the values with the others to develop her priority list. When the call came through, she was ready. Kimbry had a round smiling face and her dark hair was in cornrows. El smiled back and was glad she looked friendly. El appreciated PJ's connections but some of them were intimidating.

"Hello, you must be El. It's so nice to meet you. PJ told me about your Master's Degree in Relationships. I'm intrigued and happy to help you with your studies."

El felt herself starting to blush. "Well, I'm just starting. I'm not sure where I'm going with it."

Kimbry held up a hand to stop her, and El noticed her many silver bracelets and rings. "Please, it sounds like fun. Let me introduce myself. I'm Kimbry Stone and I teach women how to be authentic."

"That sounds amazing," said El. She quickly introduced herself and said, "I did the pre-work. Do you want to start with that?"

Kimbry grinned and said, "Let's look at the big picture first." She gestured with both hands, palms out. "Let me tell you what I tell my students: before you get into a relationship and try to understand someone else, you need to understand who you really are. In my classes, women spend time understanding how their backgrounds, their families, their experiences, and their beliefs have brought them to where they are now.

"People have their brains, their hearts, and their bodies, and it's important for all three to be aligned. So many times, I see women and their hearts are at war with their brains and they wonder why they're not happy.

"Brene Brown has a wonderful book, *The Gifts of Imperfection: Let Go of Who You Think You're Supposed To Be And Embrace Who You Are*. Think about that for a minute. We all have an idea of who we think we should be, but why? Why do we think that? Is it something our parents said when we were small and we never questioned it? Did we come up with a picture of an ideal person from what we learned in school or from society? What makes that persona perfect and us not? Once you can let go of the idea that you need to be some sort of perfect person and you can relax, life gets a whole lot easier." She paused and looked at El. "Questions? What do you think?"

El looked off to the side, "I guess I never really thought about it. Are you saying that striving to be perfect isn't a good idea?"

"I'm saying that you should be the best you, not some plastic version of yourself that you imagine would be perfect because of some stories you're telling yourself."

"Huh, I'll have to think about that a little more," said El sipping her tea.

"Let's tie it to relationships. If we're focused on being a perfect ideal person then we won't allow ourselves the opportunity to understand who we really are. And if we don't know who we really are, we can't actually get close to someone else, because we'll be afraid that they'll see that we're not the perfect ideal person."

El nodded. "That makes sense. But what's the alternative?"

"The alternative is really understanding who you are and what you value, not what you think other people or society is telling you."

El tipped her head. "But what if other people don't like that?"

"Exactly. That's exactly what you want." She paused and waited for El's reaction.

"That's what you want?" El was confused.

"Yes. You don't need to have everyone like you. If you're true to yourself, you'll be able to connect with people who are naturally like you and you can relax and be yourself. This can help you to think about the question, what is your main assignment of life? Why are you here?" She paused. "Maybe I'm getting ahead of myself. Let's get back to relationships. You need to know who you are so you can let people know the real you. Let me tell you about my first husband. I got married young and I didn't really know who I was. My husband was a nice guy and a big sports fan. I was not. Frankly, I didn't care at all and I barely knew the names of the teams he was rooting for, but it was really important to him and I went along with it. And I'm not proud of this, but I cared about him so much that I told him I was a big sports fan and I tried to learn everything I could about sports so we could share it. But the problem was that after I learned about it, I still didn't care. I kept up the charade though and we went to games and I started to feel more and more disconnected. And then I felt annoyed and resentful when he would want to go to games and I started arguing with him, telling him that the tickets cost too much and were taking up too much of his time." She looked serious. "I said everything but what was really bothering me. I didn't care about this and I told him I did. When I think about it now, I realize I was lying to myself."

El thought about Derek. She had tried to get excited about his business deals, but they really weren't what she cared about. "That sounds good but what would have happened if you had told him you didn't like sports?"

"Either we would have built a relationship based on truth or we would have stopped dating. Because my truth was that wasn't important to me and it would have been better if I'd recognized that and let him know."

"And when would you have told him?"

"That brings me to my most important relationship advice. Let the other person know right away who you are and what you value. Then you can both decide if you want to move forward. So many people spend the first few months hiding themselves and only sharing the best about them. I think they figure if they only share the good stuff, they'll get the other person to like them enough so that the other stuff won't matter as much. Of course, part of the problem is that both people are doing it at the same time so you don't know what's real. It's such a waste of time and energy."

"It does sound silly when you say it like that," agreed El.

"Yes, one of my friends started dating someone and she told him on the first or second date that she was planning to move as soon as her company would transfer her. She wanted to let him know right away that if living in that city was important to him, then it didn't make sense to keep dating. It worked out because he didn't mind moving so he moved with her when she got transferred and they've been married twelve years now."

"Yes, but that's an easy one. It's not like you're sharing something about yourself."

"Good point. If he had said he didn't want to move, she wouldn't have taken it personally. He might have really loved living in that city. But if she shared that she suffered from anxiety and he decided to stop seeing her, it would have hurt because it would have been about her."

El sipped her tea and thought of Derek. When she talked about the things she cared about, he dismissed them so she stopped talking about them. "I know it's a good idea to be authentic, but it's not easy."

Kimbry nodded and put her hands up. "Absolutely. It's difficult. But what's the alternative? Wouldn't you rather deal with being uncomfortable early on instead of dealing with small hurts over years when you feel you can't be yourself?"

El nodded. "What do you suggest?"

"A radical approach to dating. Don't spend time trying to be perfect. Be you, with your flaws. The guys who don't match you will quickly leave. But the ones that stay…" She smiled. "They're worth it."

El gritted her teeth. "Scary."

Kimbry nodded. "But when you're authentic then he can be who he is too and you can decide if that's right for you. Let me tell you about my husband, Joseph." She grinned broadly. "When I met him, I was very clear about what I liked and didn't like and I told him I wanted to know the same about him." She laughed. "He was a little surprised, to say the least. But he went along. And we didn't agree on everything; there are things he likes that I don't and that's okay. The key is that we're aligned on the important things. We have the same values. That's why I wanted you to do the values exercise. What's really important to you. And to get back to my original comments, not the values you think you should have, not your parents' values or society's values," she said as she pointed to El, "but what do you care most passionately about?"

Kimbry asked about El's values and they talked about her priorities. After they reviewed them, Kimbry asked if she had any questions. El said, "Plenty, but I need to think about it some more." Kimbry laughed and said that they could talk again when she was ready. When El got off the call, she put her head back and closed her eyes. Why was it all so complicated?

Bernie texted her throughout the week and they planned to get together on Friday night. Owen texted her on Tuesday and said he would be training for a marathon on Saturday morning but wanted to see her Saturday night. El was glad that she could see both of them, but what if at some point they both wanted to see her on the same day? She shook her head and thought sarcastically, what a tough problem to have.

On Thursday night, El met Teresa at the pole dancing studio, Dancing Spirits. It was a small office space in a busy strip mall. When El got there, Teresa was sitting in the waiting area with two other women. El filled out the paperwork and quietly chatted with her friend about what was going on with work. She wasn't sure how she felt about this class but she knew she wanted to support Teresa.

As they waited, she looked around at the comfortable surroundings and framed affirmations on the walls including "Love yourself" and "Dance Like No One Is Looking." A few more women walked in and El was surprised that several of them were much older.

The door opened and women from the previous class walked out, El noticed that they were smiling and talking to each other. That was a good sign. A few minutes later, a short brunette with a pixie cut came out to welcome them and introduced herself as Sarah. The room was dark with no mirrors and had six poles. Yoga mats were spread on the floor and Sarah told them to each find a mat and get comfortable. She sat cross-legged in a large overstuffed chair and looked at a notebook.

She welcomed the ten women to Dancing Spirits and explained that their philosophy was for everyone to have a special time. She explained it was a judgment-free zone, which is why there were no mirrors and the lights were low. It helped to make it a more relaxing and fun experience. El looked at Teresa and smiled.

This was the introduction teaser class and if they liked it, they could sign up for a beginner class. After that, there were eight more levels of classes. She explained that only some of the dancing was going to be on the poles; they would also learn wall dancing that they could do at home and how to give a lap dance. El laughed nervously; this was not what she had expected.

"Let's start with a meditation," said Sarah. They closed their eyes and they listened to a relaxing message. When they opened their eyes, she instructed them to start with some simple stretching exercises. They did that for a few minutes and then put their mats away.

She told them to have a seat on the benches and she went to the pole and showed them how to do a slow slutty strut around the pole while holding onto it. Then she split the class into two groups and had the first group go to the poles and try it. El was glad she and Teresa were in the second group so they could watch it a few more times before attempting what was expected. Sarah was very complimentary to everyone and cheered them on.

Sarah showed some more moves and each time had the groups practice. El surprised herself by being able to swing around the pole. When she did it the first time, she let out a "whooo" and started laughing.

Then it was time to practice moves against the wall. Sarah said that these were the moves they could take home with them. She turned up the music and they practiced their slutty struts to the wall, turned around, did a flirty dance, and then slid down the wall for the finale.

When they were finished, Sarah said she had something for them and went into the other room. One woman said to the others, "That was fun. How'd you like it?"

Another woman agreed and took a sip from her water bottle. "I tried this at another studio and it was too serious. Women there were real pole dancers. This was way more fun. I'm going to come back."

Teresa looked anxiously at El, "Well?"

"We'll talk," said El. Teresa looked so concerned that El felt bad about keeping her guessing, so she said, "Okay, I'm in," and smiled.

Sarah came back and handed each one a discount coupon for the next class and a small flower. "This is to remind you all of how special you are."

Teresa and El agreed to connect the next day and coordinate which of the beginner classes they would sign up for.

Since Friday was Carl's last day, Kate and the rest of the team threw a lunch in his honor at a nearby restaurant. Kate thanked him for his years of service to the company. She told the team that they were still evaluating Carl's replacement and they might re-structure the groups a bit and that she'd make an announcement about the decision by the end of the following week.

Carl, rocking a royal blue and black plaid suit with a black silk shirt and black-on-black wingtips, sat next to El. He leaned towards her and whispered, "Drink directly after work?"

El said, "Sure, Carl. I'd love to." While she loved having both of their teams together and this big Carl-send-off, El coveted time spent with him one-on-one. She had learned so much from him and valued his unofficial championing, mentorship, and friendship. She was truly sad that she wouldn't be seeing him daily.

After the lunch and in between meetings, El texted Owen a message to say she was looking forward to seeing him tomorrow night, and asked where he'd like to meet. He promptly responded: "May I pick you up at 6 and can where we are going remain a surprise?"

El smiled. Few men had ever taken her on a surprise date. "Absolutely," she texted, along with her address.

At exactly 5 p.m., El and Carl met at the elevator bank. "I already moved my personal effects out of my office and gave security my ID badge," he said by way of greeting. He was solemn.

El put a hand on his arm. "Sad, I will mourn with you over cocktails. But we will also celebrate your success and your opportunity. I'm devastated to see you go but I am very happy for you."

"Thank you, El," he said.

After exiting their building, they walked a few blocks to a trendy martini bar. When they had been seated on high black leather stools that flanked a high-top walnut and steel table and had ordered the house specialty drink of the day, Carl said, "I didn't ask you here just to say good-bye and to celebrate. I had a long talk with Kate, El, about the future and structure of the two teams. I told her I thought the teams could be combined, or kept separate, and that you could lead them both."

El started to say, "But—" before cutting herself off because she heard PJ and her friends in her head telling her to seize opportunities for growth and promotion.

Carl held up his hand like a cop stopping oncoming cars. "No but. You're an excellent leader. And so you know, I'm not advocating you to take on twice the workload. What I told Kate is that instead of you being a manager, I think she could promote you to director or some title like that and give you a staff person or two to handle the busy work that you do yourself now. There's no reason you should schedule your own meetings, draft your own presentations and letters and things. This would let you manage the people who report to you and let them do the work on the projects. You'd have more of a steering and advisory role."

Their artfully decorated drinks arrived and Carl lifted his martini glass towards El before she even had a chance to process what he had just said. "To both of our success," Carl said. "Cheers."

They gently clinked their glasses together.

"So you're saying I might get a promotion because you decided to leave?"

Carl laughed. "That's what I've been advocating. I mean, think about it, if they cut the payroll line item that is *moi*, they have money to promote you and pay you more and to hire an admin or two. Financially, it could be a savings or a wash. And you, you deserve both a raise and a promotion, El. You work your butt off and save the company so much money and keep clients happy, happy, happy."

El giggled. She took another sip of her lemon and gingery drink and then said, "To happiness" while raising her glass. She couldn't believe she might actually get another promotion and raise. That would be amazing. But, she told herself, it hasn't happened yet. Don't go counting chickens and all of that.

El made eye contact with Carl. "Thank you so much, Carl. For your mentorship of me, for your advocating for me, for helping me get my current job. I'd be in such a different place without you. Truly."

"My pleasure and you're welcome. And remember, we all succeed when we help others succeed." He eyed an ahi tuna appetizer that had been delivered to the next table. "You eat fish, right?"

El chuckled. "Yes, I do, but I'm going out to supper with Bernie tonight."

"One appetizer won't spoil your appetite. And besides you still have time. How's it going with Bernie?"

"Good, I think. It's our second date, or third if you count baking that cake shortly after your party."

"He's a good guy. You know we met years ago when he and Stu first got together, right?"

El's drink was partway to her mouth. "He and Stu were a couple?"

"Yes, ages ago, before Annie and before that hot doctor that he dated. Garrett had invited Stu to a party we threw and Stu brought Bernie. To be honest, I couldn't see it. Stu will go after anyone who appeals to him, any time. Bernie is more old-soul. He's creative and awesome for sure but he's also more mature and others-centered. Like I said, he's a good guy."

"Interesting," El said. "Stu did strike me as more of a party-guy."

"Yes. Don't get me wrong, I like Stu. I just don't like Bernie and Stu as a couple. They're much better as roommates and friends. Anyway, it will be interesting to see how your relationship develops. To romance," Carl said, holding up the last swallow of his drink.

El laughed as she clinked her drink to his. She felt nervous energy regarding her dates, both of them. "Can we schedule regular happy hours to catch up now that I won't see you every day?"

"Of course, El. I'd love that. Let's try a new place each month. In fact, let's schedule the first four weeks from today." Carl pulled out his phone and opened his calendar, booked the block of time and invited El. In the location was "TBD." "And of course you can text me anytime. I'm leaving the company, but I'm still going to watch you skyrocket your career and cheer you from the sidelines every step of the way."

He popped a bite of ahi tuna in his mouth. "This is delicious. Do you have time for one more round?" He motioned the waiter. And then launched into a story of the crazy things his dog had done, and what was new with him and Garrett. And El admitted to taking the pole dancing class and that she actually had fun.

"Getting your sexy on. Good for you," Carl joked.

El blushed. "I feel kind of silly telling anyone. But Teresa wants to surprise Jordan, so I guess I'll go again and support her."

Carl said, "El, it's okay to like it. And you could also consider doing it for yourself, too. My other friends who have gone talked about how empowering it was. All of us could use a little more empowerment. It's important to embrace what makes you happy."

"I guess," El said, thinking of Kimbry's whole lecture on authenticity.

Chapter 15

El pulled into the parking garage where Bernie had suggested they meet and texted him. She thought about how to be authentic on a date. Instead of going along with someone else's interests, she was going to think of her needs first. She inwardly cringed at the thought; it didn't seem nice. But she realized it was something she had to learn.

She got a text right back and Bernie told her where to meet him. They were going to a monthly local art walk and there were plenty of restaurants in the area.

El smiled when she saw Bernie. He was wearing a bright purple shirt, tight black jeans, and boots. He hugged her and kissed her on the mouth twice. "It's so great to see you," he said. He quickly slipped his hand into hers and said, "Let's find a place to eat. I'm starving. How about a fun little Indian place I heard about? They're supposed to have wonderful tandoori chicken and shrimp curry."

El was about to agree and thought, is this what I really want? "You know, I'm not really in the mood for curry. How about something else?"

Bernie grinned and paused. "Sure. There's a quirky Mexican-Chinese place on the next street over or some great burgers a few blocks away."

El laughed and shook her head. "Mexican-Chinese? I have to try that."

"Your wish is my command, Cinderella," he said as they started to walk.

She opened her mouth to protest and stopped. She actually enjoyed it a little when he called her that.

Bernie asked how her week had been and she told him about Carl's last day and their meeting after work. By the time they had gotten to the restaurant, she had described Carl's suggestion to Kate and how excited she was about the opportunity.

China Cinco was busy so they found seats at the bar. The menu explained that it had been started by a Mexican husband and Chinese wife more than fifteen years ago.

"Do you want to share?" asked Bernie looking at the options.

"Sure. What are you thinking?"

"How about the egg foo young quesadilla or Chinese barbecue pork?"

"I like the idea of Chinese barbecue pork. How about that and the jade chicken burrito?

"You got a deal. Are you okay if we start with some carnitas pot stickers?" She agreed and he put down the menu and turned to her. His brown eyes looked into hers as he put his hand on her arm. "Tell me more about what Carl said."

El liked that he was such a good listener. She told him more about Carl's comments. "And he said some very nice things about you."

"Carl's a good guy. What'd he say?"

"He said you are an old soul."

Bernie nodded. "Yes, yes. That's how I feel."

The bartender asked for their order and El wondered if she should say what she was thinking.

When Bernie turned back to her she said, "He also told me how he met you."

Bernie ran his fingers through his hair. "Oh yeah, that was a while ago."

El decided to continue. "He said Stu brought you to a party." She paused. "And you and Stu were going out."

Bernie shrugged. "Ancient history. But yes, we dated for a short time. Stu is great but he's better as a friend." He looked carefully at her. "Does that bother you?"

El said, "I was surprised. It is a little odd that you're roommates. I mean you're not still…"

"No, no, no," interrupted Bernie, waving his hand. "We haven't had sex in years but we've been friends since then, and when we both needed a place to live a few years ago, it made a lot of sense." He

123

launched into a story about Carl and El wondered if he was changing the subject on purpose.

The food was delicious, but they decided to skip the tempting dessert so they could find something sweet on the art walk. Bernie started to reach for the check and El stopped him and suggested they split it.

They joined others walking down the streets and visiting the open art galleries and antique stores. One gallery was dominated by paintings and sculptures inspired by Star Wars characters. Bernie enthusiastically commented on the paintings as he walked around.

While El appreciated the technique, she didn't know who most of the characters were and frankly didn't care. She thought back to what she might have done with Derek in the past. He wouldn't have taken her to a gallery, but there were other things he did in which she tried to act interested. She thought, I'm not going to make believe I care about something when I really don't. Not anymore.

When Bernie paused in front of a giant painting of a character all in black who foisted a glowing sword, she leaned over and quietly said, "This is not really my thing."

He looked aghast. "Not a fan?"

She shook her head, "I've never seen any of the movies. Sorry. Not a sci-fi person. I never really got into the whole Star Trek thing."

"Star Wars not Star Trek. That's blasphemy." He looked so shocked that she started to laugh.

"Seriously, I've never really been interested."

"I don't even know if I can talk to you anymore," he said shaking his head. They walked out of the gallery. "I've seen every Star Wars movie at least two or three times. They tell universal stories of life and love, good and evil, loss and redemption." Bernie stopped and turned to her. "How about this? A movie marathon next weekend and maybe the weekend after. We can start with the original ones and bring you up to speed."

He looked so happy that she almost felt bad to tell him no. "Really, I'm just not interested." Other friends of hers had tried to show her how amazing it was and it hadn't worked. The authentic El really wasn't interested in this, didn't want to spend the time on it, and that was okay.

Bernie put his arm around her shoulders and gave her a quick hug.

124

"Well, it's your loss. But it's your opinion and I'm fine with that."

They continued to walk into different galleries. They quickly left one gallery that had death as the main theme. El lingered in a gallery with paintings from the southwest desert. She told Bernie that they made her think of her grandparent's house in Arizona. They admired the pictures of cactus, sunsets, and roadrunners. She told Bernie stories of visiting there when she was younger. Her grandfather had asthma and had moved there because the climate would be easier on him. She told stories about swimming in their pool in December and seeing snakes when they went for walks.

Bernie told her about his family. He'd grown up in the Chicago area and most of his family was still there. He said he tried to get back to visit them once a year. El enjoyed hearing him talk about his early years.

The time passed quickly and it seemed too soon when they arrived at El's car. Bernie leaned back against the side of the car and pulled her close, kissing her gently while stroking her hair. El felt a little breathless when they pulled apart. He whispered into her ear, "Thanks for a wonderful evening." His hand traced down her spine. "When can I see you again?"

El was dreading this part. She had felt guilty about seeing Bernie after making plans with Owen and now she was feeling guilty about the date with Owen on Saturday night. "How about Sunday?" She whispered into his ear.

"Sunday it is." He kissed her again. "Why don't you drive me to my car?" When they got to his car, he leaned over and kissed her again more passionately. He pulled back and cupped her face with his hands. "I'll see you Sunday," he said and went to his car.

When El awoke on Saturday morning, she lingered in bed thinking about the kisses. Teresa had already texted her to ask how the date was. She texted back one big grinning emoji and decided she needed a workout after all of that Chinese-Mexican food. She grabbed her yoga mat and stretched as Mr. Fluffy groomed himself nearby.

When she was done, there was a message from Todd from The Ink Spot checking to make sure she was ready to run the book club on Wednesday night. The thought made her nervous but she realized that being a Badass meant taking chances. She said yes and he let her know that seventeen attendees had signed up, which was more than he had hoped but for, but that probably only eight or ten would show up.

She read through the questions he had sent and reviewed her notes. She flipped through the book and added some more ideas. He had assured her that she didn't need to present the material, she just needed to facilitate the discussion. But she wanted to be ready. El ended up spending two hours preparing for the discussion. She had kind of lost track of time but when Mr. Fluffy kneaded his claw into her foot, she realized she hadn't fed him or herself yet. All she had had was her morning coffee.

She hopped off the sofa and padded barefoot into the kitchen. She gave him a can of tuna since she felt a bit guilty leaving him alone while being out two nights in a row with plans for two more. She scrambled herself an egg and cut up a melon for a late brunch.

As she was loading the dishwasher, a group text appeared from Teresa, "Hey are you guys bringing dates to the rehearsal dinner?"

El stared at the text. Teresa's wedding was in a month. It never registered with her that she might bring a date. She had been so caught up in the wedding planning and co-maid of honor duties that she never thought beyond the ceremony, the dresses, the shower, and the bachelorette party. And at the moment, she had no idea whether to bring Bernie or Owen.

"I don't know," El texted. "May I get back to you?" at the same time Leticia's "Yes," popped onto El's screen.

El and Teresa simultaneously texted, "Who?"

"Happy hour at the Gecko tomorrow at 5. I'll introduce you," Leticia texted.

"I have a date," El responded.

Leticia said, "Bring him...Or cancel."

Teresa texted El privately, "What the hell?"

"No idea. But it's about time she's coming clean." El texted to Teresa. To the group, she wrote, "See you at 5." She texted Teresa, "You bringing Jordan?"

Teresa called El who answered, "Yes?"

Teresa answered with, "I don't think so. I think this is something for us to handle first. All this secrecy and always busy. And I think she's been lying. Something just feels off. Leticia's always been driven but she's also carefree. Or she used to be."

"I think she's definitely involved with someone," El said. "I guess tomorrow we find out with whom. Maybe once it is out in the open, we will get the old Leticia back. I miss her."

"Me, too. And El, just say yes to bringing a date. You don't have to decide who it has to be until the day of. Just bring whomever feels right in the moment. It's not like we'll have place cards or anything." Teresa chuckled.

"Thank you. I appreciate your flexibility. I have a date with Owen in a few hours, and Bernie wanted to see me again tomorrow."

"Third official date. Some guys think that's the sex date, if you haven't already."

"No. No, of course we haven't."

"Where's Owen taking you?"

"I have no idea. He is coming to get me at six. Oh, I should probably text him to find out what to wear."

"Good idea. Don't want to be underdressed. Have fun. Please kiss and tell." Teresa blew a kiss into the phone and disconnected.

El chuckled, and then texted Owen. "How informal or formal should I be this evening?"

He responded immediately, "Definitely wear a dress. If you want to be fancy, go for it. I can be fancy, too." He then sent a gif of a pug in a tuxedo.

El laughed. She walked into her bedroom and opened the closet door and flipped through her four fanciest dresses. The dress she felt the sexiest in still had the tags on it and was for Teresa's wedding. For a split second El actually considered wearing it anyway.

Instead, she decided on a royal blue silk strapless dress with a sweetheart neckline and a fitted bodice. The skirt had shimmery blue tuille over the underlay silk and was almost knee length. She decided her nude heels went best with it. She hooked a crystal necklace over the hanger and put it all back in the closet away from the curious Mr. Fluffy. He had been watching her from atop the bed as she took things in and out of the closet to try them on.

It was still too early to get dressed yet. So El decided to flip through Teresa and Jordan's wedding registry to see what was still left. She needed gifts for the shower and the wedding. As she scrolled through the towels and sheet sets she felt uninspired. She wanted gifts that were memorable, and that celebrated Teresa's unique style.

El followed one link to another and somewhere along the search ended up eyeing agate cheese boards. They were about one foot in length and seven inches in width and came in a variety of natural stones and were exquisite...and reasonably priced, too. El read the online reviews and only one or two people said the color that arrived wasn't as vibrant as on the website. One person recommended picking it out at the store in person since the colors varied depending on where from the big slab it was cut.

El noted that they were in stock at the store closest to her but El didn't think she had enough time to run over there and back and be ready in time for her date. She decided to go first thing in the morning when they opened. She took a screenshot of the blue agate tray and the green agate tray and sent them to Leticia. "For T's wedding gift?"

"Stunning," Leticia texted back.

El smiled at her phone, pleased at the find. Her stomach growled. She grabbed an apple, a knife and a jar of peanut butter in the kitchen and had a snack and made a cup of tea. She needed to get moving and in the shower and start getting ready. She put some kibble in Mr. Fluffy's bowl in case he got hungry this evening.

She cranked up her GirlPower Play List before she got into the shower so she could hear it over the spray. She sung along as she washed her hair and shaved her legs. She wanted her skin silky smooth just in case Owen touched her. She grinned at the thought.

El's hair and makeup were done and she was dressed and ready to go by 5:45, which was a good thing because at 5:47, her phone rang.

"Hi, El. I'm downstairs and early. I wanted to see if it was okay to be so early or if you want me to wait until 6 to ring the buzzer." Owen's voice made El's heart beat faster.

She laughed nervously. "I'm ready so it's fine." She pushed the buzzer to open the building's door. "Come on up." El consciously had to wipe the huge grin from her face.

"Wish me luck, Mr. Fluffy," she said. The cat was perched on the back of the sofa eyeing her at the door.

Owen knocked once on the door, and El opened it. His mouth was agape as he saw her. "Oh my god. You look gorgeous," he said, quickly followed by, "I didn't mean to sound surprised."

El laughed. "Thank you."

"You're breathtaking."

"So are you," El said, before consciously knowing what was coming from her mouth.

Owen wore a black tuxedo with a white shirt and an emerald green bowtie. "Thank you," he said, and he bent and kissed her lips. Then he handed her a single long stem yellow rose.

El's eyes widened. "A yellow rose is my favorite. How did you—"

"Jack," Owen said. "I asked him, and he knew. I don't know too many other brothers who know that kind of information about their sisters. But he's one amazing guy."

El nodded her head. "He is. Thank you."

Mr. Fluffy let loose a big, "Meow" because no one was paying attention to him. Owen took a step towards him and asked, "Who do we have here?" at the same time the cat launched himself at Owen, who caught him right before Mr. Fluffy crashed into his chest. He cradled the cat, and said "That's a good boy," and Mr. Fluffy purred in a way that made El think he had found his soulmate.

El said, "I'm sorry about the cat hair."

"Not a problem at all. It's why lint rollers were made."

Mr. Fluffy closed his eyes like he was going to sleep in Owen's arms. El rolled her eyes. "We may never get out of here now."

"No rush," Owen said and sat on the sofa with Mr. Fluffy. After a minute, he moved a throw pillow to his elbow and seamlessly slid the sleeping cat onto the pillow cushion. Then he stood up, reached for El's hand, and said, "To the chariot, mi'lady," as he guided her to the door.

El marveled that the cat stayed right where Owen put him. She thought, he's hot and a cat whisperer, too. OMG. Life couldn't get much better.

But El was wrong. Owen drove them to his apartment in one of the swanky new buildings in the city. And when they entered through the front door, El discovered the whole place was decorated in fairy lights and streamers and balloons in their high school's colors, and music from a decade ago was playing throughout the apartment. After he shut the front door behind them, he tapped El's shoulder and said, "El, may I have this dance," just as a slow song started.

El grinned in response and looped her hands behind his neck.

He started with his hands at her waist but then pulled her tight against him as they swayed to the song. As it was ending, he pulled back a bit, looked into her eyes, and kissed her deeply. El felt her stomach drop and she kissed him back with need that caught her off-guard.

When they broke apart, she was breathless. Owen took her hand and pulled her towards the dining room. "Before we dance again, let's dine."

The table had been set for two, with white place settings and shiny stainless flatware atop a blue tablecloth with coordinated cloth napkins. A champagne flute and a wineglass as well as glasses of water with a single lemon slice in each were at both place settings. Owen went into the kitchen and returned with a bottle of rosé champagne, and he popped the cork and filled both of their glasses.

"To the dance we never had," he said.

El clinked her glass against his and added, "To the more adult version. I had no idea pink champagne existed when I was in high school or that the smaller the bubbles, the better the bubbly. And this is one fine bubbly." She peered into her glass as she took her first sip. "Delicious."

"Like you," Owen said, as he bent to kiss her again.

She kissed him quickly and laughed nervously.

"You can sit down if you want. I'll go get the appetizer." But before he left the room, Owen pulled out a chair for her, and after she sat, pushed her towards the table. Wow. Manners, she thought, as he went into the kitchen.

He returned bearing a tray of bacon-wrapped, goat cheese-stuffed dates and a wide-mouthed bowl filled with some of the largest prawns on ice that El had ever seen. She adored stuffed dates and realized that Jack must have struck again.

Owen put the tray and bowl on the table between them. "I confess to making none of these."

El laughed. "They look delicious." She helped herself to a date and popped it into her mouth. It was sweet, salty, bacony, and cheesy all at the same time and she was so happy, she actually sighed after she swallowed.

Owen laughed. "That good, huh?"

"Yes, that good." El reached for a prawn and dunked it into cocktail sauce. It was firm, meaty, and just a tad sweet. So fresh. "I'm so glad we eat better than we did when we were kids. We missed out on a lot of great food."

Owen swallowed a prawn he ate in one bite, had a sip of champagne, and said, "When I was four, I was in a fish stick phase. Fish sticks, french fries, and you remember those little mandarin oranges in the syrup? I would have eaten those three things three meals a day if my mom would have let me."

El laughed. "For me, it was Spaghetti O's. I couldn't get enough of them. And they are SO GROSS."

Owen laughed, then held up his glass, "To refined taste."

"Hear, hear," El said. She looked around the room and realized it must have taken him hours to put up all of the lights and blow up the balloons and hang the streamers. "This is really incredible, Owen. I can't believe you went to all of this trouble."

"It wasn't trouble at all. I wanted it to be memorable. And besides, El, you're worth it."

He leaned towards her and kissed her softly and sweetly on the lips. "So worth it," he said afterwards.

The salad course was next and Owen had artfully arranged a few pieces of bibb lettuce sprinkled with fresh herbs, a bit of feta, and dried cranberries with an olive oil and vinegar drizzle. Owen said, "I wanted everything to be smaller portioned so we could make it through all of the courses without feeling stuffed."

"Good plan," El said, refilling their champagne flutes.

While they ate the salads, they talked about both of their jobs and their aspirations in the workplace. And quickly they made it to the entrees. Owen served chicken marbella over jasmine rice. He poured an unoaked Chardonnay to accompany the chicken.

When he placed the plate in front of El, she said, "Wow. Marbella is so many ingredients and takes so much time."

"Yes, but the slow cooker does all of the work." Owen grinned at her.

El stabbed an olive with her fork and popped it into her mouth. OMG! It was so yummy. Hot. Mr. Fluffy whisperer and he could cook?

Oh and he can kiss, too, she reminded herself as she ate another bite. She broke into a huge grin at the thought.

"What's so funny?" Owen gazed at her with amusement and desire.

"Nothing. Just thinking. This is delicious. Thank you so much."

Just at the moment, Mariah Carey's "We Belong Together" came on Owen's sound system, and he looked a bit squirmy. That was when El realized he might be as nervous as she was. Maybe that's why he went all out, El thought.

She felt herself soften towards him even more. She took a sip of wine, and then, did what authentic El wanted. She leaned towards him and put her hand on his. She looked up and into his eyes and said, "Owen, kiss me."

As they kissed, she slipped out of her chair and slid onto his lap. And she lost track of time and place.

When they pulled apart, they were both breathless. The song was over and Beyonce's "Irreplaceable" was on, which was totally wrong for their moods. Owen said, "Alexa, play romantic ballads."

"Playing romantic ballads," Alexa said back.

El smiled at Owen. "We should probably finish this fabulous supper you made."

"Or we could reheat it." Owen grinned as El slid back to her own chair.

Owen made chocolate mousse for dessert, but El begged off dessert until the food digested a bit and they danced away some calories.

Two hours later with one and a half wine bottles emptied and the champagne gone, and countless dances both slow and fast, El realized she was kind of drunk. She said so aloud. "I think I drank too much."

Owen's arms were around her and they were swaying to the music. "Are you okay?"

"I think so. I don't feel sick. But the room is swaying a little."

Owen chuckled. "So are we."

But he led her to the leather sofa and had her sit. "I'm going to get us both more water."

He returned quickly and held her water glass to her lips as she drank, before he drank his own glass. He undid his bowtie and pulled it from his shirt. He had removed his jacket sometime before, El had no idea when. He undid the top few buttons of his shirt and then he leaned back against the sofa and pulled her so her back was against his chest and she sat in between his legs. They rested like this, content and silent.

Eventually El fell asleep.

Chapter 16

She awoke as a sunbeam hit her face through the window; she was lying on her side, still on the sofa. She found that her shoes had been removed, a pillow had been placed under her head, and she had been covered with a blanket. Owen was in the kitchen making coffee.

It took her a moment to remember what happened and why she was there. She briefly panicked as she wondered what time it was. She glanced at her watch and realized that it was only 8:30. She guiltily thought about her 12:30 date planned with Bernie. She snuck into the bathroom, made sure her makeup wasn't all over her face, quickly borrowed his toothbrush, and then walked into the kitchen.

Owen's back was to her and she briefly admired his shoulders and sexy ass. He turned around and saw her smiling at him. "Good morning, beautiful," he said giving her a kiss and pulling her close.

"I'm so sorry about last night. It was all so wonderful and I didn't mean to fall asleep."

Owen looked at her and grinned. "Don't be silly. There's no one I would rather fall asleep with."

El could feel herself blushing. "You're so sweet."

"So are you." He held her close again and she felt his warmth.

"That was an incredible night. Thank you so much," she said.

"Does that mean I get a second date?" he teased.

"I think we can arrange that," she teased back.

"Or we could just keep the date going," he said. "Spend the day with me."

"I think I need to get home and take a shower."

He looked at her and said, "There's a shower here and you're welcome to use it."

She grinned, "I should go home and feed Mr. Fluffy."

He stepped back and held onto her hands. "Oh all right. But if you change your mind, you're welcome to spend the afternoon with me. I was planning to prepare for the marathon but I would put it off for you." Then he added, "Or you could join me."

She shook her head and said, "Not today." And to herself she said, "And not ever." She had no desire to run a marathon. Just the thought of it sounded tiring.

As they had coffee, she again marveled at the decorations and let him know how much she appreciated it. They talked about high school and Jack, and then Owen reluctantly drove her home.

When they got to her place, Owen leaned over and softly kissed her. El briefly wondered if she was making a mistake. Maybe she should spend the day with him but she had to deal with Bernie and the confusion that was going on in her brain.

Mr. Fluffy yowled his displeasure as soon as she walked in the door. "Sorry, buddy. I didn't expect to be out all night." She quickly gave him cat food and sat down to text Bernie. There was still time to meet him but she didn't think she wanted to. She could not stop thinking about Owen. She apologized and said she needed to reschedule. He quickly responded with, "R you ok?"

She didn't want to explain so she just told him that she was okay but she had some things that had come up. That was true, as she thought about Leticia. Though she didn't have to see Leticia until later but it was still bothering her.

She promised that they could get together again soon. He said he'd had a great time on Friday night and was looking forward to seeing her again.

She put her head back on the couch cushion. What was she going to do? This was so confusing. Seeing Bernie on Friday night was wonderful. And last night with Owen was also wonderful. She decided she needed a good hot shower and some breakfast. When she got out of the shower, she saw a message from Teresa asking about her date. She texted that it was so incredible and she would tell her all about it when they got together later. She wanted to sort some things out first.

As she poured cereal, she thought about both Bernie and Owen and started to list their good points. She shook her head as if to clear away some of the cobwebs. This was not helping. "Okay, I need to focus," she said to herself. She thought about her Master's Degree. It was time to review some of the things she'd learned. Was it midterms already? She wondered.

She went to her bookshelf and pulled out the Byron Katie book, *I Need Your Love–Is That True?* She reread some parts and finally looked at the last chapter with the four questions listed.

She closed her eyes and carefully considered what was bothering her. The thought that was causing her the most pain was, "I need to choose between Bernie and Owen." She asked herself the first question from the book, "Is it true?" Of course not, she thought. I don't need to choose. I've just started dating both of them. Leticia and Teresa already told her that she shouldn't worry so much about it.

When she asked herself the third question, "How do you react when you believe that thought?" she thought about how rotten it made her feel. She felt confused and unhappy.

The fourth question made her pause. She asked, "Who would you be without the thought?" That would be so nice. I wouldn't be so stressed and I wouldn't worry about who I should pick. I could just enjoy. These thoughts made her shoulders feel less tight.

It made sense, but how could she do it? She looked at the next step in the book which was to turn that thought around. She said to herself, "I don't need to choose between Bernie and Owen." That made her smile. The book said to find some other possible turnarounds so she thought, Bernie and Owen need to choose me. Bernie and Owen don't need to choose me. Hmmm. She was so focused on trying to decide if she wanted to keep dating them that she hadn't thought if they would want to keep dating her. Maybe one of them would decide that it wasn't working for him. Not a pleasant thought, El realized, but possible.

She got herself another cup of tea and wondered why this was so stressful now. Teresa's wedding was part of it. It was a reminder that she hadn't found the love of her life. When she really thought about it that way, it seemed so silly. She didn't need to decide if either Bernie or Owen was the love of her life.

Thinking about Teresa's wedding and the rehearsal dinner made her feel like she had to find the "right" man. In reality, she didn't. Instead she needed to remind herself that going out with both of them was helping her to understand what was important to her.

She closed her eyes and reminded herself that this was a Master's Degree. She needed to learn as much as she could. But how could she do that? She thought back to what Kimbry told her. She needed to practice being authentic. She could tell both of them that she didn't want to jump into anything. As Teresa had reminded her, she didn't want to be stuck in another relationship. She was going to take it slow and learn more about herself.

The thought that she needed to find the love of her life was not helping her. She thought about a turnaround. I don't need to find the love of my life was her first turnaround thought. Then she smiled and thought, I'm the love of my life. That felt true. If she didn't love herself first, how could she be in a great relationship?

She briefly flipped through the *You Are A Badass* book and found that it also reminded her of the importance of loving yourself. She looked at Mr. Fluffy, who was washing his back leg. "What do I want to do to love myself?" she asked him. She grabbed her yoga mat and turned on some soothing music and started to stretch.

Forty-five minutes later, she felt better but decided she was still feeling restless. She put on a 20-minute guided meditation. She promised herself to stop worrying about other people and she reminded herself that she needed to take care of herself. She started some laundry, straightened up, and decided to take a short nap. When she got up, she picked up the book about the cupcake bakers. Since one of the characters was getting married, El thought that she could count that as research.

After a few chapters, she stretched and thought about the romance she was reading. Why was it that all the men in cozy mysteries were terrific? Even though there were obstacles, you knew in the end it would be okay. Sure, she knew it was all part of the story, but she wanted to be in one. She needed to write her own story, her own amazing story where she was authentic and happy. She briefly considered what that story would be like.

Then she looked at her watch and realized it was getting late. It would be time to go soon to see Leticia and Teresa and find out the truth.

She quickly changed into jeans and a sweater and left for the Gecko.

When El walked through the door, she spied Teresa perched on a stool behind a high-top table. Chips and salsa were in front of her and a glass of water. Teresa was facing the door and she grinned when she saw El.

"You're glowing," Teresa said as El approached.

"Oh yeah?" El hugged her friend and plopped on the next stool. "Have you ordered?"

"No, I was waiting for you. But I told the waitress we would probably get a pitcher. Cheaper for the three of us and we may need that much margarita for whatever Leticia will say." El chuckled and agreed.

"So, do tell, what happened with Owen?"

El started with, "Well, he brought me home at 8:30 this morning?"

Teresa's eyebrows shot towards her scalp. "Really now?"

"But not for that reason. It was magical. The fairy lights and our high school colored streamers all over his apartment. His tuxedo—"

Teresa interrupted, "Damn, I'm sure he looks extra fine in a tux."

"You have no idea," El dreamily said, looking off into the distance. "And the sumptuous food he made—including some of my favorites— and the kisses. Oh my God, can he kiss. And he even showed up with a long-stem yellow rose."

"Perfect."

"Well, Jack helped him with that."

"So you'll see him again. And maybe again and again," Teresa joked.

"I will see him again," El said. She faced Teresa then and said, "He's awesome. But the best part is that I'm learning about myself and who I am and what I want."

Teresa said, "That is the most important part. Is Bernie helping you learn the same thing?"

"Yes. I admitted to him that I had no interest in Star Wars and Star Trek and his first thought was to try to convert me, but I stood my ground—"

Teresa interrupted, "Something you rarely did with Derek."

"Exactly." El waved at the waitress and told her they wanted a pitcher of house margaritas and three glasses. But then she saw Leticia at the door and Jack behind her so she said, "Four glasses actually."

Teresa followed the direction of El's eyes. "Why is Leticia bringing Ja—Oh my god!"

El was momentarily confused but instantly understood.

"Hey, Rella. Hi, Teresa." Jack greeted them both before handing out bear hugs.

Leticia eyed her friends warily, and then blurted, "T, I'm bringing Jack to the rehearsal dinner and the wedding. We're a couple and thought it is time you two know."

"Since when?" El asked, so grateful the pitcher and glasses arrived. Jack poured the round.

Leticia looked at Jack and they locked eyes in some kind of silent acknowledgment. She said, "We got together six, maybe eight months ago. Ran into each other at a restaurant, both on dates that weren't going well. Ended up commiserating together. Joked that maybe we should go on a date together." Leticia eyed Jack again. He nodded his head for her to continue.

El wasn't used to Leticia seeking permission from anyone. That rocked her more than knowing one half of her BFF was dating her brother.

"I didn't take it very seriously. But well, you know Jack. He got to thinking about it and a month or six weeks later called me and asked me to go explore a hot new restaurant that was opening. And we had the best time." Leticia grinned at Jack, who grinned back and draped his arm around her.

"We did," he agreed. "But we also weren't sure where it was going and didn't want to ruin what seems like our lifelong friendship."

"But we definitely had chemistry. And serious sexual chemistry," Leticia said, which made Jack's cheeks color.

Leticia continued, "So we waited to see where it went. And we're telling you today because a we want you both to know that we've been seeing each other exclusively and b I didn't want to wait and spring Jack on you at the rehearsal dinner or wedding. It's your weekend, T, and you need no bombshells to upstage you."

Teresa squealed, "I'm so happy for you guys. Two of my favorite people in love." She raised her glass. "Thank you for your thoughtfulness regarding my and Jordan's wedding. To love."

The others raised their glasses in the toast. El remained silent for a beat and looked from Leticia to Jack. She was a bit miffed they hadn't told her sooner.

"So all of those times when you said you were hooking up with—"

"Yes," Leticia stopped her. "Yes, I was hooking up with Jack."

Jack grinned.

"So, Jack's the reason you've been so tired and secretive and distant?" El probed.

"Yes." Leticia confirmed. "I hated that and you know that isn't me. But I wanted to be clear how I felt about him and he felt about me. You know how foreign this love stuff is for me, El. And I wanted to tell you, but he's your brother. It's not like I could lockerroom talk with you about him." She took a sip of her drink, and more quietly said, "And besides, I didn't want to talk about him to anyone. For once what I was doing with someone felt private, kind of sacred. I needed to figure shit out for myself. It all felt so different. Like I finally found my equal, someone who was like me, who understood me."

El said, "I get it. You're equally ambitious and driven, have similar dating histories, and you like a lot of the same things. Like me, for example." El grinned and laughed and raised her glass. "To my brother and my best friend. May your love continue to grow." But before they clinked glasses, El asked Jack, "Have you broken the news yet to Mom and Dad?"

He laughed. "No. It was more important to tell you and T first. Now that that is over and done with, let's order some food. And then El, we want to hear about your dates. Owen sent us photos of himself being dressed to impress."

El laughed. "Can you send me that photo?"

She didn't have a photo of Owen and wished that she had taken a picture with him the night before.

"Only if you tell us about it," said Jack.

After El described the evening with Owen, Teresa said, "I think he's a keeper."

El grinned. "We'll see."

As they ate appetizers, things seemed almost normal until Leticia looked at Jack in a certain way or Jack gently touched her arm. Then El was reminded that things had definitely changed. Before they ordered the next pitcher, El said she was tired and was going to go home. They teased her a bit for not getting enough sleep the night before.

When she hugged Jack, he looked serious for a moment and said, "You okay?" She assured him everything was fine and she gave Leticia and Teresa big hugs.

She was so busy thinking about Leticia and Jack on the way home that she almost missed her exit. She was happy for both of them, really she was. Two of her favorite people had found someone special. She felt annoyed that they had lied to her all this time. She realized that they wanted to keep it secret while they sorted it out, but seriously?

She had a busy week planned. Without Carl at work, she felt like she was putting out one fire after another for the teams. She was glad to spend the next night reviewing her *Badass* notes for the book club. Rereading sections made her feel more confident.

She arrived at The Ink Spot thirty minutes before the event was scheduled to start. She and Todd had talked the day before about the format. Todd greeted her warmly and showed her where they would be meeting. A separate room in the back of the store had chairs for twenty people set in groups of four. There was a seat in front where she placed her book, notes, and jacket.

As she and Todd chatted, they were joined by another man who Todd introduced as his brother, Keith. "I recruited him in case we needed any help." El could see the family resemblance. Keith was a little taller than Todd but had the same slender build and pale skin. His light brown hair was longer than his brother's and he didn't wear glasses.

Keith smiled and said, "I'm sure you have everything taken care of, but I'm here if you need anything."

"Will you join the discussion?" asked El.

"I have to admit I haven't read the book, but I'll be happy to hear more about it from you. It sounds really interesting."

As Todd went to get some snacks from the Ink Link, El walked around and tried to channel her nervousness. What was she so worried about? She didn't know any of the people who would show up; this was just for fun. She looked over at Keith and he waved at her. "Yes, this is going to be fun," she said to herself.

Keith walked over and asked, "How are you doing?"

She glanced at Todd and leaned closer to Keith as she said, "Frankly, I'm a little nervous. I've never done anything like this before, but your brother sort of talked me into it."

Keith laughed. "Yeah, he does stuff like that. But I'm sure you'll be terrific. He told me about how much you like the book and about the questions you prepared. I think what you're doing is amazing and will really help people who want to discuss it."

El thanked him. His comments made her feel a little less nervous.

As Todd set up the snacks, the first attendees arrived and El welcomed them. Eighteen women joined the discussion and at the end, El wished that they had more time. Todd thanked everyone who had come and promoted the next book club event that was scheduled for the following month.

After the event, Todd told her what a great job she'd done. He asked her if she'd like some tea and dessert. She hesitated, since she'd filled up on snacks during the talk.

"We have a new delicious flourless chocolate cake," he said.

She laughed. "How can I say no to that?"

Keith joined them in the café and the three of them chatted about the book.

Todd looked to the side and saw an employee gesturing to him. "Excuse me, I'll be back."

"Todd told me about your Master's Degree in Relationships. That sounds really interesting," said Keith sipping a soda.

El felt embarrassed and said, "It's really not a big deal."

"Are you kidding? It sounds like a great idea. I want to hear what you've learned. Maybe I'll have to get my own Master's Degree."

She took a bite of the cake. "Wow, this really is amazing." El considered PJ's mentorship contingency that she share information with others and always pay it forward, so she said, "Okay, what do you want to know?"

"Well, let's say, I wanted to get my own degree, what kinds of things would I study? How would I get information?"

She thought back to some of her insights. She told him about the books she read and the people she talked to and added, "I learned that you have to be yourself. And it helps to work on what's inside before you start to look outside at someone else."

He tipped his head to the side and smiled. "Okay," he said, "I'm hearing the theory but what about the practical information. How do you actually use it?"

"You mean how it actually helps me with my relationships?"

"Yeah, sort of what I asked myself about history classes in college, very interesting but what am I really going to do with it?"

"Are you trying to quiz me?"

"No, no," he said, waving his fork. "I'd like to be a fellow student and I want to find out what I'll learn."

El sat back and looked at him. She'd already noticed that he had no wedding band. "Okay, let me ask you, if you're thinking of applying to this school, what would you put on your essay? What do you want to get out of your studies?"

He nodded and smiled. "Good one. Well, professor..."

El interrupted and said, "No, just another student who started a little ahead of you."

"Okay." He briefly looked off to the side and stopped smiling. He turned back to El. "Really, I'd like to learn how to have a great relationship. I was married and it didn't work out, and I don't want to go through that again." He paused and smiled again. "I'd like to apply to a program to learn how to do things differently." He leaned forward. "Todd told me about what you were doing and I was really curious. I'd like to figure out relationships. I'm an engineer and I understand facts. Relationships, though, are not so easy," he said. "What would you say to a study group? I'd really like to hear more about what you think."

Todd came back at that point and apologized and said he needed to get back to work. He thanked El again and asked if she would consider doing another book club. El glanced at Keith, who was smiling, and said she'd be happy to. When Todd walked away, El looked at her watch and realized how late it was. She exchanged numbers with Keith and said they could meet and discuss. She felt kind of funny giving her number to Keith but she said to herself, "It is just a study group, right?"

Thursday night was the next pole dancing class. The class started with a mindful meditation about forgiving others and forgiving yourself. El felt her shoulders relax and her tension reduce. They were practicing the pole dancing moves wearing high platform shoes. They had plenty of shoes to choose from and El picked a red pair with a two inch platform in the front and the back heel looked to be about five inches. Teresa picked a sexy black pair and they laughed as they tried to strut across the room.

After class, they chatted for a few minutes outside their cars about Jack and Leticia. They were still processing it. Teresa admitted to being hurt since she felt like Leticia had lied to them. El said she felt the same way, though on a logical level, she understood the secrecy.

Teresa said, "Now that you know Jack is Leticia's plus one, does that make you feel more pressure to bring Owen to the rehearsal dinner and wedding?"

El admitted that it had crossed her mind that it would be make life easier since Jack and Owen could hang out while she and Leticia did the bridesmaid thing. The wedding was coming up soon and this weekend was her last free one. The others would be filled with Teresa's shower, a girls' trip to Tahoe for a bachelorette weekend, and then the wedding weekend itself. And speaking of secrets, it suddenly hit El that Teresa had never told them where they planned to honeymoon. She and Jordan had considered Hawaii, some resort in Mexico El had never heard of, and an eco-resort in Costa Rica. When El asked, Teresa said, "I actually don't know. Jordan decided he wanted to plan it and surprise me. That's why I never told you. And that's why I decided to study pole dancing, so I'd have a honeymoon surprise of my own."

"Oh that's so sweet," El said. "Wherever you go, I'm sure you'll have a great time."

"Yes," Teresa agreed. "But I hope he doesn't pick somewhere with cold weather. I'd prefer to hang out near a beach." She grinned.

"I can't blame you there," El said. "Well, I should get home. I've got a super busy day at work tomorrow."

"And a date tomorrow night," Teresa added.

"Yes, I'm hanging out with Owen. He asked if we could keep it low key because he's running the marathon on Sunday."

"Better him than us," Teresa said.

"Totally."

They hugged goodbye and parted. As El drove home, her phone lit up with a text. At a light, she glanced down at it. Keith asked if she had any time on Saturday or Sunday to study.

After El got home, pet Mr. Fluffy, washed her face, and changed into her pajamas, she texted Keith and said, "I'm still figuring out my weekend. I'll text you tomorrow. Thank you."

She put down her phone on the nightstand and crawled into bed, thinking she'd read ten minutes of her cozy mystery novel before going to sleep, but just as she picked up the book, Bernie texted. "Legion of Honor has a new Gothic exhibit, a film and installation. Wanna go see it on Sunday afternoon?"

El stared at the phone. Gothic? She thought of architecture. She Googled Legion of Honor and gothic to see what he was talking about.

The photo was a close-up of a face with blood shot eyes and blood coming from the mouth. Yuck. El made a disgusted face. Why would I want to see that, she wondered. And she immediately thought of Kimbry and the sports example.

"Be authentic," El told herself aloud. Mr. Fluffy raised his head from the bed and gave her the eye. Then he sighed and flattened back down. She texted, "Thank you for the invitation. I would like to see you. But I have no interest in going to that."

Bernie responded almost instantaneously with, "Meet me for lunch then after I see it." He named a restaurant in the Marina District and suggested one o'clock.

El smiled at the message. "That sounds great. See you then."

In that moment, El felt great about her whole life. She skipped the novel and turned off the light, saying, "Good night, Mr. Fluffy. I love you."

Chapter 17

When El got to work on Friday morning, there was a message from Kate asking her to meet at eleven. As she grabbed her cup of coffee, she tried to stop the butterflies in her stomach. She pulled out the notes she had made about her ideas for the two teams.

There was a voice in the back of her head that said that she wasn't ready for a senior manager role. She stepped into an empty conference room, closed her eyes for a minute, and thought back to what she had learned earlier from her friend and mentor, PJ. She thought about the power of mind movies and she needed to have a clear picture in her head about how it would look when she was running both areas. She also imagined what it would be like when she met with Kate, how she would look confident, and how Kate would believe in her abilities. El took a few deep breaths. Yes, she could see it. She reviewed her notes again and arrived at Kate's office a few minutes early.

Kate was seated at her desk when El walked in and gestured to the seating area. El noticed her stylishly cut black suit with a turquoise blouse accented with gold a heavy gold necklace. Kate got right to the point.

"El, thanks for meeting with me on short notice. How are things going?"

El smiled and briefly mentioned the status of two key projects they were working on.

Kate thanked her and let her know how much she appreciated El taking on the extra work. "I've been very pleased with how you've stepped up since Carl left and I'd like you to take on both groups for the next quarter as we decide what direction to go in." Kate told her that she had faith in her and was going to have an assistant from another group help her with one of the projects. She was also scheduling El for the upcoming company's leadership development programs.

El had been hoping that Kate would automatically promote her but she realized that this was her chance to show her and the higher up management what she could do. And she realized that she never asked for the promotion, so she put a smile on her face and thanked Kate for the opportunity. Then she said, "To be clear, if I lead the two groups well during the next quarter, I'd like the possibility of a promotion."

Kate smiled and said, "El, that is one possibility we are considering."

"Thank you," El said, trying not to grin. They spent the rest of the meeting discussing expectations for upcoming projects and targets her groups needed to hit or exceed.

El left the meeting feeling excited but nervous. She wished that Carl was there to go out to lunch with. Instead, she texted Carl to find out if he had some time to talk. They scheduled a time to chat that afternoon. As soon as he congratulated her, she started to say it wasn't a big deal and then she interrupted herself and said, "Thank you" instead. When she asked for his opinion, he said, "You've got this." She started to argue with him and he stopped her. "You've done this all on your own. "

She appreciated his words and his confidence, but she was nervous. When she got home, she explained it all to Mr. Fluffy as she made herself a salad. As cute as he was, it made her think how nice it would be to talk this over with someone special with a little less fur. It made her think about seeing Owen and Bernie.

She was scheduled to meet Owen in front of a local movie theater at 6:50 p.m. She changed out of her work clothes and into her favorite jeans, a navy merino wool sweater, and short brown boots. Her hair had been up all day at work so she took the pins out of it, fluffed it, and then decided to add a few curls. As the curling iron heated, she added a bit more mascara and a coat of berry lip gloss.

She gave Mr. Fluffy fresh water, a few extra bites of kibble, and told him not to wait up.

El arrived at the theater five minutes early. She stood next to the building and watched people. Love, or at least like, seemed to be all around her. She saw grey haired couples who held hands and were clearly in love. Teenagers who pushed and shoved each other but looked almost giddy to be together. Other pairs kept distance between themselves and barely made eye contact. El tried to guess which might be on awkward first dates or were long-term couples who had grown indifferent. The second type made her sad. She never wanted to be in a relationship where the spark had died and the individuals were leading separate lives within the same sphere.

She thought of her parents and the example they had set for her and Jack. They had been married for more than thirty years and her father still reached for her mother's hand and love still shown in their eyes. That's what El aspired to.

Owen was on the other side of the fountain walking towards El. He wore jeans, a chest-hugging red sweater, and chocolate leather driving moccasins. His face lit up when he saw her. He picked her up in a bear hug before putting her on the ground to kiss her lightly on the lips.

"I Fandango-ed the tickets so we wouldn't have to stand in line," he said.

"Oh, thank you," said El.

He kept his arm around her, steering her into the doors of the theater. "Popcorn? Nachos? Candy?" he asked.

"Popcorn is fine," El said. "I'll buy it. You bought the tickets. Do you want anything else?"

El bought a large popcorn and two bottles of water, and then they went into theater two. Owen directed her to the center of the theater and asked if it was okay to sit there. El said, "Of course." She hated to sit in the first few rows.

They participated in the movie trivia questions before the start of the film, laughing at some of the answer options, and enjoyed the popcorn, which El held on her left leg since Owen was on her left. Once the lights dimmed and the movie began, Owen snuggled closer to her and put his arm around her shoulder.

Halfway through the movie, after the popcorn was finished and El had moved the bucket to the floor, he repositioned so his hand was near her left knee. El mirrored his action. And that's how they stayed until the movie ended.

El whispered, "I like to watch the credits."

"Really? Me too," Owen said.

After they finished but before they left their seats, El explained, "I'm always curious about where the movie has been filmed."

Owen admitted that he had friends who went into sound engineering and videography so he was forever on the lookout for names of people he knew. "Stupid, right?" he asked El.

"Not at all," she said. "Some day you may be able to say 'hey, I went to school with that person' when you see them thanking the Academy." El grinned.

Owen laughed. His arm went around her as they exited the theater. "I'd love to ask you to get a drink or get dessert but I'm not consuming either until after the race."

"Do you drink tea?" El asked, not wanting the date to end so soon.

"I do," Owen said. "Want to go find some?"

"I was thinking we could drink some at my place," El said, but then realized the implication when she saw a huge smile on his face. She quickly added, "When I said tea, I meant tea." She giggled. "It wasn't a euphemism."

Owen laughed and said, "That's too bad, but I'll happily drink tea with you and hang out with Mr. Fluffy."

"I'm sure he'll be thrilled," El said.

Twenty minutes later when they entered her apartment, Mr. Fluffy greeted them at the door. He wove himself around Owen's ankles purring his happiness. Owen picked him up and cradled him like last time. El took off her boots and then went into the kitchen to heat water. "Herbal okay with you? It's too late for me to drink caffeine," she said.

"Herbal's fine." Owen made himself at home on El's sofa and removed his shoes. Mr. Fluffy parked himself on Owen's lap.

When El returned with a ceramic teapot that had tea brewing inside and two mugs and took in the scene, she said, "That's so weird. I've never seen him like this with anyone, not even Jack. Are you really a cat whisperer?"

"Nah. But animals do love me. When I was little any bird or furry thing that was hurt I brought home. My mother hated it because she never knew what I'd walk in the door with. Sometimes I'd have a snake in my pocket, or one time it was two squirrel babies that a hawk had swooped in on and I tried to save." Owen looked sad when he added,

"The talon marks were too deep and they didn't make it."

"Oh wow," El said. "Dr. Doolittle in training."

Owen smiled. "I loved Dr. Doolittle. I probably would have become a vet or a zoologist or something, but I never wanted to help an animal die." Owen stared off at the far wall. Quietly he added, "That's one of my weaknesses."

El could relate. She reached for his hand and held it. "I could never be a vet either."

They had a few moments of silence, lost in their own thoughts, and then El let go of his hand to pour the tea. She handed a mug to Owen, and asked how long he had been running.

"I've done it on and off since I was a teenager," he said. "But usually just a couple of miles at a time." He explained that after his last relationship ended and he was feeling a bit depressed, he started running more earnestly and daily. It created endorphins that chased away his blues. Then he started to do races, 5K, 10K, half marathons for fun, but found them a bit addicting also. The race on Sunday would be his first full marathon. He had been practicing with Team in Training for it and felt ready, but also felt ready to get it over with.

He laughed. "You know when you plan and prep for something for a long time that you're also sick of it by the time the event arrives?"

El immediately thought of Teresa's wedding. She was happy for T and Jordan but so much of their friendship and time over the last few months had been devoted to Teresa's wedding that she couldn't wait for it to be past them. "Absolutely," El said and took a sip of the tea.

"That's kind of where I am right now. But I'd also love to be able to say, 'Yeah, I've run a marathon.'" Owen shrugged his shoulders.

"It is quite an accomplishment," El said, though she, herself, had no aspirations to ever run one.

She took another sip of tea, when suddenly she wondered something. "Hey, did you know Jack has a girlfriend?"

Owen looked her in the eyes and responded, "Yes, I know he's been dating one of your best friends."

"And you knew I didn't know?"

Owen still gazed into her eyes. "Yes, El. Jack asked me not to tell you. At first he thought they were just hooking up and having fun. Then he told me they were both scared shitless when they realized it might be something more. I told him it was about time he had genuine deep feelings for someone." Owen smiled. "And I'm so glad that cat is out of the proverbial bag."

At the word cat, Mr. Fluffy opened his eyes and peered at Owen.

"Not you, cat." He pet Mr. Fluffy causing him to loudly purr. "Oh, you like that, huh?" Owen said to the cat.

El sighed and admitted to herself that she'd like to be pet by Owen in a similar fashion. She was sure she might purr, too. Aloud, she said, "You're a good friend."

Owen stopped petting Mr. Fluffy, set his tea on a coaster on the end table, and directed his full attention to El once again. He put a hand on her neck near her ear and looked into her eyes. "El, are you okay with Jack and Leticia?"

"Yes. It was a shock at first, but then I realized it made sense. Both them being together and the secrecy. Though I never thought either of them would really settle down."

Owen stroked her cheek with his thumb. "Settled isn't a word I'd use for Jack. I don't think being with someone means monotony or even a routine. Or it doesn't have to. Jack is still the same guy, full of life, always going somewhere or doing something. He's always been a combo of the life of the party and extremely driven. From what I understand, your friend Leticia is the same way. The only thing that has changed is that they have agreed to only have sex with each other, as opposed to changing partners whenever the urge hit them, like they did before."

El wondered if that would eventually grow old for them. She hoped not as she didn't want to see either heartbroken. "It seems like a big change for them," El almost whispered.

"It may be," Owen said, "but that's what love does. Sneaks up on you and makes you rethink your life. Jack said he knew he was in trouble when he wanted to be with Leticia more than he wanted his space." He paused and took a breath. He moved his face just a tad closer to hers and then said, "And right now I'm glad to be in your space, El."

He kissed her sweetly at first and then more hungrily.

El felt the electric jolt of the kiss all the way to her toes. She returned his kiss with fervor and when he ran his hand on the outside of her sweater, she kissed him more deeply.

After a few moments, she broke away from his lips. Breathless, she searched his eyes and all she saw was the same flame that had been stoked within her.

"Mr. Fluffy, please move," El said, dumping the cat from Owen's lap. "Now where were we?" she said to Owen, pushing him back onto the sofa cushions and planting herself, fully clothed, lengthwise on top of him.

After twenty more minutes of making out with roving hands and gasps and a few moans, Owen asked if she wanted to relocate to her bedroom.

Still atop him and a bit disheveled, she hesitated and thought of Bernie. And then she wondered what the pre-Jack Leticia would do. *Ah, hell, she'd go for it,* she thought. But El wasn't Leticia and she wasn't sure about sleeping with a guy she really liked while she was still dating other guys she really liked. Before she answered, Owen, who had been watching her closely, said, "El, it's okay. Your hesitation is your answer. Plus you made it clear from the beginning that your invitation for tea wasn't a booty call."

El felt relief followed quickly by disappointment. "It's not that I don't want to," she started. "I am SO attracted to you, and I'm loving getting to know you, the adult you as opposed to Jack's teenage friend." She sat up and made some space between them. "But I've been in relationships on and off for years and I've never taken the time to date or find out who I am and what I want. It would be so easy for me to say yes to sex with you right now. I mean, you are one terrific kisser and definitely have my juices flowing..." El blushed that she admitted the last part.

Owen smiled.

"But unlike Jack and Leticia, I've never been one to have sex for having sex's sake."

"I respect that," Owen said. He massaged her hand and maintained eye contact.

El realized he might be thinking she was hinting for a relationship so she added, "That said, I'm not asking for a relationship. I'm just saying I need to figure some things out before we get that intimate."

"Okay," Owen said. "El, I like you. I have since we were kids. I'm not going anywhere."

El had been holding her breath and she finally let it out. She felt relief that she stated what she needed and he wasn't angry or dismissive. What she felt emanating from him was love and patience.

"Thank you," she said, and snuggled closer to him and hugged him. He encircled her in his arms and kissed the top of her head. She breathed in his spicy scent and felt so relaxed and at peace in his arms. That's what she really missed about being in a relationship: the regular physical contact and falling asleep in someone's arms. And if she were going to be authentic about her own needs, that's what she wanted.

She pulled back a little so she could see his face. "Owen, would you think I was a cock tease if I asked you to spend the night but not have sex? I'd love to fall asleep with us holding each other."

Owen grinned. "As long as you're okay if I sleep in my boxer briefs and you understand being so close to you may arouse the beast."

El chuckled. "I get it. And I'll make you breakfast in the morning but you can't stay too late as I have something at ten o'clock."

"Deal," he said, kissing her lightly. Then he picked up their mugs and the teapot and carried them into the kitchen. "Hey, you wouldn't happen to have an extra toothbrush, would you?"

"No...oh wait. I have extra replacement heads for my Sonicare." El ran into the bathroom, grabbed the box and the toothbrush, and then met him in the kitchen. "Here, there's a blue banded one and a grey banded one. Which do you want? I'm using the pink one."

"Either. Thank you." El unscrewed her toothbrush head and replaced it with the blue one and handed the whole toothbrush to Owen. "Toothpaste is in my medicine cabinet. Help yourself to that or anything else you need."

El loaded the dishwasher while Owen used her bathroom. El changed into her pajama bottoms and tank top in her walk-in closet. When she emerged Owen was staring at the bed. He asked, "Which side do you usually sleep on?"

"The right," El said. "Or sometimes the middle." El went into the bathroom to clean her face and teeth.

Owen pulled off his jeans and sweater and folded them neatly and put them on El's dresser. When El emerged from the bathroom, he said, "Thank you for inviting me to spend the night with you. I read somewhere that sleeping with someone is more intimate than sex and can mean a person trusts you since we can be at our most vulnerable when we sleep." He slipped into the left side of El's bed.

She had never thought of sleeping with someone that way, but it made sense. She snuggled closer to Owen, facing him. They kissed a few times, softly and sweetly, careful not to let passion overpower them.

At one point the kiss deepened and El could feel Owen's arousal. But suddenly they felt all eighteen pounds of cat and claws on their heads. Mr. Fluffy had pounced onto the pillow where he usually slept, not caring that it was occupied.

Owen moved the furball from their heads and plopped him onto El's pillow. Then he pulled El partway onto him on the left side of the bed. "Good night, beautiful," he said, "and pleasant dreams." He encircled her in his arms and they both drifted off to sleep.

Chapter 18

Around six, El awoke and found that they were still snuggled close together and that Mr. Fluffy was in a ball against her shoulder blades. Owen snored lightly. She didn't want to disturb either of them but she really had to pee, so she moved as carefully as possible to disentangle herself. Once in the bathroom, she decided to shower, shave, and put on just a touch of make-up before Owen woke up.

When she exited the bathroom in her black terry cloth robe, she found him sitting up in bed, Mr. Fluffy on his lap again, reading the mystery novel that had been on her dresser. "Enjoying that?" she asked.

"Actually, yes. Have you read Diane Mott Davidson's Goldilock's Catering series?" The question coming from Owen's mouth seemed incongruent with the masculinity of his chest, El thought. He was certainly a man of surprises.

"Yes, the whole series. But why have you?"

"She includes great recipes," Owen said, not answering the question.

"Agreed. But you're male. And a very hot one at that," El added.

Owen grinned. "Thank you. But are you saying hot males can't read mysteries?"

"They don't usually read cozies. They read Patterson and police procedurals and thrillers. At least I think so." El realized that Derek never read fiction and any other guy she been in relationships with hadn't either.

"I have read Patterson and police procedurals. I also read a lot of nonfiction, whatever wins The National Book Award and the Pulitzer each year, and any books on science and nature. I don't know if you remember or even knew but my mother is a literature professor and my dad is an economist. From the time we were young, they made us read for thirty minutes each day. At times I hated it because I'd rather ride bikes or run around with my friends. But as I got older, I saw its advantages so I've kept up the daily practice. Hell, I've even forwarded recipes in books to your brother." Owen grinned again.

"I did not know that. But in my defense, when we were kids, I thought you were one of Jack's annoying friends." They both laughed.

"And now?" Owen prompted.

"And now, you're partly naked and in my bed and…" we're talking about books is how El's mind finished that sentence, followed by the thought, *Are you crazy? Most women would be jumping him right now.*

"And?" Owen prompted again with a slight smile.

"And I'm torn between wanting to lick your nipple and delivering on that breakfast I promised you."

Owen's face broke into a full grin. "You could do both."

El returned his grin. "I could. But I also have a deadline this morning."

"True," Owen said. "And I'd rather we have unlimited time. If we're going to get together, I want to take it slow and for it to be the most pleasurable and memorable experience of your life."

His face was so serious, and that combined with the words, sent a jolt through El that made her knees weak. No man had ever mentioned her pleasure, except in comments like, "You like that, huh?" that seemed more about the man than her actual enjoyment.

"I'd like that," she squeaked, before walking to her closet and shutting herself in so she could catch her breath. She heard Owen go into the bathroom and close the door. She quickly dressed in black jeans and a mustard colored sweater, and then went into the kitchen to start the coffee.

When she heard Owen exit the bathroom, she asked if he wanted eggs and toast or yogurt and fruit. He came up behind her and wrapped his arms around her as she stood in front of the coffeemaker. He kissed her neck. "Thank you, El, for such a great night. I'll have coffee with some fruit. We can make a frittata together. Do you have some cheese and veggies?"

They joked around and enjoyed chopping tomatoes and mushrooms and then broccoli into almost dust. Owen whipped the veggies into the eggs and then poured it all into a pan that El had greased. They sat in the living room drinking their coffee while the egg mixture cooked in the toaster oven. Owen asked about her work and how busy she'd be in the coming week and when he could see her again.

El fed Mr. Fluffy so that the three of them could sit down to breakfast. And then Owen loaded the dishwasher and ran it before kissing El good-bye and thanking her once again for spending the night with him.

After El shut the front door after his departure, she asked Mr. Fluffy, "Did I do the right thing?"

She swore the cat rolled his eyes before licking his paw.

She said aloud, "To thine own self be true."

She grabbed her wallet and keys and headed out the door. El had agreed to meet Keith for coffee at The Ink Spot. He was already waiting there for her with a cup in front of him. She greeted him and went to get her coffee and thought about Owen. Maybe she should have cancelled the coffee with Keith.

She wasn't sure what they were going to talk about. She had been so focused on work and Owen that she hadn't thought much about this. As she sat down and saw Keith's big smile and bright blue eyes, she realized that it didn't matter what they talked about. It would be nice to have someone with whom to share ideas.

He said, "Tell me more about what the program is like. If I decide to enroll, what would I be learning?"

She talked to him about some of the books she had read and he wrote them down and promised to get them. He asked her about what started her on this journey so she told him about Derek and why she was trying to figure it out. It was easy to talk to Keith. He didn't interrupt and seemed genuinely interested about what she had to say.

She was curious about his divorce and finally asked him about it.

He looked down at his cup and took a breath. He looked back at her and smiled ruefully. "I was wondering when you'd ask," he said. "There's not much to tell. She was my high school sweetheart. We decided to go to the same college and after that got married." He paused. "We grew apart, and when she got offered a transfer to Chicago, we decided to split."

"Oh, I'm sorry to hear that."

"Yeah, well it was not the direction I expected my life to take."

"I can imagine."

"I haven't been interested in going through that again. But then Todd told me about talking to you and I was intrigued. It sounds like I can learn some things."

"You really want to have a study group?"

"Oh yeah, I'm great at studying, but I'd really appreciate a woman's point of view to really help me understand." He smiled. "I mean, I want to get good grades and I think that can help me make the dean's list."

El laughed. "Okay, I'm in," she said. They decided that he'd read one of the books and they'd get back together to discuss it.

They chatted about other things and El found herself telling Keith about what was going on at work. He listened to her concerns about the new opportunity, and unlike Mr. Fluffy, he asked good questions and told her it sounded impressive.

Owen was a good listener, too, but this was different. There was no pressure or nervousness about talking to Keith because it didn't feel like there was anything at stake. She didn't need to impress him or worry what he thought. He was a nice friendly guy and she could be herself. Hmm she thought, how can I get that same relaxed feeling with guys I'm interested in?

She realized that the tables around them had turned over several times and they'd been chatting for almost two hours. Keith said he'd check his schedule and would get back to her for their next study group. This is going to be fun, she thought.

When she got back home, she texted Leticia and Teresa that she had another fabulous date with Owen. Teresa responded right away with "Details!?"

El texted, "Too hot to text, call me." The phone rang a few minutes later and her friend said, "What happened?"

El laughed. "Whatever do you mean?" Then she told Teresa all about the wonderful evening. She left out a few details but Teresa got the message.

"Whoa. I told you. He's a keeper."

"Okay, it's only our second date...or maybe our third if you count that first meal. I think I need to know him a little longer."

"Yes, but it's the second time you've fallen asleep with him."

"Good point."

They continued to talk about Owen until Teresa had to get off to meet her mom to talk about some final wedding details.

As El cleaned the kitchen, she thought about Owen and what a special night it had been. Leticia called her a little while later, and El went through the whole story again. It was even more fun telling it again.

She spent the rest of the day grocery shopping and running errands that she didn't have time for during the week. When she finally got home to Mr. Fluffy, she stretched out on the couch and was reminded again of what a wonderful night it had been. Then she started thinking about seeing Bernie the next day and wondered if she should cancel. She felt kind of bad. Did she want to cancel it? No, she realized that she really had fun with Bernie. He made her laugh.

After dinner, she reached for the cozy mystery and made a bag of popcorn. Owen texted her and said he was going to bed soon and missed her company. They texted back and forth for a bit before he said good night. When she slid into bed, she imagined him next to her again and grabbed an extra pillow to hold onto. The thought of his warm skin against hers made her sigh.

The next morning, she wondered how he was doing in the marathon. She started to imagine his sexy shoulders and shook her head to clear her thoughts. She spent some of the morning checking work emails just to make sure things would not be too overwhelming on Monday. She didn't like giving up part of her weekend, but it was a way to reduce stress a little.

She arrived at Sugar and Spice on time, but there was no sign of Bernie. He texted that he'd be right there and because there were only a few tables open, she decided to take one. According to the menu, the restaurant was a local favorite for giant cinnamon rolls but she wasn't sure she was in the mood for that. The place was noisy and she didn't notice Bernie until he put his hand on her shoulder. "Hello, Cinderella." He leaned over and kissed her. He really does have such nice soft lips, she thought. He sat down across from her and reached out his hand to touch her fingertips. He was wearing a blue shirt with pink flamingos on it and a grey fedora.

"How was the movie?"

"Amazing. You might have hated it. It had even more blood than I expected."

"Glad I passed."

As they chatted about the menu, El realized that she was feeling relaxed. She wasn't sure if it was because of Bernie's personality or because going out with Owen took some pressure off—it meant she didn't have to obsess if Bernie was "the one" for her. It surprised her so much that she momentarily missed what Bernie was saying about the pancakes and had to ask him to repeat it. She had expected that it might be an uncomfortable lunch because she was feeling guilty about seeing both of them. She still felt a little bad but realized that it was easier to relax when she wasn't worrying if someone was her true love or not.

Bernie rested his hand on hers as they waited for their food. He told some stories about Stu, who had apparently decided to go on a caveman diet and was driving him crazy. He wanted to throw out all Bernie's food, calling it poison and made snotty remarks when he cooked. El laughed along with Bernie who didn't seem to be too upset about it. It sounded like Stu started fads like that regularly.

El enjoyed the rest of lunch. She told Bernie about her brother and Leticia and what a surprise that had been. Bernie wanted to hear more and then they told stories about their families. After lunch, they walked hand in hand down the street window shopping. Bernie suggested a local street fair and El said she was a little tired and needed to get back home. Bernie stopped and looked at her. "Big date last night?"

El could feel herself blushing. "No," she said a little too loudly but glad that it was the truth. "It's just been a really long week at work." She proceeded to tell him about what had happened with Kate and ignored the obvious point of the question. They talked for a few more minutes and headed back to the restaurant.

They stopped in front of her car and Bernie put his arms around her and she felt his lips on hers. Then he kissed the top of her head and held her close before saying goodbye.

When she got home, she checked her phone for messages. One was from Keith and commented on some things he read in the book El suggested. One was from Owen stating, "I'm now a marathon finisher. Want to come over and congratulate me with a kiss?" El smiled at that.

She responded, "How about a celebratory dinner Tuesday night? My treat."

"Great," Owen said. "Tell me when and where and I'll be there."

The third text was from Jack confirming the time and address for Saturday. Jack had offered Jack's Victorious Veggies truck to cater Teresa's shower, at cost, since he knew being in the wedding and throwing the shower and the bachelorette weekend was a lot of expense for El and Leticia. Teresa's aunt had offered to host the shower at her home in Walnut Creek, which had much more space for all of the guests than either El or Leticia's one-bedroom apartments.

Chapter 19

On Monday evening at 6:30, Leticia buzzed El's apartment. She brought with her a cauliflower crust pizza and a bottle of pinot noir. El had dozens of small glass bowls, boxes of sugar, an assortment of essential oils, markers, labels, and ribbons spread over the living room floor. She also had the invite list in an Excel spreadsheet, with notes on responses, a stack of index cards, and a list of potential games printed from a bridal website.

After inhaling a slice of pizza, Leticia asked, "Have I told you how much I hate showers? Bridal, baby, it doesn't matter."

"Many, many times," El said. "Just think of how much you love Teresa." She looked through the list of women coming to the shower. Thirty-six had responded, "Yes." Three hadn't responded at all. "Should we include the non-responders in the count just in case?"

"I guess," Leticia said. "Do we have enough for them?"

"Plenty," El said. She would lead the group through creating their own bottles of sugar scrub as their take-home favor. She had assigned Leticia to lead a game called Fantasy Date. El hated shower games so she was determined to keep it to just one, to satisfy Teresa's older relatives, of which there were many. Fantasy Date required every woman to write on an index card which celebrity would be their dream date. And then everyone else had to match the celebrity with the woman who wrote it.

Leticia read the directions from a website, and said, "I like the flip idea of writing who would be your celebrity date from hell. That would be more fun."

"We can do both, if you want. We'll have time and we have plenty of index cards." El drained her glass of pinot noir. Then she grabbed the spool of blue tulle and measured and cut six-inch squares. Leticia took each square, put a spoonful of Jordan almonds in it, and tied it with a white ribbon.

"When you said Jordan almonds, I thought why? So old school. But then I got it. Teresa and Jordan. Duh." Leticia laughed.

"Exactly," El said. She laughed at her own joke. "So, what did you end up getting T, besides this shower?"

Leticia looked at El but didn't say anything at first, then she said, "Don't laugh, but I ordered them a personalized bride and groom Christmas ornament. I figured it could be the first ornament they own together."

"Oh my God. That's romantic." El wished she had thought of that, and she was a bit surprised that Leticia did. She had never considered that Leticia had any romantic bones in her body.

"Thank you."

El ran into her bedroom and pulled out the agate cutting board she had bought Teresa and the silk nightie. "This is for their wedding gift," El said, nodding her head towards the board, "and this is for the shower."

"They are both gorgeous," Leticia said. She had about half of the packets of almonds put together so she took a break to eat more pizza.

As El bit into a slice, Leticia asked, "Are you really okay with me and Jack?"

"Absolutely," El said. "I mean part of me feels like I would have rather known earlier, but the other part of me totally gets it. And I love you both so much and I can totally see you together. But no pressure. He's my brother and all but I want you to be happy." El suddenly felt like a shift could be happening in their friendship. "You'd tell me if you weren't right, even though he's my brother?"

"Yes, El," Leticia said. "No more secrets. You know, I've never wanted or needed a guy before. I mean for beyond sex. I thought relationships weren't for me. I loved my life, my work, my friends. And when I needed more, booty calls were so easy and drama-free." She took a sip of wine. "But with Jack, things are different. I want to know everything about him and I'm okay with him knowing everything about me. I want to build something with him. Hell, if I accidentally got pregnant, I might even consider having his baby."

"Whoa!" El exclaimed. She knew how adamant Leticia was against having children. All through college she played that Harvey Danger song and sang along super loudly, "Been around the world and found / That only stupid people are breeding." "That's huge," El said.

"I know." Leticia looked a bit disappointed in herself with her mouth turned down and her brow furrowed.

El raised her glass. "I'm happy for you. Happy for the both of you. The world needs more love and I'm glad the bug bit you and Jack." She grinned.

"Cheers," Leticia said, smiling again. "So, things are heating up with Owen. How'd your date with Bernie go? Anyone else I need to know about?"

El filled her in on the date, on the two-person study group with Keith, and that she was taking Owen to a celebratory dinner tomorrow night.

"Do you think you'll finally do it?" Leticia asked.

"Not sure. I have this little Leticia devil on my one shoulder saying, 'Go for it! He's hot. Be like Nike and just do it.'"

Leticia laughed. "I've been called worse things and have given worse advice."

El chuckled. "And then this little angel from somewhere in my childhood or Sunday school or something says, 'No. Wait.'"

"What's holding you back?"

"Dating two guys at once. Not knowing if Owen is dating or sleeping with other people. I figured Bernie probably is, which is one reason I haven't gone there with him. Do you remember at some point in high school health class or somewhere hearing that by having sex with someone you're also being intimate with all of the people they've had sex with?"

"That's a disgusting concept."

"I know. But I think it is holding me back. You know me. I've never had a one night stand. All of my sexual partners have been either someone who was a very close friend or whom I've dated long term."

"Which may be why you need to cut loose and have some fun. Look, I'm not saying be reckless. But you like Owen and he likes you. See how compatible you are. Give it a chance to see where it goes. And if you decide to do the same thing with Bernie, that's great. Grab life, or the guys, by the balls." Leticia grinned like a piranha. "Be empowered. Tap into the El that is kicking ass at work. She's the same El that can excel in her Master's Degree in Relationships. Then again, if you get all A's, maybe you should go on for a Ph.D." Leticia laughed. Then as if something just occurred to her, she reached for her giant purse, and pulled out a box of condoms and tossed them to El. "But use these," she said.

"Thanks, but I have some. And don't you need them?"

"Nah. When Jack and I decided to be exclusive, we got tested, and then stopped using condoms."

"That's a HUGE step for you," El said. For years Leticia had preached the importance of always using a condom and having back up protection such as the pill. She wanted there to be no chance at all of pregnancy.

"I know. But if you're going to listen to my little devil on your shoulder advice, be safe."

"So you really think I should do it?"

"Yes. In fact, call him right now and say you're coming over. Don't wait until tomorrow. A surprise booty call would blow his mind."

"Ha ha. That's too much." The thought of that sent a surge of energy straight to her vagina but also made her nervous and lightheaded. She drained the rest of her glass. "Let's get this shower crap over with so we can call it a night."

The next morning did not start off well. El spilled a coffee on her desk and barely missed dousing her laptop. Then the fire alarm went off in the building and they had to evacuate until they got the all clear. Is it going to be one of those days? she wondered.

That night she met Owen at a local restaurant that he suggested, a casual barbeque place, BBQ Baby, that had picnic tables with plastic tablecloths. She thought it would be safer than cooking for him at her place. As she waited, she got a text that he was running late. He showed up fifteen minutes later and apologized as he hugged and kissed her. "Work was really crazy today. Hard to leave. So sorry." He smiled at her and she told him not to worry. But there was a little voice in her brain that reminded her that Derek also would get stuck at work and make her wait. They ordered their food at a counter and got a plastic number to put on their table.

Owen steered her to a table in the corner and sat next to her. He rested his hand on her leg as he turned to her and asked her how she was doing. As she told him about planning the shower with Leticia, he seemed a little distracted. The server brought over Owen's tall Blue Moon with an orange and El's Sea Glass cabernet. His phone beeped and he apologized and looked at it. He frowned.

"Nothing important," he said. "So sorry."

"No worries. Tell me about the marathon."

He ran his fingers through his hair, and El heard his phone beep again but he ignored it. As he talked about the marathon, he seemed to relax a little. He was really proud that he had finished and showed her some pictures of him at the finish line with his group.

When the food arrived, it smelled delicious. Owen had ordered the brisket plate with jalapeno cornbread and mac and cheese. El had picked the pulled pork sandwich and coleslaw and it was much bigger and messier than she had expected. The first bite was delicious, and El thanked Owen for suggesting it. "But, I'm going to need a lot more napkins," she said trying not to lose any of the pork from the bun. She offered Owen some and held it out for him to bite. He happily took a bite and offered her some of his.

Owen held up his beer and pointed to his plate. "I earned this and now I can enjoy it."

As they continued to talk, El heard his phone beep a few more times but he didn't look at it. She was having fun but something felt a little off. She tried to ignore it. Having Owen's leg pressed against her own was making her feel very warm.

El was trying to decide what to do next, when Owen said, "Listen, I'm really sorry. It's been a very long day. I have a lot of things going on. Can we call it a night?"

El tried not to show how disappointed she was but said that was fine.

"Thanks, I appreciate you understanding," he said as he rubbed her arm.

At her car, Owen wrapped his arms around her and kissed her. Before he let her go, he squeezed her tightly. On the drive home she wondered if she had done something wrong or if he was just having a bad day.

"What do you think, Mr. Fluffy?" she asked when she got home. "Why are men so hard to figure out? At least you're easy to understand."

She got a text from Owen saying thanks for dinner and sorry he had to go. Then she got a text from Keith asking if she'd like to meet for coffee again on Saturday. She texted back that she had a bridal shower so it wouldn't work. He said he was busy Sunday so what about Thursday night? She didn't want to tell him that would be her next pole dancing class so she suggested Wednesday night. She thought it would be fun and might keep her mind off what was going on with Owen.

The next morning Leticia texted her, "How was last night???"

El sighed and texted back that he'd had a long day and so they just had dinner. She realized that even though she'd told him it was fine, she was disappointed. How could he be so amazing and then... She really didn't feel like thinking about it. Fortunately, work was packed with meetings and she barely had time to eat a quick yogurt at her desk for lunch.

At the end of the day, she rushed to The Ink Spot and found Keith waiting for her in the Ink Link. He'd suggested that they get a sandwich there so they could spend more time talking about the book. He had a sandwich and water in front of him and she went to order. She came back to the table with a ham sandwich and iced tea.

They chatted for a few minutes and El said, "So study buddy, what did you read?"

"I decided to start with *Attached*."

"Good choice," she said. "What'd you learn? Did you take the quiz?"

"Yes," he said and paused.

"Well?"

"I'm not being graded on this right?"

She laughed. "No grades."

"Okay, I had a hard time with the quiz. I was high on the Secure style and the Avoidant style."

"Which means?"

"It seems like I'm okay at understanding someone else's moods and responding to them so that's the Secure. But then I don't like feeling controlled by someone else and my independence is important to me so that's Avoidant."

El thought about Derek, the poster child for the Avoidant style.

"And what do you think about that?"

"Well, it wasn't what I wanted to see. The Secure style sounds much better. And what about you, where did you score?"

"Oh, I scored higher on Anxious and Secure. Hardly at all on Avoidant."

"Interesting," he said, looking at her and unwrapping his sandwich. "Why?"

"I would have thought that you would have been higher on the Secure style." Keith looked at her and smiled. "I figured that you were a TA for this class so you had all the answers. What did you learn?" He took a bite.

"I thought it was a great book. What I found most interesting was taking the quiz about your partner's style and thinking about my ex-boyfriend. Understanding the Avoidant style really put things into place."

Keith nodded. "Yeah, I thought about my ex-wife and realized that she was Anxious style. She was very sensitive and there was a lot of drama." He paused. "I guess I could have handled it better. I just really didn't understand what was going on though. She just seemed really moody. And when she was emotional, I tried to be logical. Acted Avoidant."

"Sounds tough." She took a bite of her sandwich and they both sat in silence.

Keith looked up from his sandwich. "One thing I found really interesting is the notion that we may be drawn to opposite styles so we keep running the same bad script again over and over. Unless we understand it and stop. Which is why I want this degree. I don't want to do this again."

El nodded and took a sip of iced tea. "I agree."

They chatted more about the styles and El said, "Okay, study buddy. I have a question for you. What is it about guys that they are so Avoidant? First you start off so nice and sweet and then you stop."

Keith stopped chewing and looked at El. He swallowed. "Are you mad at all guys or just me?"

"I'm not mad at you or all guys."

"Well you certainly sound like it."

El sighed. "I didn't mean to. It's just that…" and then she told Keith briefly about the date with Owen the night before. She ended with, "I don't know what happened. I mean did he decide he doesn't like me? Did his ex-girlfriend call him? What's going on?" She covered her hands with her eyes. "I'm so sorry. I shouldn't have told you all that."

Keith said, "It's okay. Don't be upset." He paused. "All right, study buddy, what would someone with a Secure style do?"

El tipped her head back and sighed again. "Someone with a Secure style would stop making up stories and would focus on the problem at hand."

Keith smiled. "Good. And then?"

"And then, someone with a Secure style would show concern for the other person and be there for them."

"Bingo."

She said, "And that person would text the other person and see how he's doing without being snotty or passive aggressive." She looked at Keith and smiled. "Did I pass?"

He nodded. "Impressive. I think you did great on the quiz."

"Thank you. I really needed to hear that."

"That's what a Secure style does," he said smiling.

They talked for a little while longer about the book and then agreed to meet again the next week.

When El got to her car, she texted Owen. "It was nice to see you yesterday. I hope you're having a better day today. Let me know if I can help with anything."

Owen texted back almost immediately. "Thanks. Still at work. May I call you when I get home?"

El immediately thought of Derek again and his long hours. Then she checked herself. "Only you can rewrite the script," she said aloud to herself. "Owen isn't Derek and you don't know what is going on." In fact, El realized, Owen was courteous enough to ask if he could call; he didn't assume she'd be available to him whenever he wanted.

As El was about to drive out of the parking lot, she spotted Bernie and another man. The guy held the door open for Bernie and Bernie grinned at him in a similar way he looked happily at El. El wondered if they were on a date.

When she got home, Mr. Fluffy greeted her with a loud "Meow." He then raced into the kitchen and banged his empty bowl with his paw. "Point taken," El said to him as she dumped kibble into his bowl. Mr. Fluffy was the epitome of Secure, and he was very demanding. El shook her head. After Mr. Fluffy gobbled his food, he jumped onto her bed and watched her change out of her work clothes. When she sat next to him, he snuggled close.

"I wish cats could come to the wedding," El said. "You'd be a great date." Mr. Fluffy rolled his eyes up at her. "And you'd be cute in a little tux." El giggled, acknowledging to herself that she sounded a bit like a crazy cat lady.

She pulled on her pajamas, washed her face and brushed her teeth, and then she settled into bed with Mr. Fluffy, her mystery novel, and her phone.

At nine, Owen called and the first words out of his mouth were, "Is it too late for you to talk?"

"No. It's fine." El appreciated his consideration.

"I wanted to apologize for how distracted I was last night and how disconnected from you. Work turned into a dramafest this week, with so many fires that need to be either put out or managed. My head wasn't on the date despite you being sweet enough to take me out to celebrate the marathon."

El wished they were on video so she could see his face. "Thank you for the apology," she said. Then she took a deep breath and decided to speak her truth. "I was disappointed with how things went. And I owe you an apology for mentally comparing you to my ex."

"Will you permit me to make it up to you on Friday night?" Owen asked. "You'll have my undivided attention. I give you my word."

"Your word, huh? That's pretty serious," El joked. "At least it wasn't an Unbreakable Vow." El figured since Owen was a reader, he'd get the Harry Potter reference.

Owen chuckled. "You know at the age I read that series, I dreamed that you'd be my Ginny Weasley."

"That's sweet," El said, truly touched. "So are we going to a

Quidditch match on Friday?"

"That's not the kind of game I had in mind," Owen almost whispered.

El's stomach did a flip flop. "Oh," she said as more of an exhale than a word. And then she decided to be bolder than she ever had. It was time to write a new story. "So strip poker then?"

Owen laughed heartily. "Only if you want. But I'll let you know getting me naked wouldn't be much of a challenge because I suck at poker."

El grinned from ear to ear even though he couldn't see her. "So no poker then," she said.

"Uh...no." Owen said as El realized the entendre of what she said. "I was thinking more of a romantic, homecooked dinner. But without the tux and fancy dress this time. What do you say? You can even bring Mr. Fluffy, if he's a cat that travels."

El smiled again, and then said, "Thank you. He doesn't. And I have a bridal shower in Walnut Creek on Saturday and I need to leave for it in the late morning. Would you be willing to come here instead, that way if this turns into another sleepover, I don't have so much running around to do?"

"Absolutely," Owen said. "But I'll still handle dinner. Does six-thirty work?"

"That sounds great. Thank you for being flexible. Good night."

"Pleasant dreams, El. I wish I were there holding you right now."

After El ended the call, she said to Mr. Fluffy, "Owen isn't Derek. He's way more self-aware. Derek would have never apologized or even thought he needed to." The cat stretched out a paw in response and kneaded her.

Chapter 20

El's Thursday at the office sailed by. She ran from meeting to meeting in the morning, had twenty minutes to scarf a salad for lunch, and then worked with her new assistant on and off for most of the afternoon.

Around 2 p.m. Bernie texted and asked if she wanted to go to brunch with him on Sunday. She sent back a "Yes. What time and where?"

At 2:30 p.m. Owen texted, "Miss you. Can't wait to kiss you." El smiled at that, and responded with "me too."

At 3 p.m. Keith texted, "What are your two most important values?"

El smiled at the phone. "Doing homework, are you?"

"I have a very strict TA"

"Oh really?"

"Yes. But's she's also pretty so I'm trying to impress her."

El stared at the phone. Was he flirting or teasing? She wasn't sure how to respond. Then she texted, "She thinks you're her best student. But then again, you're her only student."

"Touché." Keith wrote with a grinning emoji.

El shook her head to clear it. She needed to concentrate on work. She turned her phone facedown on her desk. She approved one team member's expense report, scheduled three team meetings for next week, and wrote updated status reports on two projects. Before she knew it, it was five o'clock. She sent a quick text to Teresa as she waited for the elevator. "Need to talk about all three guys. Starbucks next to class 30 min. before?"

Teresa said, "3? Sure."

El grabbed a smoothie with added protein powder at one of Jack's trucks before racing home to feed Mr. Fluffy and to change from her work clothes into yoga clothes for the pole dancing class. This week they were going to learn how to peel off tops in a sexy way so the instructors had told students to wear a sports bra or tight shirt under the top they were going to strip off.

She got to Starbucks just as Teresa was walking in. Teresa gave her a hug and said, "Three guys now. I just can't keep up with you. What's going on?"

El rolled her eyes and said, "Tea first." They got their drinks and sat at a table in the corner.

"Who's bachelor number three? Some cute guy at work?"

"Ewwww, no," said El. "I would never date anyone at work. I do not want to have to see someone at work after a break up. That's a problem just waiting to blow up."

"So?"

"It's Keith, the guy I told you about that wanted to learn more about my Master's Degree."

Teresa looked confused. "I thought he was the bookstore manager's brother and you were helping him out. And he's divorced. Why are you dating him?"

"No, I'm not dating him. He is Todd's brother. He wanted to discuss the material and it was fun talking to him about it. He read one of the books and we had a really good discussion. I wasn't interested in him." She paused.

"And...?" Teresa gestured for her to go on.

"And he texted me today with a question and he said I was pretty so I think he has begun flirting with me." When El said it aloud she realized that it sounded a little silly.

"So what? Good for you that he's flirting with you."

"Yes, but it made me wonder..." She paused again.

"Yes?"

"I wonder if maybe I should think about it."

"But you've got Owen and he's soooo hot and so sweet. And aren't you still seeing Bernie?"

"I know, I know, but there's something about Keith." El looked off to the side. "He's really nice to talk to. And it feels really relaxed and easy when I'm with him."

"Duh, of course it's easy to talk to him because he's just a guy, not someone you're interested in. That takes all the stress out of it."

El thought about it. "Maybe. But it seems different. He's a really nice and secure guy in a way I've never felt. It's so comfortable." She described some of the things they had talked about during their last meeting and described how he helped her to figure out what to do with Owen."

"Okay so keep talking to him. But tell me more about Owen."

Teresa frowned as El told her about the bad dinner date. Then El told her about the phone call and their plans for tomorrow night. Teresa sat back and smiled at her friend. "That's more like it." They talked for a few more minutes and realized they needed to get to the studio a few doors down the strip mall.

As the instructor, went through some announcements, El thought more about Keith. It's true she hadn't considered dating him because she was focused on Owen and Bernie. The thought of Bernie bothered her. Was he dating someone else? Should it bother her? After all, she was dating Owen. Maybe that's why he only asked to see her on Sunday. Ugh, that did bother her. She knew it wasn't fair but she didn't like it.

The first exercise for pole dancing class was a short meditation to relax and let go of the cares of the day. As she breathed out, El released her worries and told herself to stop thinking about guys. She needed to think about herself. She smiled and decided to focus on enjoying the class.

She was glad that the lighting in the studio was dim and there were no mirrors as she practiced the sexy moves. The instructor showed them how to grind their hips in a sensual dance while holding the bottom of the shirt and gently twisting it. She modeled how to slowly pull the shirt off and the group practiced it a few times. They then practiced a floor routine they had learned the week before and added the sexy shirt strip at the end. When they finished with that, they learned two new ways to spin around the pole.

El struggled with spins, but it didn't bother her. Even though they were fun, El didn't envision buying a pole for her living room. She could imagine showing Owen the floor routine and the shirt strip though so she was glad she'd learned that.

Teresa was more athletic than El and had an easier time practicing the spins. El smiled and hoped that Jordan would enjoy his surprise.

As they walked out of class, Teresa asked El. "So have you decided if you want to bring Owen to the wedding? Or Bernie?" she added when she saw the look on El's face.

El felt all the frustration that she had worked out during the class return to her shoulders. She knew that Teresa didn't mean to upset her but trying to decide who she would invite was stressful. Though if Bernie was seeing someone else maybe that was an easy way to decide. But El wasn't sure she wanted to bring Owen. She knew that Teresa was just trying to get everything taken care of for the wedding but she wished she would just give her some time.

She didn't want to upset her friend, so she said, "I'm still thinking about it."

When she got home she wondered why she was hesitating about bringing Owen. He was hot and fun and hot and sweet and hot…

But there was something that bothered her. A little voice in her head wondered if he really cared about her or if he still thought of her as that seventeen-year-old he'd had a crush on. His words, that he imagined that she'd be his Ginny Weasley, made her worry that he might still be crushing on her the way he did when they were in high school. But that was silly, she told herself as she put her pajamas on. After all, she didn't think of him as that annoying fifteen-year-old any more.

Friday at work was another busy day. She texted Leticia between meetings to make sure everything was set for the shower. In a way, she was glad the day was busy, that way she didn't have time to spend thinking about her date with Owen. At a few minutes to five, she texted Carl and asked if he had time to get a drink the following week. She regretted that though they had promised to get together regularly, that they had yet to make that a reality, and she missed him.

By quarter to six she was home, had sorted her mail, and had fed Mr. Fluffy. El stood staring into the closet unsure what to wear. She wanted to be comfortable and look sexy but not wear something that screamed "I wanna screw."

She texted Leticia and Teresa, "Do you think this sweater and jeans are okay for this date?"

She put on her lightest weight cashmere sweater with a deep V that showed just a hint of cleavage and took a photo and sent it.

"Hot," responded Leticia. "If I liked girls, I'd do you."

"Of course," texted Teresa.

"Very funny, L." El texted back while wearing a huge grin on her face. She took off the sweater and stripped nude and hopped into the shower. After a quick wash and one more swipe with the razor over her legs, she turned off the water and dried off.

Then she slipped on the jeans, a push-up bra, and the sweater; decided to go barefoot; fluffed up her hair and added a bit more mascara and some tinted lip balm. She also spritzed a light perfume behind her ear.

By the time she returned to the living room, Owen buzzed from downstairs asking to be let in. The scent of curry and cumin preceded his ringing of El's bell. She opened the door; his hands were full. He had a bouquet of purple irises in one hand and the bag of Indian take-out in the other. El stepped aside so he could enter her apartment.

"You look gorgeous," he said, as he made his way into the kitchen and set down the bag of food. "Jack said you liked Indian. I hope he is correct."

"I love it. Thank you," El said.

"And these are for you." Owen held out the flowers to her. "They were out of yellow roses, but I thought these looked happy."

El smiled, took the flowers, and got a glass vase from the cupboard.

Owen wrapped his arms around her from behind and kissed the top of her head. She leaned into him, relishing his warmth and his masculine scent.

He turned her around and kissed her, exploring her mouth with his tongue. He tasted slightly minty and cool, like he had been chewing gum.

When they broke apart he said, "Oh, and I forgot." He reached around El to the food bag and pulled out a can. "I couldn't forget about my fine, furry friend." Owen held up a can of salmon, which was way more food than the cat needed for one meal.

El grinned. She marveled at how thoughtful Owen was. "He'll be thrilled." She handed Owen a can opener from one of her drawers. "You do the honors, but just give him a quarter of that can. He's already had his supper. We'll save the rest."

El pulled some aluminum foil from a drawer to cover the rest of the can. Then she turned back to Owen, "Red or white wine?"

"Either. Lady's choice," he said. He started spooning food onto two plates.

As they ate, they reminisced about teachers they had had from kindergarten to grade twelve, about fellow students they had known and what they had seen on Facebook or LinkedIn that they were up to now.

El asked Owen about his past travels and if he had a bucket list of places he'd like to see. "Paris is supposed to be so romantic," he said. "We should go. And if I decide to keep at this marathon thing, a great one is supposed to be on The Great Wall in China. That'd be cool."

"It might," El said. She didn't respond to the Paris comment. She wasn't sure how she felt. To her, it seemed a little cliched. Romance could be had anywhere.

When they finished the food—long after Mr. Fluffy had scarfed his salmon and curled up on Owen's feet—El cleared the table. They all relocated to the living room sofa, with Mr. Fluffy parking himself between El and Owen. She asked Owen if he wanted to watch a movie, play a computer or board game, or listen to music.

"I love Cards Against Humanity," he said, "but it isn't fun without a group."

"Agreed," El said. She picked up Mr. Fluffy and set him down on the other side of Owen so she could snuggle closer to him. Her hormones felt like they were surging. She really wanted to kiss him again, so she did. Long, slow, and lingering, their kiss went on until they were breathless.

When they parted, Owen gazed at her with an intensity El had never seen before. "What?" she asked.

"You. You're just so…I mean, I've dreamed of you, this, us for so long. Come here." Owen pulled El onto his lap. He stroked the sleeve of her sweater. "And you're so soft. You feel so amazing."

Emboldened, El said, "And you are so freaking hot." She bit his bottom lip and purred.

He laughed. "*That* was hot."

She ran her hands over his biceps and down his chest. The T-shirt he wore was almost molded to his muscles, and she really, really wanted to touch those muscles, to feel their strength under her fingertips. "May I remove your shirt?" she asked.

"Absolutely." Owen grinned at her and held his hands over his head to facilitate the shirt's removal.

El shifted so she faced him and pulled the shirt up and off. "Hmmm," she said, first running her hands over him and then kissing his collarbone and his pec.

He grasped her waist and made encouraging sounds. When El bent down to kiss his belly and lick his abs, a small groan escaped his lips. He gently coaxed her head back up to his and engaged her in a deep, passionate kiss, while he used his hands to explore the front of her sweater and then her skin under the sweater and under her bra. El gasped as he played with her nipple while gently sucking her tongue.

When they came up for air, El said, "Maybe we should relocate," and led him into her bedroom.

Atop the bed, they continued kissing, caressing, and exploring one another's bodies. At some point—El lost track of time—she realized they were both mostly naked. Owen's head was between her legs and he was touching and probing with fingers and tongue and El was no longer caught up in the moment.

Words from Leticia flashed like neon in her head. "It goes from pleasure to annoying if a guy doesn't know what he's doing down there." El felt a bit like a science experiment. Sure, she acknowledged to herself that it was their first time together. They didn't know what the other liked. But right there, at that moment, she just wanted him to stop, wanted them to go back to how they were. So, she grabbed his arm and said, "Hey come back up here. I miss your lips."

And when he complied, she opened her mouth wide to him to show how much she still wanted him. She was determined to feel the magic again, the connection that they shared so strongly. She kissed him deeper, with more urgency. She ran her hands over his back and his buttocks, and she squeezed one of his ass cheeks. He moaned into their kiss.

She loved how strong and hard he felt and she was once again in the mood and in the moment, so she grabbed a condom from her nightstand and rolled it onto him. Then she tilted her hips just a little and invited him inside.

At first, he felt marvelous. It had been so long, and he was a little bigger than Derek. Owen moving inside her took her breath away.

But then he started short thrusts and jerking his hips in a way that banged against her. Try as she might, she couldn't match his rhythm. His eyes were closed and he seemed to really be into it. She looked up at the ceiling over his shoulder. She was unsure what to do. So she tried to move a bit, and she waited. And when he finally came and collapsed on top of her, she felt sadness. She had expected so much more.

He caught his breath and moved onto his side and next to her. "El, I'm sorry I couldn't wait for you, but that was amazing. Do you know how many years I've waited to do that with you?"

El forced a smile. "Probably too many."

"Next time I promise, we'll get you off first." He stroked her stomach and grinned at her.

"Okay," El said, telling herself that the first time for people together is often not good. But then she wondered if that was horseshit. She tried to remember the first time with Derek, but it was so many years ago. She did know that her first time ever was mediocre at best. Maybe she and Owen just needed more practice.

She kissed his lips and then padded barefoot into the bathroom to throw away the condom, to pee, and to brush her teeth. By the time she returned to the bed, Owen was already sound asleep with a smile on his face, and Mr. Fluffy was curled around his head.

Chapter 21

The next morning, El awoke to Owen drawing imaginary circles around her nipples and stomach. "Good morning, beautiful," he whispered.

"Morning," she said. Her body was responding to the stimulation, so she returned his caresses. Within minutes, she was slick and ready, so she pushed him onto his back on the bed and after putting a condom on him, she climbed on. Better for me to set the rhythm, she thought.

Owen cupped her butt and seemed to enjoy her grinding on him but when he tried to buck and jerk and become a more active participant, El lost the crescendo ride she had been on.

Dammit, she thought. She would have to be assertive to get what she needed. She put a hand in the middle of his chest. "Owen, may I use you for a few minutes? All you have to do is be here and stay hard."

He grinned. "I can do that."

"Good." El closed her eyes and moved in a way that brought her pleasure. She focused one hundred percent on herself and what she was feeling, and within two minutes, she came crashing hard and was breathless. She collapsed on his chest.

"Oh my God. You're so hot when you orgasm."

She smiled to herself.

Owen asked, "Would you mind finishing me off?"

"Sure. Come shower with me," El said, scooting off of him. She raced him to the bathroom.

Later, while they cooked breakfast, El texted Leticia, "Can you ride with me to the shower? I need to debrief ASAP."

"You okay?"

"Yes. No. IDK."

"I'll have Jack drop me off. xoxo."

"TY."

Leticia arrived at El's apartment ten minutes after Owen had kissed her goodbye, thanking her for such an awesome time. He asked to see her again after Teresa's shower, but El said it would be too late. And when he asked about Sunday, she said she already had plans. He left looking very disappointed though they made tentative plans for Monday.

Leticia helped El finish loading the party supplies in her car. Leticia offered to drive and El happily gave her the keys. They chatted about the party, going over some details. At a pause, Leticia said, "So what are we debriefing?"

"Ugh," said El slumping in her seat. "Last night. It was soooo..." She paused. "Okay, were you ever with a guy the first time and you just didn't seem to click?"

"Oh so that's what it was."

"Yeah." El sighed. "He's so hot and sexy but we weren't connecting. It just wasn't what I was expecting. I couldn't wait for him to leave this morning."

"Ouch. Sorry to hear that. Was he upset?"

"He was fine," said El loudly. "He didn't seem to notice that it was terrible and I didn't say anything."

"Whew, not good. What are you going to do?"

"I just don't know. I really like him," said El, twisting her hands. "He's sweet and adorable. I mean no one's ever done anything for me like that dance dinner. It was A-MA-ZING. And I normally have a great time with him. He's so hot and Mr. Fluffy LOVES him. He's like a cat whisperer. And Jack likes him. He's a great person."

Leticia said, "It doesn't matter who else likes him. This is about how you feel. If he's not the guy who lights your fire, he's not the one for you."

"That's just the thing! He was sooooo hot until we got into bed. Seriously, after the way I felt when he kissed me, I really expected something waaaay better," said El.

"Maybe you were expecting fabulous and he was only okay."

"I wish. He wasn't even okay."

"Yikes."

"And I'm not sure he even realized. Ugh. What am I going to do?" El closed her eyes.

"Do you think he's teachable?"

"I feel like I shouldn't have to teach him what to do."

"Maybe you just have to teach him how you like it. Everyone's a little different."

"Maybe. I just don't know."

"You don't have to decide now," said Leticia.

"Have you ever had bad sex?"

"Oh yeah. But I'm pretty clear about what I want and don't want." Leticia paused and said, "But you know my motto. Life's too short for bad sex."

El smiled. "Normally I would so agree with you! But I don't know. I've got to think about it." She paused. "But right now, we've got to think about Teresa."

"Yes, she's having great sex."

"Shut up," said El, laughing.

"Got you to laugh."

During the rest of the drive, they talked about the shower and the people who would be there. They wanted to make sure that Teresa had a great time.

Once at the house, they hurried to put things into place. El stopped thinking about Owen and focused on Teresa. She loved seeing her friend look so happy surrounded by her family and Jordan's family.

When El found a free moment and herself near Teresa's mom, she told her how glad she was that her chemo was over and that she looked good. Teresa's mom hugged her, and said she was feeling much better than she had a few months ago. She thanked El for helping Teresa find such a perfect wedding gown and for being such a great friend.

Jack's food was a big hit. After eating, they put Teresa in a large chair in the middle of the group and opened presents. The group had a great time playing games and El saw Leticia roll her eyes only once. At the end, Teresa gave El and Leticia big hugs and told them she was so lucky to have friends like them.

On the way home, Leticia brought up the subject again. "Any more thoughts about Owen?"

"Well, the old El would have been silently miserable or would have decided that this wasn't working. I realize though that I have to be authentic and talk to him about this."

"Good for you. How?"

"I don't know. I'm going to have to work on that a little bit. I don't want to hurt him but I need to say it in a way that's true for me. I could talk about what I want, not what I don't want."

"Sounds like a plan."

"I'm a bit concerned he won't take it well. But I'm not responsible for other people's responses. I'll say it the best way I can and be kind and sincere, but if he gets upset about it, that's going to be his problem."

"I agree. It's not up to you to make him feel better. He has a choice: he can listen to you or get upset at you."

"Yeah, well, we'll see what happens."

When they got back to El's apartment, they talked about the wedding. El said, "Teresa asked me again who I'm bringing to the wedding."

"And?"

She pointed to the cat asleep on the couch. "Right now, my first choice is Mr. Fluffy."

Leticia laughed. "I wouldn't. Someone might be allergic."

"Come on. He'd look so cute in a little tux."

"If not Owen, what about Bernie?"

"I'm not sure about Bernie." El told her friend about briefly seeing Bernie with someone who looked like a date when she was leaving the The Ink Spot. Leticia started to respond and El interrupted. "Wait, I didn't tell you about the other guy, Keith, who started flirting with me."

"What! You waited this long to tell me about another guy! Spill it!"

El told her about their last meeting and the phone call.

"I wonder how he is in the sack?"

"Oooh. you're so bad," said El, smiling.

"Come on, I just said what you're thinking."

They talked some more and Leticia asked, "What are you going to do about Bernie tomorrow?"

"Not sure, I need to practice being authentic and secure. Bernie's a really good guy and I have a lot of fun with him. I think I need to stop making up stories in my head and focus on being in the present."

Leticia looked at her watch. "Jack should be here to pick me up in a few minutes. Do you want to go out with us tonight?"

El briefly thought about it and then told her friend that she'd like a little quiet time on her own. Leticia nodded and told her to text or call if she wanted to talk about anything.

A little later, El got a text from Owen asking how the shower was. They texted on and off during the evening. When she was about to go to sleep, he texted that he wished he was holding her. She smiled and thought back to the previous weekend when he had stayed over without sex. She texted back, "Yes, that would be nice. Sweet dreams."

The next morning, Mr. Fluffy hit El in the face with his paw and that woke her up. "Damn, cat. It's six-thirty on a Sunday. What's your deal?"

He hopped off the bed and stood in her bedroom doorway waiting for her. "Can't you wait to eat?" she grumbled.

Mr. Fluffy let loose a loud meow in response.

She threw a robe over her pajamas to ward off the chill and followed him. To her surprise, he scratched at the front door. "What the…"

She opened the door and there, on her doormat, was a dozen yellow roses with a note. "How in the hell…" Her building was supposed to be secure.

"Thank you for some of the best nights of my life. Love, Owen."

"Ugh," El said aloud. Some of the nights were really special. But Friday night overshadowed that in her mind.

The roses had such a fragrant scent. She took them to the kitchen and put them in a vase. She also poured Mr. Fluffy some kibble in case he was hungry, but he just marched past her and returned to the bedroom. El followed him with the vase, which she put on her nightstand.

She crawled back under the covers and texted Owen. "The flowers are gorgeous. Thank you."

"Beautiful like you," he responded.

El smiled at her phone. She debated if she should wait until tomorrow to see him or if she should try to see him this evening. "What's your day like?" she texted.

"Going for a run soon. Watching the 49ers play this afternoon with Jack."

"Oh okay," El texted.

"Why? You have something else in mind?"

El could hear the tease and hopefulness in his text.

"Not sure," she admitted. "I have something that starts at 10. Not sure how long it will last."

"Let me know when you're done and if you want to get together."

"Okay," El said. "And thanks again for the roses."

She picked up her mystery novel and read for a half an hour, but then her phone chimed. Bernie had texted, "Got food poisoning or something. Been up all night. Can't eat. Raincheck?"

"Oh no!" El responded. "Want me to bring Gatorade, ginger ale, and chicken soup for later?"

"You're an angel," he answered. "I'll leave the door unlocked."

El got out of bed, raced to the kitchen to put some coffee on, and then went into the shower. Afterwards, she dressed in leggings, an oversized sweater, and boots. She put her hair into a ponytail. She put her coffee in a to-go cup, and then drove to Safeway.

She bought a bag of croissants from the bakery, some soup from the deli, and the drinks, and then drove to Bernie's apartment. It was almost nine by then. The door was unlocked like he promised. He was lying on the living room sofa covered in a colorful afghan that El was certain someone's grandmother had made.

He looked pale and his hair was a bit matted. He opened his eyes and smiled at her. "You really are an angel." She poured him some ginger ale and gave it to him to sip. "What happened?"

"I went out with a doctoral student last night to a Chinese restaurant. Thirty minutes after we finished the meal, I got sick. Digestive pyrotechnics aren't very sexy." He grimaced.

"I'd think not." El chuckled. "How are you feeling now?"

"Worn out. But better now that you're here."

"Where's Stu?"

"Sonoma. Weekend wine tasting."

"Ah. And I'm sure Remington and Qwerty haven't been much help." The cats were nowhere to be seen. El figured they were holed up in a bedroom.

"Nope. Though they knew enough to stay out of the way as I ran back and forth from the bathroom."

"Smart cats. Can I get you anything else? Want a croissant?"

"Not yet. Do you mind sitting with me? We could talk or watch a movie."

"Either is fine."

Bernie repositioned himself so he was sitting upright towards the middle of the sofa and El sat down next to him. He snuggled against her and held her hand. With his other hand, he turned on the TV with the remote and went immediately to Netflix. "The Great British Baking Show okay with you? I'm using it as schooling for our next Saturday morning bake-date."

El smiled. "That sounds fine."

They binged through three episodes and Bernie fell asleep with his head on her shoulder. Eventually, she switched off the TV, slid him into a prone position, adjusted the afghan around him, and then went into the kitchen. She noticed the empty cat dishes so she searched the cupboards for their food, and then fed them and gave them fresh water. She left a note for Bernie that said, *"Thank you for allowing me to help you. Give me a call when you're well and I'll plan a date for us. xoxo El."*

Then she let herself out of his apartment, locking it behind her.

When she got to her car, she sat for a moment. The old El would have stayed all day and clucked over him like a mother hen. She had certainly done that to Derek when he was sick. The new El had a desire to give and help but knew she had to balance that with having her own life. She smiled to herself, proud of how far she had come.

She asked herself, "What do I want to do now?" as a text from Keith appeared.

"I know it is last minute, but Deborah Tannen is speaking at the university at 2. Wanna go?"

She had thirty minutes to drive there, which was totally doable. "Sounds good. I'll meet you there."

When she got to the campus, she spotted one of Jack's trucks. "Thank God for small favors," El said to herself. She parked and rushed to the truck to get a couple of tacos. Woman does not live on coffee and croissant alone, she thought, smiling to herself.

After inhaling the food, she raced to the auditorium for the lecture. She spotted Keith immediately. He was wearing jeans and a forest green cashmere sweater. He grinned when he saw her and gave her a hug when she got to where he was sitting and saving her a seat. "Thank you for being so spontaneous. I was reading the paper and saw the announcement about this and thought it could count as a lecture towards our degree."

"Absolutely," El said as the house lights went down and the MC took the stage to thank everyone for coming to hear one of the world's foremost experts on men's and women's communication patterns and differences.

Two hours later, when the lecture was over and people were exiting the auditorium, Keith asked, "Would you like to grab an early supper?"

"Sure," El said. She wanted more time to talk to him about the lecture and to learn more about him personally. They walked to a nearby cafe that served California fusion cuisine, in this case locally grown food with a slightly Asian interpretation.

As they reviewed the menu, El thanked Keith for suggesting the lecture.

"You should also thank Todd. When I saw it, I texted him to see what he suggested and he said it would be great."

"He was so right. A few years ago, I read her book about moms and daughters titled, *You're Wearing That?* The name of it cracked me up but reading it helped me to understand some things my mom does that drive me crazy. And once I understood what was going on, it helped me to not get so upset and adjust what I was saying to her."

Keith laughed. "Families can be so difficult sometimes."

"I also read her *Talking From 9 to 5* book about what to say at work. That really helped me to think about how so many guys are focused on competition and women tend to be more cooperative. I know that describes me." El smiled.

Keith sipped his water. "I thought it was really interesting that she's a linguist and records real conversations so you can see what's actually happening."

"Yeah, when she takes it apart, it makes so much sense. I guess I didn't realize that she'd also written about men and women in relationships. I need to get those books."

"I think you just chose a future homework assignment," said Keith, smiling.

"That sounds like a great plan to me," agreed El.

After the waiter took their order, El continued. "I loved the stories she told. Her points about directness and indirectness really made so much sense. I'm a lot more indirect and that was a real problem with Derek. He would directly tell me what to do and it would upset me sometimes. I've realized though that my indirectness used to bug him also. I thought he'd be upset if I disagreed with him and directly told him what I thought. I felt it was more appropriate to suggest."

"And you hoped he would pick up on your cues," said Keith.

El nodded. "I'm afraid so. When you look at it like that, it would have made a lot more sense to discuss what we each wanted so we could understand each other better. But we made assumptions."

"The story about the couple who fought about where to go for dinner really resonated with me."

"That was a great example."

"I thought it was really interesting how she described the way the wife started off the conversation by asking her husband where he wanted to go to dinner. She expected to start vague and figure it out. And then the husband named a specific restaurant because he expected the negotiation to start specific and work it out from there. But she took it that he wanted to go to that restaurant. And then got upset at him for telling her what restaurant to go to." Keith shook his head. "I know I've been guilty of that before. When my ex would ask me something like that, I would do the same thing. I guess I need to learn to understand what the other person is looking for."

"I really liked her point that you have to communicate about communicating instead of making assumptions. But that's so hard."

"But that's what we're doing now," said Keith. "Maybe it's not that hard if you start off with that foundation and are willing to be curious and learn."

They continued to chat about the speech and their food soon arrived, Yaki Udon for El with stir fried thick noodles with chicken and vegetables. Keith had the House Special with beef and vegetables.

Keith said, "I have another book to add to our reading list."

"What?"

He paused. "How about *The Five Love Languages*?"

El considered that. "Hmm. We could. I know a little about it but I've never actually read it."

"Have you taken the quiz?"

"Oh yeah."

Keith smiled and quietly asked, "And would you be willing to share your Love Languages with me?"

El felt herself blush. It didn't seem like a study group any more. "Um, sure. I mean if you're willing to share yours."

Keith nodded as he took a bite of his beef.

El looked off to the side as she thought. "Remind me of the languages."

He ticked them off on his fingers. "Words of Affirmation, Acts of Service, Gifts, Quality Time, and Touch."

"Okay. I remember. My primary language is Words of Affirmation and secondary is Acts of Service." She pointed to Keith as she said, "And you?"

"I'm Quality Time and Words of Affirmation." He paused. "So Words of Affirmation are important to you, too. You like it when other people let you know how much they appreciate you."

El nodded.

Keith looked into her eyes and said, "Well, that shouldn't be too hard. I'm sure your friends and family really appreciate you."

El thought about how nice that sounded when he said it. She felt herself getting red again and joked about it. "Sometimes."

Keith said, "Well, I can tell you I appreciate our conversations. I enjoy discussing ideas with you and hearing your insights. Getting together with you is the high point of my week."

"Well…well, thank you. That's really sweet of you. And I appreciate having you to talk to also. It's really easy to discuss things with you."

"You're welcome."

They both sat quietly for a minute. Then Keith said, "So shall we add that to our reading list?" El readily agreed.

When the waiter asked about dessert, El declined but ordered a hot tea. She was full but didn't want it to end. A little while later, she reluctantly said they should probably go. Keith smiled and said that he was willing to spend whatever time needed studying to make sure they both got good grades. El thanked him, but she needed some time to debrief from her crazy weekend. They agreed to meet at the bookstore later in the week.

As El crawled into bed with Mr. Fluffy by her side, she thought again about the Deborah Tannen lecture and the discussion with Keith and the importance of not making assumptions. She had definitely made assumptions based on the Friday night experience with Owen, but she had done little to communicate with him. He was a decent guy. She owed it to herself and him to have the conversation, despite how awkward and intimidating it felt. She determined that she would talk to him all about it when she saw him after work tomorrow. She texted him, "Will you come to my house tomorrow night at 6:30? I'll order a pizza and have wine."

Owen texted back, "Is 7 okay?"

"Sure."

"Great. Can't wait to see you tomorrow."

"Thank you, Owen, and once again for the flowers, too." They brightened up her nightstand. She sniffed them one last time before turning off her bedroom light and going to sleep. "Good night, Mr. Fluffy," she said before snuggling into the comforter and pillows.

Chapter 22

First thing Monday morning, El had to fill out her performance self-evaluation and send it to Kate. El's team members had been sending theirs to her over the last two weeks and El had scheduled a one-on-one with each of them. The first one was with her newest team member, Maria, and happened in the late morning in a conference room that El had commandeered for the occasion.

As El reviewed Maria's goals with her and how she thought she had met those, and as they discussed things Maria had done well, El had an epiphany. Talking about sensitive subjects in a relationship could be structured a lot like performance reviews were: start with talking about the goals and what was done well before approaching the areas for improvement, and then set a course of action to reach the goals. While this approach seemed left-brained and nerdy to El, it was also what she realized she needed to do to communicate with the guys she was dating who were very logical. And even Bernie, who was definitely more creative and free-spirited than Owen and Keith seemed, definitely seemed to value a straight-forward, open approach.

During her lunch break, El jotted some notes to get her thoughts coherent regarding how she'd talk to Owen that evening. And though broaching the subject of not very satisfying sex was still a bit terrifying, El felt calmer and more grounded by her game plan. She also texted Bernie to see if he was feeling better. He responded, "Yes. At work. Drinks Wednesday?"

She said, "Sounds good."

When she arrived home a little before six, El fed Mr. Fluffy, drank a big glass of water, and then changed into yoga clothes. She unrolled her mat and sat in front of a YouTube video, stretching and channeling calmness through all of her chakras for half an hour. Then she ordered a cauliflower crust pizza and a house salad from her favorite place down the street from her apartment. Its delivery coincided with Owen's arrival so she buzzed them both into her building at the same time.

She took the food from the delivery woman and put it on the dining room table, and when she returned with plates, silverware, and the wine, she found Mr. Fluffy once again in Owen's arms. "This cat is so funny," Owen said. "He launched himself at me from the back of the couch again."

El shook her head. "I've never seen him do that before. You have strange cat powers."

"I'd prefer El powers," Owen said, grinning.

El smiled.

He set Mr. Fluffy on the sofa and promised he'd sit with him soon. Then Owen approached El and wrapped his arms around her and bent down for a very long kiss.

El's stomach flipped and she lost track of time in the kiss. When they broke apart, she wondered again why that chemistry hadn't infused the actual act of intercourse.

They sat at the table and El said, "Do you want me to serve you some salad or do we just want to eat it from the take-out container?"

"The container is fine," Owen said, spearing a cucumber slice with his fork. "I already share my germs with you." He smiled.

El poured two glasses of wine and handed one to him.

He asked how the rest of her weekend had been and how her day was. El told him the highlights from the shower and about taking food to a sick friend on Sunday morning, neglecting to mention the scheduled date, and how she met another friend for the Tannen lecture. She decided that was a good way to segue into what she wanted to talk about.

So she said, "That lecture got me thinking about the ways women and men communicate and how everyone starts off with assumptions instead of actually communicating and being curious and asking what may be tough questions."

Owen nodded his head in agreement while taking a large bite of pizza.

"For example, you've said you had a crush on me in high school and always wanted to go to a formal school dance with me. So you created a first date where we could do that. And it was so much fun and I adored the whole night. Then this past weekend, you compared me to Ginny and referenced your fantasies about me from your teen years. I used that information to make an assumption that you are dating me to fulfill a fantasy—"

Owen interrupted, "No—"

El interrupted him back, "—instead of getting to know the late 20-something version of me." She took a sip of wine, and he took that as an opportunity to speak.

"Yes, I admit at first the idea of going out with you appealed to me because I had always wanted to go out with you. But then I saw you and I was blown away by your adult beauty, and I loved your intelligence and your drive and your sense of humor. Yes, it helped that we had a shared history and had things in common, I admit that. But El, I want to know everything about you. I'm falling for the very adult version of you."

El maintained his eye contact. She felt elated by the "falling for" but saddened by how they were in bed. That needed to be addressed. "Owen, when you kiss me, I get all tingly and am so caught up in the moment that my mind goes blank. All I can feel is your heat and our combined want and a sense of urgency. But something happened on Friday when we went from the sofa to the bed. I don't know how else to say it but some of the chemistry and connection disappeared. I mean, we haven't ever talked about what you like and don't like and how I can make sure I please you and vice versa." El took a sip of wine.

Owen was nodding his head in agreement again, while consuming more pizza.

"My goal for us, especially while we are still learning about each other, is to figure out what turns you on and what turns you off. And I want you to learn the same things about me."

"I want to learn those things about you, El. I want to know how to touch you and where, and where and how you like to be kissed. I want to know your secret turn-ons. I want to know what turns you off and shuts you down so I can avoid doing that." He took a sip of wine before he continued. "In hindsight, I get that Friday night didn't work so well for you and that Saturday morning you were determined to get yourself off." He grinned at the memory.

El felt her face blush to the roots of her hair.

"But if you're willing," Owen said, "maybe tonight we explore each other's bodies, learn some of each other's favorite things, and work towards the same goal." He reached for her hand and stroked it with his thumb.

El smiled at him and then leaned forward and kissed his lips. "Only if we are both one hundred percent honest with each other."

"It's a deal," he said, "and if we're being honest, I need to ask you something."

"Yes?" El said between bites of salad.

"Are you seeing just me or are you dating lots of people?" Owen was looking at her intently.

She swallowed the salad and cleared her throat. "I am dating you and one other person, but I am not having sex with him."

"Do you plan to?"

"No. I don't know. I don't think so." El maintained Owen's eye contact and tried to gauge his reaction. He had a poker face.

"If you decide to, can you please let me know?"

"Yes," El said, a bit surprised at how calm Owen was.

"It is up to you who you date and sleep with," Owen said, "but I prefer not to have sex with a woman who is sleeping with other people."

"I understand," El said quietly.

He rubbed her hand again with his thumb and added, "I am crazy about you, El. And I don't like the thought of you and someone else. And I have no desire to be with someone else. But I'm not sure either of us is ready for an exclusive relationship yet."

El was astounded by the wisdom and maturity in his statement. Maybe he knew her better than she gave him credit for. "Owen, you're amazing," she said. "I love being in your arms and kissing you. I've enjoyed the times we've woken up together. But you're right. I read an interview Emma Watson did recently where she described herself as being 'self-partnered' instead of single. That resonated with me because I've had so much to learn about myself these past few months."

As they finished the food and drank the rest of the bottle of wine, El divulged to him that she was on the quest for a personalized Master's Degree in Relationships, and talked about what she had learned so far about herself, how she interacted with others, and what she wanted from her relationships, romantic and otherwise. Owen asked questions and joked that he could be both guinea pig for any experiments she wanted to conduct as well as an assignment for any sexual exploration.

They cleaned up the dining room and decided to start on El's homework.

Chapter 23

El awoke Tuesday morning with a smile on her face. Once they had transferred to the bedroom, things with Owen were a bit awkward at first with a lot of touching and kissing and questions and answers. But after a lot of back and forth, they had explored almost every inch of each other's bodies and knew the ticklish spots, the sensitive places, and where and how they could rev each other's engines.

El was so grateful she had been willing to squash her pride and have the difficult conversation. Owen was a special guy. He had left her place around four-thirty that morning since he hadn't brought his work clothes to her house. Mr. Fluffy had seen him to the door and had been mewing in sadness ever since.

"Silly cat," El said, as she ruffled his fur. But unlike on Saturday morning when she couldn't wait for Owen to leave, she too was sad he was gone. El felt capable of playing hooky and spending the day in bed. But alas, duty awaited. She had four one-on-one performance evaluation meetings with her team members today. So she made twice as much coffee as usual, set the pot to brew, and went to shower.

At noon, El debated texting Leticia something like "OMG last night didn't suck," but then she suddenly felt protective of what she and Owen had shared. El wasn't sure if the sex was a foundation for something bigger and longer term, but she did feel like their communication was a foundation for her, the groundwork she needed to lay (no pun intended) in any relationship she had going forward. Communication—talking and listening and being curious—was really the key to success.

Around three, the gray haired receptionist at the front desk on the ground floor showed up at El's office doorway. She was carrying a bouquet of red roses in a clear vase. "You're lucky," she said, handing the vase to El. The woman eyed the roses wistfully. "No one has sent me flowers in years."

El felt sad for the woman. "Would you like a rose or two for your desk?" Before the woman answered, El plucked two from the vase and handed them to her.

The woman's eyes were big like she was shocked. "Thank *you,* " she said to El before going back downstairs.

El already knew who they were from. And she grinned thinking, no one has ever given me this many flowers. The card read: THANK YOU FOR GIVING US ANOTHER CHANCE and it was signed the cat whisperer

El laughed aloud. Then she texted Leticia and Teresa, "Drinks at Gecko at 5:30?" The hell with it. Her joy needed to be shared.

Teresa arrived last and when she saw Leticia and El, she gave them both hugs. "Thank you, thank you, thank you!" She gushed about how much she loved the shower and what it meant to her. El was glad that her friend was so happy. It had been a lot of work, but it had been worth it.

They ordered appetizers and Leticia asked El what was going on.

She briefly told them about Bernie and then talked about Keith and his surprise invitation to the lecture. Both of her friends wanted to hear more about what the speaker had to say but El held up her hand and said, "But wait, there's more." She then told about her dinner and frank conversation with Owen.

"You go girl!" said Leticia.

"And things were better this time," El said coyly. "He left early this morning and I was sorry to see him go. And today I got these at work." She pulled out her phone and shared pictures of the roses and the card.

"Just what I said before. He's a keeper," said Teresa.

El appreciated her friend's focus on making sure she was part of a happy couple. She realized that was really important to Teresa. El wasn't sure it was as important to her at this time.

"He may be," said El smiling, "but I don't know that I'm ready for that kind of relationship yet. I thought that's what I wanted but learning more about me and what I really want has been amazing. It's been really freeing."

"Hear hear," said Leticia, raising her glass. "To amazing women loving ourselves first." Her friends raised their glasses.

"This whole situation has made me realize I don't want to jump into anything yet. And Owen seems to understand that and I really appreciate that about him."

The friends talked more about Owen. Then Leticia asked about Bernie. El said that she really liked Bernie, too. He made her laugh and gave her different perspectives. She'd never met anyone like him before.

El told them she'd need to make it an early night and Leticia teased her. "That's what happens when you stay up too late."

"So worth it," said El.

They all laughed, and El hugged them and left.

El was distracted at work the next day and found it hard to concentrate at times. She was thinking about Bernie. She'd had an honest conversation with Owen and it went well. Was it time to do the same with Bernie?

She met him after work at a local bar that he recommended. Seating at the bar was full but they easily found a table in the corner. Bernie thanked her again for taking care of him. "That was really sweet of you. It meant a lot to me." He put his hand on hers. "I'll make it up to you."

"I was happy to help. I felt so bad for you."

He looked into her eyes and said, "It's not often when someone takes care of me. Thank you."

El joked, "Yes, I bet you're the one who takes care of others." He agreed.

After their drink order was taken, El decided she had to say what was on her mind. "So I was at The Ink Spot last week and I saw you and a friend of yours going to your car when I was driving away." She paused.

He looked a little surprised. "Oh yeah, I was near there having dinner."

"So Bernie, you know I've been working on my Master's Degree and thinking about relationships and one thing I'm learning is how important it is to be willing to talk about things instead of making assumptions. So I hope you understand when I ask you this, are you seeing him?"

Bernie sat back in his chair and bit his lip. "Since you asked, yes I'm seeing him. Does that bother you?"

El paused. "We've never said that we're exclusive so I knew you could be seeing other people." She paused again. "It is a little weird for me. I didn't expect to actually see you with someone else."

"And the fact that he's a guy?"

"Yes, also a little weird."

Bernie shrugged his shoulders. "El I told you, I see people for who they are. What's underneath. Their essence. Their soul. Not societal gender norms."

"I hear you. That's just not something I'm used to."

Bernie leaned forward again. "Is that a problem for us?"

"No, I'm just trying to figure it out."

"And what about you? Are you seeing other people?"

"I am. Look, I have a lot of fun with you. You're a great guy who makes me laugh."

"But?" he interrupted.

El shook her head. "No buts."

"But I like your butt."

She laughed. "I mean I enjoy spending time with you and I want to keep doing that."

He put his hand on hers again and said, "I'd like that, too."

El was relieved that she had brought up the topic. They kept the rest of the evening on a light note and El felt that something had changed, but she wasn't sure if it was her relationship with Bernie or if she had changed. She was glad she'd been able to have a difficult conversation without getting upset or blaming. It felt good. Bernie walked her to her car, hugged her, then kissed her, and then hugged her again, before wishing her a good night.

Keith had set up another study group with El for Thursday night and she was looking forward to it. When she got there, she got a bottle of water and chicken salad and sat at their usual table. She had brought her copy of Deborah Tannen's book, *That's Not What I Meant,* and flipped through it as she waited.

She waved at Keith when she saw him and he waved back with a grin. He said hello and left his backpack as he went to get food.

"How is your week going?"

"Great! I told my friends all about the lecture. They were very envious. Thanks again for suggesting it. I really enjoyed it."

They spoke for a few minutes about it and Keith pulled out the books that he had bought.

"And what have you done with it this week?" El asked.

"Actually, it came in very handy. I had to deal with my ex and instead of making assumptions, I tried to use the information in the book to have a better outcome."

"And?"

"It went better. I didn't expect it would be perfect. I just tried to make sure I didn't fall into the usual patterns, and when I started to, I recognized it and stopped myself. I thought about sending her a copy of the book, but I don't think that would go over too well." He smiled.

"Why'd you have to deal with your ex? You've been divorced a while right?"

He sighed. "Yes, but her side of the family always really liked me. Her grandmother went to the hospital and my ex-mother-in-law sent me a message letting me know."

"Oh, I'm so sorry to hear that."

"Yeah, she fell and broke her arm. The good news is she's doing much better now. Of course, she's going to need time to heal. Anyway, I was trying to decide what to do and I expected that my ex might be angry that her mother let me know. So I decided to call her and say I was sorry to hear about her grandmother and try to defuse any problems with her mom. Also, instead of assuming that she didn't want me to contact her grandmother, I just asked her and let her know it was up to her. I think she really appreciated it and said she was fine with it so I sent flowers. I know there are going to be times when I have to have tough conversations and that helped me to be less stressed about this one." He took a sip of water. "How about you? What have you done?"

El expected the question and she had been trying to figure out how much to reveal but she had decided that she needed to be authentic, so she said, "I used it to talk with a guy I'm seeing, Owen. He and I just started seeing each other and instead of making assumptions about some things, I brought them up and started talking about it."

Keith chewed his sandwich and nodded. "Good for you."

El decided to continue. "And I also used the information with another guy I had started to see, Bernie, to talk to him about something I was concerned about."

"Well, well. Two guys? Any others?"

El felt herself blushing. "No."

"I'm just saying," said Keith smiling.

"Hey, I am doing a Master's Degree in Relationships. I need to go out with some guys."

"Oh so they're homework?"

"No." She started to laugh. "You're such a jerk." El tried to playfully slap his hand but he grabbed hers in his and warned, "I wouldn't do that. I know the manager. I can get you tossed out."

"Okay, okay." She pulled her hands out of his grasp then realized she kind of liked the way her hand felt in his. She gazed into his eyes for a couple of seconds and then said, " Seriously, I haven't gone out with anyone since breaking up with my ex six months ago and I happened to meet both of them." She briefly told him about meeting Bernie and being set up with Owen. "What about you? Haven't you been seeing anyone?"

"No, I wanted to figure things out first." He shrugged. "That's why I like working on this material with you." He looked straight at her as if he was trying to make her understand a point he wasn't saying. "And I'm not going to go out with someone until the time is right and the person is special."

El nodded her head once and felt herself blush again. "I get it."

"Do you?" He was holding her gaze.

"Yes," El's voice came out weaker than she had planned so she cleared her throat and began again. "While I have been using dating to better understand myself and what I want and need, you want time alone...or I guess with me sometimes to study...before jumping into dating or a relationship."

"Yes. And I believe that when I'm ready, the right person for me will be there and be ready, too."

"Did you date a lot of people when you were younger?" El took a sip of her water.

"Well, I'm not sure what a lot is. But I went out and did a bit of partying, partly because I was young and stupid and partly because it was what my friends did and was expected of me, or at least that's what I thought at the time. The truth is, I rarely felt great about it the next day, on a bunch of different levels. Deep down, I've always preferred to connect strongly with someone. I guess that's why I got married younger than many of my friends did. Hell, some of them still haven't stopped sleeping around." Keith shook his head.

"How old are you?" El asked. It had been on her mind and she finally felt like that was a good segue to ask.

Keith smiled and chuckled. "Thirty-three. Ancient, right?"

El grinned. "I'm twenty-eight, soon to be twenty-nine. I'm sure at one point in my life a five-year difference seemed huge, but now it seems like we're practically the same age."

"You're kind."

"Said the man I tried to slap a few moments ago."

"It was all in good fun. Hey, we should probably wrap this up. I know you have a big day tomorrow."

Keith was correct; she hadn't even begun to pack. El had taken tomorrow off from work so she, Leticia, and Teresa could drive to Incline Village, Nevada, for a Lake Tahoe spa relaxation weekend. Jack had agreed to move into El's apartment for the weekend and Mr. Fluffy sit.

As they walked to the parking lot, Keith asked, "So which of the lucky dates are you taking to the wedding?"

El stopped in her tracks and turned to him. "I haven't asked either."

He stopped too. "Why?"

"I honestly have no idea. Owen, I have known for more than half of my life as he was close friends with my brother. And my brother is now dating my best friend so he's coming to the wedding. Owen would have been an easy choice. But...I just wasn't feeling it."

"And Bernie?"

"Wasn't feeling that either." El scrunched up her face, then said, "And my cat wasn't a legitimate option."

Keith laughed. "But I'm sure he'd look great in a tux."

El's eyes widened. "Hey, that's the same thing I said."

"So you're going solo?"

"Yes…No…I don't know. Isn't that crazy?"

"I don't think so. I think you're trying to do what feels right for you. Not what your friends think or your brother or anyone else, and maybe sometimes you don't know what that is, like it's easier to know what isn't the right choice but harder to know what or who is."

"Oh my God. That's exactly it, but I haven't been able to articulate it." El was elated, and without thinking, she grabbed Keith and hugged him.

He returned her embrace, and then when they parted, he said, "El, no pressure, but if you'd rather go with someone than go alone, I'd be willing to go."

El paused, trying to gauge how she felt about the suggestion. It really did feel like no pressure. If she took Owen or Bernie, it felt like it meant something about their relationships moving forward. With Keith, it felt like she was taking a friend. She said, "As a friend, not a date?"

"As anyway you want to classify it." Keith gave a little chuckle.

"That's really nice of you. Thank you. I appreciate your offer."

"El, I enjoy our time together and it will give me a chance to meet your friends and see other sides of you besides the strict TA" He laughed and so did El.

"Oh yes, I'm so strict," she said.

He continued, "And a wedding would give me a chance to think about relationships in a different way."

El smiled. "I'll think about it and let you know. I might just decide to go by myself and do my own studying."

"Whatever works for you," said Keith.

El got in her car and Keith shut her door. He stepped back when she started the engine, but then she wound down the window. "Hey, did I just become *your* homework?"

"Maybe." He shrugged while grinning from ear to ear.

"Huh," she said aloud and then mumbled to herself, "The teacher becomes the schooled or something like that."

She waved and yelled, "Have a great weekend," before driving home.

After feeding Mr. Fluffy yet again—the cat seemed to have a bottomless pit of a stomach—and making herself a cup of herbal tea,

El checked her phone. Bernie texted asking if she was free for a concert on Saturday night. She texted back, "No. I'm in Tahoe this weekend."

He responded, "Can I come with?"

She laughed. "Nope. Weekend before the wedding girls' trip."

"Did you buy a big inflatable penis?"

El laughed. "Not that kind of weekend."

"Too bad. That could be fun. See you when you return?"

"Maybe dinner on Tuesday?"

"Can't. Wednesday?"

"Let me call you when I return."

"K. Have fun!"

Owen had left a voicemail. "Hey, El. Just wanted to say I'm thinking of you. I know you're leaving tomorrow. Want me to come over tonight?"

El paused and checked the time on the message. Did she want Owen to come over? Hmmm. Actually, a booty call did kind of appeal to her. The old El would have been embarassed to say to some guy, "Yes, I want to get laid right now." But the new El, well, she called Owen and said, "Can you get here in twenty minutes?"

Chapter 24

Owen left El's apartment five hours before Jack and Leticia showed up. She hadn't slept the recommended eight hours but somehow she felt energized. She was packed and raring to go. She loved the whole Tahoe area; the air felt so fresh and clean. The water was a gorgeous blue that she had never seen elsewhere. El loved to hike and do the obstacle course that was within walking distance from their resort. She couldn't wait to relax at the spa, drink cocktails by the fire, and talk with her best friends in their last weekend together. It was hard to believe one of them would be married next Saturday. El knew that event would change the dynamics of their trio; even the engagement had caused shifts that sometimes felt seismic.

As she tucked a bottle of bubbly into her backpack (why pay resort prices?), Teresa arrived at her door. Leticia let her in. El went over final instructions with Jack saying, "Don't let Mr. Fluffy bully you into giving him too much food."

Jack ruffled the cat's fur as he stood on the kitchen counter. "Don't worry. It's caviar and steak tartare for us both all weekend, Your Royal Highness."

"Very funny," El said.

"Hey, is it okay if Owen comes over on Sunday to watch the game with me and the furball?" Jack asked.

"Sure," El joked, "Just keep him out of my underwear drawer."

"I'll try but I make no promises."

"Okay. Let's go!" El hugged Jack and grabbed her bag. She yelled over her shoulder to Leticia, "We'll give you privacy in case you want to be all slobbery. Come on, T." And she and Teresa headed towards the elevator.

"What's Jordan doing for his bachelor's weekend?"

"I'm not sure since no one would really tell me, but you know Jordan, most likely it is golfing and wine-tasting or something sedate."

El laughed. "It's why you two are a perfect pair. Bernie asked if I was bringing an inflatable cock."

"Good God no." Teresa winced.

"Exactly. No inflatables. No crowns. No 'I'm the bride' shirts or banners. A classy weekend of cocktails...not cocks...fine food, facials, massages, and bodywraps, hiking, and fresh mountain air."

"Hear, hear." Teresa said. Then she yelled back toward El's apartment. "Come on, Leticia. Leave his lips alone and let's go!"

El laughed and pushed the elevator button. When the elevator dinged its doors open, Leticia raced to them. "That man is all hands." She laughed.

"Eww. That man is my brother," El said.

"He is," Leticia said. "Hard to believe he was here all this time."

El said, "Yep. But neither of you were ready."

As they got into El's car, she said, "I have news. Now my friend Keith has offered to accompany me to your wedding."

"Really?" Teresa said. "You couldn't decide between two so a third decided to throw his proverbial hat into the mix?"

"Yep. I told him I'd think about it over the weekend. Oh, and Owen and I were kind of like rabbits much of the night. Things are *so much* bettter there after we talked about what we wanted and found mutual goals."

Teresa and Leticia looked at each other with open mouths. Their shock was evident. "Whoa, whoa, whoa," Leticia said. "Back up. You might bring Keith to the wedding, but you're banging Owen's brains out?"

El grinned. "Yes, I guess I am. And Bernie and I talked. He likes my butt." El laughed, and continued, "And he's dating me and at least one other person, a dude. And he knows I'm dating men besides him. And we'll continue to see each other. It feels so good to be honest and authentic and...to be me."

"Hallelujah!" Leticia said, "She's finally seen the light."

Teresa's face was slightly pinched. "But are you happy?"

"Ecstatic," El said. "I feel loved. All different kinds. And I'm getting laid. And I love myself. That's the most important part for me."

"Hear hear." Leticia toasted with an imaginary glass.

"But it isn't about me. This weekend is about T. That's why I wanted to let you guys know now, upfront, my latest news. So the rest of this weekend, we can focus on Teresa and Jordan. So, T, for your first act on the last weekend of your single life, you get to pick the tunes. What'll it be?"

Teresa laughed and put on a Top 40 station and they sang along until they moved out of range of the station around Sacramento and Teresa had to pick a new one. An hour outside of Nevada, El pulled up an iTunes mixlist on her phone and had Girl Power music play through her car speakers. After all, Girl Power was what the weekend was about, and they were feeling pretty freaking powerful by the time they arrived in Incline Village.

The hotel front desk manager personally showed them to the suite they had reserved. A bottle of champagne was chilling on the coffee table next to three crystal flutes, a bowl of strawberries, and box of chocolate truffles. "Compliments of the house," the manager said.

The suite was bigger than any El had stayed in and so elegant. El made a mental note to request the same thing for her last single's weekend, if it ever came.

The best friends relaxed on the sofa sipping the champagne and eating the chocolates and deciding where to go for dinner. They picked a local casual vegetarian restaurant to make sure Teresa could have whatever she wanted. After dinner, El pulled out the card games she had brought. "Let's start with Twosomes, Threesomes, Foursomes. I've never played it but my cousin said it's hilarious. Especially with drinks."

Leticia poured three glasses of wine and said, "I'll drink to that."

They each got ten cards and they had to put them in fun combinations of two, three, or four cards. If they couldn't make a combination, they had to draw extra cards. The first one to get rid of all her cards would win.

El looked over her cards which included "Brad Pitt's sexy ass," "Cover it in chocolate," "In an elevator." She played the cards and wrote down her points. "Yes, that sounds delicious."

Teresa put her hand over her eyes and said, "It's the only combination I have." She played "Dwayne 'The Rock' Johnson," "With my mouth," "On television."

Leticia said, "That sounds good to me."

"On television?" said Teresa.

"Girl, I'd want everyone to know I was doing The Rock."

El and Teresa laughed aloud.

"I hear that," said El. "But don't let Jack know."

Leticia closed her eyes. "Let me just picture that for a moment."

After a few more rounds, El was blushing and said, "Good thing we didn't play this at your shower."

Teresa giggled. "Oh nooooooo. That would have been bad. Jordan's grandmother would have fainted."

Soon after that, El yawned a few times and her friends teased her about staying up too late.

"Or was it Owen staying up too long?" asked Leticia.

El smirked and said, "I don't kiss and tell." Then she yawned again. "I'm fine, I'm fine. I just need some more wine." She held out her glass so Teresa could pour a refill.

When they finally went to bed, El expected that she would fall asleep right away, but she was too wired. Her mind kept going back to her date for the wedding. Owen was the obvious choice. Why was she hesitating? She already knew he looked great in a tux. She smiled at the thought of the amazing dinner dance he had made for her. He could hang out with Jack when she was being a part of the big day. She really did have a wonderful time with him. She hadn't asked him, but he was probably expecting she would. And maybe wondering why she hadn't yet.

Or she could go solo. She could let him know that she was going to be really busy with wedding duties and she wouldn't be able to enjoy the time with him. She smiled again thinking that she could make that her Master's Degree homework.

Then she thought about Keith. It would be ridiculous to take him to the wedding. She barely knew him. Sure, she enjoyed their conversations. She thought back to him holding her hands and the way he looked at her. Keith, she wondered. Keith...? She fell asleep dreaming about him.

When she awoke the sun was shining through the window. She checked her phone. 7:43. A text from Owen said: I keep thinking about that amazing move you do with your hips. Text me your ETA for Sunday when you know it. I want to experience that again.

She grinned and shook her head. Sometimes men were easy. She responded with the kiss blowing emoji.

Since they were scheduled to spend half the day at the spa, El just brushed her hair and put it into a ponytail and threw on yoga clothes. When she padded into the kitchenette, El found Leticia and Teresa both up and similarly dressed, coffees in hand, and talking quietly.

"What'd I miss?" El asked, pouring herself a mug of the rich black stimulant.

"Jack sent a cute photo of Mr. Fluffy. He apparently made fish tacos for supper last night and he made one for Mr. Fluffy, too." Leticia held up her phone.

El laughed. "That cat is so spoiled. Hey, did I ever tell you how he launches himself at Owen? It's the craziest thing. He literally makes himself into a projectile as soon as Owen walks into the door. I'm thankful Owen has fast reflexes otherwise the cat might bounce off his chest and drop to the floor."

Teresa said, "So what you're saying is the cat is in love with Owen?"

"I think so."

Teresa tilted her head like some dogs do when trying to hear better and she asked, "And you?"

"What? In love with Owen?" El took a sip of coffee to stall.

"Yes." Teresa stared at her.

"No, I'm in like with Owen. I'm in heat with Owen. He's got such a hot body. Must be all that running."

"But you aren't in love with him? Are you sure?" Teresa broke eye contact with El to look at Leticia.

"Wait," El said. "Are you both asking or just you, T?"

Leticia responded, "I told her you were just having some fun. You don't have to be in love with the man to want to ride him every night." Leticia grinned like a Cheshire cat at her own comment.

"But it helps," Teresa said.

"Helps what?" Leticia and El asked in unison.

"It helps the bond. Makes you feel more secure," Teresa replied.

"Hmmph," Leticia said.

"We have a great bond," El said. "And I'm secure in myself." As the words escaped her lips she realized how true they were. "I may not have always been. But I am now. I'm doing what I want, seeing the men I want. I'm having fun, and I'm not ready to commit to one man right now. I'm committed to myself."

"So, you're bringing yourself to my wedding?" No malice was in Teresa's question; she was smiling.

"I am. But last night before I fell asleep, I thought about bringing Owen. I also dreamt of Keith at the start of the night. But not in regards to your wedding."

"Sex dream?" Leticia asked, eyebrows raised.

"Nope." She drank more coffee to signal an end to that discussion.

"So what's the agenda for today?" Teresa asked, helping herself to more coffee from the pot. She also put a bunch of fruit on the table, a jar of peanut butter, and some cheese, along with a loaf of gluten-free bread. "Light breakfast," she explained.

"Good idea," El said. "We have to check in at the spa at eight-fifty. Our services start at nine. Facials, wraps, massages, plus we can soak in the sauna or whirlpool as much as we want. We'll be done around one so I figured come back here and change and go for a late, casual lunch, then maybe an afternoon hike to enjoy scenery and smell the pines. We have dinner reservations at seven, but can go earlier to get a drink beforehand, if you want."

"Sounds heavenly," Teresa said.

"Yes," Leticia added. "I could really use the destress. Work has been brutal."

"Do you want to tell us about it now so we don't carry work talk into the serene space?" El asked.

"I don't want to talk about it at all. This weekend is all about us. So who wants some toast?" Leticia opened the bag and started loading slices into the toaster. Then she quartered an apple and an orange and started pulling clumps of grapes from a bigger bunch. She pulled three plates from the cupboard and arranged fruit on each.

Teresa cut slices of cheese and added them to each of the plates.

"Anyone want peanut butter for the apple or bread?"

Both Leticia and El passed. Teresa put a blob on her apple slice. As they ate, El asked Teresa, "What's your favorite thing about Jordan?"

Teresa didn't even pause before answering, "The way he looks at me."

"Which is how?" El asked.

"Like I matter to him. There's always love and warmth in his eyes even when we aren't in a romantic or sexual situation. I've never experienced anything like it."

"Jack looks at me that way," Leticia said. She frowned at her food and added, "And I hope he feels that coming from me, too." She looked up at her best friends. "This is so new for me. I'm concerned I'm going to fuck it up."

El laughed. "You? When's the last time you fucked something up? You're always Ms. Confident and know just what to do or say."

"I agree with El," Teresa added. "But I also know that true love can make you feel vulnerable."

"True love," El said in a voice that imitated the minister in *The Princess Bride*. And then she laughed.

Her friends chuckled too, but Teresa said, "I'm serious. When you really connect with someone, like your souls are intertwined like me and Jordan, you suddenly become vulnerable in a way that is scary and exhilarating simultaneously. You want that person to know you on the deepest level and you them, while understanding that what they end up knowing isn't always pretty. It can be scary. And it takes a lot of trust."

"Exactly," Leticia said. "And I'm so used to not feeling enough for any man that in the back of my mind a voice is saying I'm not loving Jack enough even though I love him so very much I don't have the vocabulary to express it." Leticia's eyes welled with tears.

El was completely taken aback. She had never seen Leticia so wrapped up in a man and so expressive. She looked so beautiful.

And five seconds later, El realized that was what she wanted for herself. Yes, she wanted the fun and the "schooling" she was getting right now. But eventually, she wanted to feel so strongly about one man that the thought of him made her as radiant as Leticia and Teresa looked this morning.

Chapter 25

After the hours at the spa and a quick lunch of veggie gluten-free pizza and iced tea, the best friends set out on a hike from their resort. They took a trail map from the concierge and decided to follow the trail through the woods that also had the obstacle course. El hung upside down from the chin-up bar like she had as a child and flipped around the bar and dismounted. Teresa and Leticia cheered her on and took iPhone photos.

Leticia vaulted over a slanted metal bar, and Teresa shimmed along the parallel bars. El shouted, "Olympics, here we come," as she laughed and did a cartwheel on the dirt trail. At one point, they found a downed tree that bisected a standing tree so El ran up the downed tree as far as it went into the other tree and then started to climb.

"What a monkey," Teresa said, laughing.

"And we thought you were more of the tree hugger," Leticia joked to Teresa.

"Yes. Who knew little El would follow in my footsteps."

"Well if you want to go up that tree, you'll be following in hers," Leticia said, holding the phone up to get ready for the photo opportunity.

"Naw, we'll let her have the fun. You know, this is the freest I've seen her in months...maybe years. She seems, well, she lacks the angst she used to have. It's like your confidence has rubbed off on her." Teresa stared as El climbed higher, then she yelled, "Not too high, El. I need you alive and not in a neck brace for my wedding."

El stopped on a branch, hugged the tree trunk with one arm while standing on the big limb, and waved down at her friends. She wore a huge grin.

As Leticia took photos, she said to Teresa, "I had nothing to do with her confidence. El decided to find it within herself. But I'm damn proud of her transformation. In work. In life. In love. And I'm so happy we're in each other's lives and on this journey together. You bitches rock!" Leticia screamed the last part.

Teresa laughed and hugged her. El yelled, "Wait for me!"as she scurried down the tree like a squirrel racing after a falling nut. They group hugged at the base of the tree.

"You guys missed the most awesome view," El said. "The mountains are amazing at that height."

"They are amazing at any height," Teresa said. "And you guys are amazing, too. I love you both."

"We love you, too," Leticia and El said in unison. They finished the last half mile of the hike in mostly silence, marveling at the birds and the autumn foliage. As the sun started to descend, they returned to their suite to rest and change into fancier clothes for supper.

At the restaurant, the manager gifted them with a bottle of bubbly to honor Teresa's nuptials, and their waiter bought them a beet and goat cheese appetizer. When they were alone, Teresa joked, "I should get married often with this kind of service and freebies."

El and Leticia were both feeling the need for meat so they ordered the filet mignon, while Teresa ordered a homemade pasta dish with a mix of colorful veggies and a garlic and cheese sauce drizzled over the top. The scent wafted across the table and El said, "Oh my God, that smells delicious, T," who then offered her a bite which she declined. "I have plenty of my own. Thank you."

Leticia said, "So, do we want a leisurely brunch or a hike to burn off these calories in the morning before check out?"

"Let's do a hike, maybe from eight until ten?" Teresa said.

"Sounds good," El said. If traffic wasn't horrible, they might get back around three, when Owen and Jack would still be watching the game. A small smile crept to El's lips.

Leticia saw it. "Spill it. Which one are you thinking about?" She was grinning at El.

"Owen. He sent a text this morning asking if we could get together tomorrow. I apparently did some move he really liked and now he wants more of it." El blushed at her admission.

Leticia high-fived her even though they weren't in that kind of restaurant. "Way to go, girl!"

"I know. Right. And to think the sex was soooo bad the first couple of times."

El tilted her head and looked at Teresa. "Have you and Jordan ever had bad sex or has it been all sunshine and roses since the beginning?" She drank a few swallows of the pinot noir she had ordered with the steak.

Teresa had her fork aloft, looking a bit deer in the headlights at the question. "No. I wouldn't say it was ever bad. I mean, it took time to get to know all of the good spots. And sometimes it was super and other times adequate, but it was never bad."

El looked at Leticia and said, "I'm not asking you because Jack's my brother."

Leticia laughed. She held up her wine glass towards El, grinned, and said, "To your brother. He's awesome at everything."

"Wow," El said.

"Lucky you," Teresa said, and they clinked their glasses together.

At the end of their meal, they were stuffed, but somehow found the space to share a flourless chocolate torte with raspberry coulis and whipped coconut cream since it was basically three bites for each of them.

Then they went outside to the Adirondack chairs and the fire and wrapped themselves in the blankets provided and ordered boozy campfire drinks and listened to the crackle of the wood and the sounds of the night, until their glasses were empty.

The next afternoon, on the drive home, with Teresa manning the playlist, she asked El, "So, are you bringing Owen to the wedding or flying solo? It will be a little weird for you not to have someone to dance with at the reception."

"Oh, I hadn't thought of that," El said. "Okay. I'm bringing Owen. Assuming he isn't already busy."

"That's great," Teresa said, and then quietly added, "especially since I had Jordan's sister create a place card for him last week."

"You what?" El asked, laughing.

"Yep. I knew you'd bring him. He's so hot and charming and so hot. And he treats you like a queen with all of the flowers and everything."

"True," El admitted. "He has given me a lot of flowers. But I've wondered if he's that guy. You know, the one who gives gifts and is so attentive at the beginning during the wooing stage, and then when he has you, you're never given anything unless it is a holiday, and maybe not even then. You know what I mean."

Leticia said from the backseat, "Totally. Can't buy my love."

"Exactly," El said. "So we'll see where this leads. But for now, I'm bringing him to the wedding."

"Well I, for one, am happy about it," Teresa said. "I can't wait to get to know him. Then the six of us can triple date."

In the rearview mirror, El saw Leticia's eyes roll. El smiled.

A couple of hours later, El pulled into her building's parking structure. Teresa hugged and kissed them both and thanked them for a great weekend. And then she hopped in her car and took off.

El and Leticia grabbed their bags and rode the elevator to El's apartment. The guys were on the sofa with Mr. Fluffy lying nestled between them, impervious to their yells at the television screen. Leticia leaned over Jack and kissed his lips, and El realized she should probably do the same with Owen.

Then she took her bag into her bedroom and while she emptied it, Owen came into her room. "God, I've missed you," he said, wrapping himself around her in a full-body hug.

"It was only two nights," El laughed.

"Longest two nights ever," he said.

"You're hopeless," she said, squirming away.

"Hopeless for you," he said, trying to pull her to him again.

"Let me go," she said, "I really need to pee."

He laughed and allowed her to escape to her bathroom. When she came out, he was sitting on her bed, flipping through something on his phone. He showed El a whole series of photos he took of Mr. Fluffy over the past few hours.

"You two are a match made in heaven," El said, before realizing what was coming out of her mouth.

"Or the three of us are." He put his arm around her and kissed her neck.

"Is there any food left?" El asked, ignoring his comment.

"Yes, on the table and some stuff got moved back into the fridge. You hungry?"

"Starving. We skipped stopping for lunch."

Owen stood up. "Want me to fix you a plate?"

"Nah. I'll get it." She left the bedroom and padded barefoot to the kitchen with Owen trailing behind her. Jack, Mr. Fluffy, and Leticia were sitting on the sofa and two of the three of them were enthralled in the game.

"You can go watch with them," El said.

"I'd rather be with you," Owen said.

"Suit yourself. Want something?" El motioned to the food she was removing from the fridge.

"I'm good," Owen said.

El loved when Jack stayed with Mr. Fluffy because he made tons of food and her refrigerator was always stocked when she returned from trips, even short ones. God bless a brother who cooked and baked.

She filled her plate and sat across the table from Owen, who moved his chair close to her and occasionally scavenged things from her plate. "You don't mind, do you?"

"No. Plenty for everyone," El said.

He asked about the weekend and El answered in between bites. Leticia, at one point, interjected, about El climbing the tree and brought over her phone to show the photos. Owen said, "Hey, we should go on a hiking trip for a weekend. The four of us, or if Jack and Leticia want to Mr. Fluffy sit…"

"Sounds like fun," El agreed.

When the game ended, Jack and Leticia said their goodbyes. El offered to let Jack take the food he made with him, but he declined. After they left Owen said, "They seem like such a great match."

"I agree," El said. They sat on her sofa and held hands. Owen asked if she wanted to watch a movie. A silly rom-com had just come out on Netflix and she wanted to see it but it wasn't exactly manly-man material. She mentioned it anyway, along with an eighties movie and a cartoon, saying she wasn't in the mood to concentrate on anything serious.

He told her to pick and he'd watch whatever, so while she started the new rom-com, he readjusted them on the sofa so that he was angled and she was between his legs with her back against his chest and he wrapped his arms around her. Of course, Mr. Fluffy parked himself atop El so that the three of them could be together.

After ninety minutes of silence, when the credits started to roll, Owen said, "The plot was a bit weak in spots, but the writing was decent. It does always seem like the perfect guy for her is right under her nose the whole time though it takes the protagonist a while to figure that out."

El hung up on his use of always. She turned to face him. "Exactly how many romantic comedies have you watched?"

"More than most dude's share. Long relationship, remember?"

"Yes. But my ex would have never sat through this with me."

"And he's an ex. Makes sense to me," Owen said. "Am I permitted to stay over and may we go to bed?"

Chapter 26

El had a lot of work crammed into her slightly shortened work week since she took half of Friday off for the rehearsal dinner and other wedding prep. Bernie and Keith had both made it clear that they'd like to see her this week, and of course Owen would be with her any time she said yes. Before he had left to change clothes before heading to his office, she had asked him to go with her to the wedding and he admitted he had kept Saturday free just in case. He asked if she needed a date for the rehearsal dinner, too. She had forgotten about that so she said she'd text Teresa and get back to him later in the day. But by the time noon arrived on Monday she had been so slammed dealing with customer issues that she hadn't had any time to text. When she paused for ten minutes to eat some fruit, nuts, and yogurt and to drink a cup of tea, she texted Teresa.

T responded almost immediately with, "Jack's coming with L so yes, bring him."

"K."

She texted Owen telling him she'd pick him up at 3:30 if he could get off early, and he agreed to the plan, but stated, "You can get me off any time."

She laughed aloud and texted, "Very funny."

There was also a text from Bernie that she had ignored all morning but she knew she had to answer. He had asked when they could get together. She thought about how nice it would be to laugh and relax with him, but she felt stressed about how much she had to get done. She decided that the message wouldn't get any easier to type if she waited. She texted Bernie an apology and said she wouldn't be able to see him this week because of wedding preparations. She suggested that they get together the next week.

Bernie sent a sad face with a happy face. "Sorry I won't see you this week. Have a great time at the wedding." El appreciated his understanding and briefly wondered how she felt about him. Before she could think much about it, an alert popped up on her computer reminding her to get to the next meeting.

She worked late that night and was glad she had some extra protein bars in her desk. She shook her head as she tried to concentrate on the budget updates she had to finish. She got a text from Keith asking how the weekend away was. Happy for a brief break, she texted back that it was great. Then she texted, "Can we schedule our next study group for next week? I'm still at work and this week is CRAZY."

"Of course, I'm happy to work around the schedule of my favorite TA," he responded.

"I'm the only TA," she texted back.

"Good point." Then he wrote, "Do you need help studying romance at the wedding this weekend?"

El smiled at the question and then paused trying to decide how to answer. She typed and re-typed it several times. "Thanks. I really appreciate your offer, but I won't need study help this weekend. I'll do the research and give you a report at our next study group." She hit send and typed. "Owen is going to the wedding with me." She paused briefly before hitting send. Then she reiterated, "My brother Jack is going too and they're old friends."

She tried to focus on the budget numbers as she waited for a response.

"Have a great time at the wedding. I look forward to your report. Let me know what day next week works for you." He ended it with a smiling face.

She was glad for the message, but part of her wondered what it would be like to take him to the wedding. She took one more look at the numbers on her screen and decided that she couldn't look at one more Excel file. She headed home.

As she fed a very annoyed Mr. Fluffy, she wondered what she was going to say at the rehearsal dinner. Making a speech made her nervous and she wanted it to be perfect. She pulled out a pad of paper to jot down notes, but she felt like her brain was empty. She shook her head as if it would help release some helpful thoughts.

What she really wanted to say was that she loved seeing how happy Teresa was and she wanted the same for herself. She grinned. Yes, she could make it all about herself and give the worst rehearsal dinner speech in history. Maybe it would go viral.

She did want to smile the way Teresa did when she talked about Jordan and feel that she had found her special someone. The weekend had helped her to realize how she wanted to feel and she knew she wasn't there yet. But somehow seeing how happy her friends were gave her hope.

She thought more about Teresa and started to write some ideas and cross things out.

Owen texted her. "I miss you. When can I come over and kiss you?"

El smiled. She wanted to see him. She leaned her head back on the top of the couch. At the same time, she really needed to get things done.

"I miss your kisses too. I'm swamped with work and wedding stuff. I may not be able to see you until Friday." She added, "I'm glad you're coming to the rehearsal dinner."

He sent back a sad face. "Friday! I don't know if I can wait that long." Another sad face.

She thought again about her schedule. She texted, "Let me see what I can get done and I'll let you know tomorrow. I was working on budgets until late tonight and I'm a little tired right now."

He sent back a happy face and a kiss.

Wednesday night she met Owen for a quick dinner and he wrapped his arms around her when he saw her. His kiss made her wonder if she should invite him to spend the night, but she had to get up extra early to get into the office for a meeting with their European team and she needed to be awake for that. He walked her to her car and slowly kissed her lips and neck. "Are you sure you don't want me to come over?" he teased.

She did. She did. Her practical side won though, and she told him she'd make it up to him after the wedding. He smiled and agreed.

After talking to Teresa, El realized that the rehearsal might be boring for Owen so she told him to meet her at the restaurant. Teresa was getting married at Jordan's family church. The location had been an interesting discussion. Teresa would have been happy to have the ceremony in the middle of a field, but her new husband's family was more religious.

The church was an imposing stone building. El headed to the main offices since she wasn't sure where she was supposed to go. A petite grey-haired woman greeted El and introduced herself as Pam, the minister. El followed her to the main church where the ceremony would be held. Teresa and her parents arrived next and her mom gave El a big hug. When Jordan arrived, El was delighted to see how happy Teresa looked.

More people arrived and El was introduced to Jordan's parents and family. The minister took charge and welcomed them all. She quickly described what would happen at the ceremony. She called people up and told them where to stand. She and Leticia stood by Teresa and two of Jordan's friends stood next to him.

El felt more nervous than Teresa. Her friend looked serene and peaceful. El hoped that she would feel that calm on her wedding day.

Pam had obviously officiated many weddings and her directions kept the rehearsal moving. After a little more than half an hour they were done. Pam spent a few more minutes with the soon-to-be bride and groom going through some final details. Then she hugged both of them and told the crowd that she would see them the next day.

The rehearsal dinner was at the restaurant where he had proposed to Teresa. They celebrated in a separate room in the back. Jack was already there and gave Leticia a big kiss. Owen arrived soon after. When he hugged El, he whispered in her ear, "Let me spend the night with you, beautiful. I'll leave early in the morning before your wedding duties. And I'll make the night super worth it."

She giggled. "Okay, but you have to promise."

"Will do," he said and kissed her.

There was no assigned seating so Leticia and El sat down at a table with some of Teresa's other friends. Jordan and Teresa sat at a long table at the front with her parents sitting next to him and his parents next to her.

El felt nervous. After everyone had been seated, Jordan's friend, Ed, clinked his spoon against his water glass to get everyone's attention. "I'd like to propose a toast. To my dear friend, Jordan and his beautiful bride-to-be Teresa. I've known Jordan since freshman year in college. And I could tell you some stories." Jordan smiled and shook his head as some people laughed. "But I'm not going to. Instead I want to congratulate you on finding someone who will put up with you." He smiled as people laughed. He turned to Teresa and said in a stage whisper, "Teresa, there's still time to get out of this."

She shook her head.

He turned back to the crowd. "Seriously, I'm really glad for both of you. To my friends, congratulations," he said, raising his glass.

After that toast, it was El's turn. She stood up and introduced herself. "I also want to say a few words about two special people. Teresa, you are my dear, dear friend. You've always been happy, but since you've met Jordan, I can see how you've changed. Being with Jordan has made you positively glow. I remember when you first told us about meeting Jordan at another wedding. There was something about the way you talked about him that made me realize he was special. I am so delighted that two such amazing people found each other and can support and love each other. I couldn't be happier for you. I wish you all the happiness in the world." She raised her glass and toasted the couple.

Leticia and Jordan's other friend, Lyle, also briefly spoke. As usual, Leticia was eloquent and articulate.

El saw Teresa lean over to Jordan and whisper something to him and then kiss him. Jordan stood up with a drink in his hands. "My friends, thank you for all your kind words, except for Ed, of course." He pointed at his friend. "I could tell some stories about you too, bud." He looked down at Teresa, "Seriously though, it means so much to both of us to have you all here. Thank you for being with us tonight. We couldn't be happier." He looked at Teresa again in a way that made El smile. "And I am the luckiest man in the world." Teresa beamed at him. He paused and looked back at the crowd. "Please help yourself to this delicious buffet to help us celebrate."

El was relieved. She had gotten through her speech and didn't have any other duties that night. Owen was very attentive and gently left his fingers on her arm as they talked with others at the table.

At the end of the evening, Teresa gave El and Leticia big hugs and thanked them. They had plans to meet at a local salon in the morning to get their hair and makeup done.

But that night, El was going to enjoy herself and not think about her wedding duties. She squeezed Owen's hand and said she'd meet him back at her place. She didn't get much sleep that night, but she was in a great mood when she got to the salon the next morning. Owen had made coffee for her when she was still asleep and had stayed for breakfast that he had cooked.

El had never gotten her hair or makeup done by anyone else, but Teresa had insisted that it was absolutely necessary and El and Leticia had agreed. As El waited for her stylist to get ready, she heard Whitney Houston's "How Will I Know" on the radio. She started singing and gestured to Leticia who stood up and started singing, too. They sang to Teresa until she joined them in singing. They clapped and cheered at the song's end.

El thought that would be a great question. Months ago, when she started her personalized Master's Degree, she had asked people how they met their significant others but now she wanted to know when and how they knew that person was the one. That could be the topic for her self-directed thesis.

"Okay, T, tell us when you knew he was the one," said Leticia.

"Oh come one, you don't want to hear."

The woman styling her hair looked amused and said, "Yeah come on, tell us."

The other stylists nodded. Teresa smiled broadly. "Okay, so Jordan and I were going out for a while and things were going great. And I got food poisoning, remember that?"

Leticia nodded and said, "Yeah, you said that was awful."

"Oh it was. He had taken me out to dinner and I think I ate something bad and I started feeling sick soon after we got back to my place. I wasn't sure if I was going to throw up or go to the bathroom. He was feeling okay and I told him to go home, but he wouldn't. He wanted to make sure I was okay. This isn't going to sound romantic at all but I remember sitting on the floor by the toilet wondering if I was going to throw up again and he put a wet towel on my forehead. He sat on the floor with me and I thought how lucky I was to have someone there by my side that was going to be there for me." She paused and said quietly.

"That's when I knew he was really special. It's easy to be around for someone when things are going well, but to me, real relationships are about being there for the other person when things are bad." She shook her head. "And believe me, things were bad. But he stayed with me all that night. He would have called in sick the next day to take care of me, but I told him not to because I was feeling better. So he went to work and rushed back at the end of the day to stay with me again. I really appreciated that and started to wonder if maybe he was the guy for me."

Teresa smiled and said, "And then, I know this is going to sound silly, but I actually realized he was the one when we were doing dishes together the week after that. I was scrubbing a pot and he was putting things in the dishwasher and it just felt so nice and right to have him by my side that night. I knew he was the one I wanted to have by my side all the time."

The hairstylist had stopped working on her and said, "Honey, that is so sweet. You are a lucky girl. Hold on to that guy!" The other stylists nodded.

At the end of the stylist appointment, the three friends went over to Teresa's house for a light lunch and to get dressed. They pulled out the gorgeous dresses they had picked out and El was again glad that she had been clear with Teresa about what she wanted.

The wedding was scheduled to start at three. A limo picked up Teresa, her mom, and her friends to take them to the side door of the church where they waited in a room so none of the guests could see the bride.

Leticia and El went to the main church to make sure everything was going as planned. When Owen arrived, El smiled broadly. He looked so sexy in his dark suit. He kissed her and said, "You look gorgeous. We should go to weddings more often."

"Silly," she said, but his comment made her smile.

The ceremony went as planned. El watched Jordan's face when he saw Teresa walk down the aisle. He looked so devoted and in love. El sighed when Teresa and Jordan exchanged rings and vows. The way they stared at each other was so loving it made her start to tear up. She didn't want to mess up her makeup so she took a few deep breaths and stopped herself. When the minister said, "You may now kiss," El cheered along with the rest of the crowd.

Jack and Owen went with the wedding party to a local park to take pictures. When they were done, they drove to Teresa's aunt and uncle's house where the reception was being held. They had a large backyard that had been transformed with a tent and rented tables and chairs.

Owen sat with El at the head table and offered to help with whatever was necessary. Fortunately for El, the family seemed to have everything taken care of, and for the first time, El felt that she could relax a little and enjoy herself. Owen smiled at her and asked her to dance. She was a little apprehensive but quickly remembered that he had great rhythm. The next song was a slow one and he took her in his arms. She leaned up against him. "I could get used to this," he whispered in her ear.

"Me too," she replied, enjoying his warmth and the earthy smell of his aftershave. She was disappointed when the next song was faster. Owen kissed her slowly before breaking apart.

El watched Teresa and Jordan go to all the tables and visit with family and friends. This is what it's all about, she thought, being with the people you love and who love you. El looked over at her brother and Leticia dancing and wondered if they would be the next ones to get married. The thought surprised her, but she wanted the best for them and hoped that it would work out.

Hours later, when the party was breaking up, Teresa and Jordan thanked El and Leticia again. Teresa hugged her friends and said, "You're the best. Thank you for making this the best day of my life!"

"I thought I did that," teased Jordan, putting his arm around her.

Teresa looked at him and said, "Dearest, my whole life is amazing with you."

"Awww," said El and Leticia in unison.

El closed her eyes briefly when Owen drove her home. She woke up when he turned off the engine. "Hey, Sleeping Beauty, we're home," he said softly.

"So sorry," she mumbled. It seemed like all the tensions of the last few weeks had left her exhausted.

She quickly fed Mr. Fluffy, who seemed to be torn between being annoyed at having to wait so long for his supper and ecstatic to see Owen.

"So sorry," she said again as she went into the bedroom. "I'm just so tired."

"Then let's get some rest," he said, as he stripped off his clothes. He slipped into bed and put his arms around her and kissed the top of her head as she fell asleep.

When El awoke, she found Owen sitting next to her with a cup of coffee in one hand and her mystery novel in the other. He seemed to be about thirty pages into it. "Good morning, my elegant El." He bent to kiss her lips.

"What time is it?" El asked.

"Close to eight. Let me get you coffee." He left the room without waiting for her to answer.

El raced into the bathroom to pee and brush her teeth. She didn't want him grossed out by her morning breath. When she returned to the bed, she kissed him again, longer and slower than their first quick kiss of the day.

As she settled back against some pillows with her coffee in hand, Owen said, "Teresa's and Jordan's wedding was nice. My sister has been planning hers since she was a little girl. What about you?"

"Uh, no," El said.

"You've never thought about your wedding?" Owen's head was turned towards her and he seemed to be searching her face.

"Not really. I mean, I always assumed I'd get married, but until we helped Teresa plan her wedding, I never really gave much thought as to what mine would be like."

"You'd make a beautiful bride," Owen said. His eyes glazed a bit like he was picturing it.

"Thanks," El said. "We already know how hot you are in a tux."

Owen grinned. "Glad you think so, but I'd wear tails to get married. I mean, when else am I going to get the chance to go that formal."

"Hmmm," El said. "You've put thought into this."

"Well, I was in a serious relationship," Owen said quietly but a bit defensively.

El nodded her head. And then it struck her: after two years of being with Derek, she had wanted a bigger commitment or to seem like she was a more important part of his life, but, if she were completely honest with herself, she never saw them as man and wife. He had been married to his job and she was more of his side hustle.

Owen, from that first day at brunch, had been more attentive to El. She was scared to ask the question that wanted to burst from her chest, but she really needed to know. She carefully worded the question in her mind, and then she reached for his hand that no longer held her book and played with his fingers. Looking down at their hands together, she asked, "You've said you wanted to be with me since we were teenagers. Owen, did you ever think about what your wedding would be like if it was with me?"

Owen laughed. "No, El. I never thought about weddings, mine or anyone else's as a teenager. I was too busy imagining nailing you and jacking off." He grinned and his eyes sparkled.

El blushed but she was grinning back at him. His answer was a relief to her.

"But now, as an adult, I'm happy to imagine that with you," Owen said, watching her reaction.

"Uhh," El said, feeling her insides clench in panic. Distraction seemed necessary. "I'd rather just get straight to the honeymoon."

She launched herself at him and covered his mouth with hers while grinding her hips into his lap.

Later, when they showered, he said, "You're way better than any of my fantasies."

El smiled and felt her heart warm.

Chapter 27

In the late afternoon, Owen and El met Jack and Leticia for happy hour at the Gecko. When their round of margaritas arrived, Jack held his aloft and said, "We have an announcement."

El thought, OMG, don't tell me they're engaged. Owen's hand rested on her thigh under the table, and he gave it a squeeze.

Leticia smiled widely and looked so lovingly at Jack. "We do," she said.

"You tell them," Jack said.

"The condo next to Jack's came up for sale. And since I'm there all of the time anyway now—" Leticia took a deep breath. "We put in an offer to buy it. And it was accepted."

That was so not what El was expecting.

Jack finished the news. "So we are moving in together and remodeling it into one, bigger place."

"That's great," Owen said, clinking his glass into Jack's and Leticia's. With his other hand, he squeezed El's thigh again, urging her to raise her glass.

"Awesome," El said. "I'm happy for both of you." To Leticia she said, "When is the move? Do you need help packing?" El really was happy for them but she was also feeling a bit like the odd man out. Teresa and Leticia had found their someones, and El was still unsure.

Leticia said, "Next month. I had to give thirty days to my building management that I was moving out. My mom and sisters said they'd come help so we can make a party out of it in a few weeks." She leaned over towards El and squeezed her saying, "I'm so freaking happy. I'm going to be a property owner plus I get to live with Jack. God, I love him."

El said, "Property ownership in this city is an accomplishment. Good for you. As for Jack, well, I can tell you as his sister…"

"Now, now, Rella," Jack said. "You don't want to start telling stories if you aren't ready for the airing of your own." And then he chuckled.

El kicked him gently under the table. "Jerk."

He grinned at her and she could feel his love. "I love you, bro," she said aloud in response.

When the waiter walked by again, Owen motioned to him and ordered a bottle of champagne. "Not sure it should be drunk after margaritas, but we need to celebrate." They all ordered some food to absorb the alcohol, too.

Later, when Owen and El were back at her apartment, and Mr. Fluffy was parked on Owen's lap, he said, "That's so great about Jack and Leticia moving their relationship forward."

"Yes, it is. It's also amazing to see after Leticia was…well, a player… for so long. And Jack too."

"That might be why they're a perfect match," Owen said, picking up her hand and threading his fingers through hers. He continued, "I was wondering, El, after this weekend and how incredible it's been, if you'd commit to being exclusive."

El felt the air leave her chest. She really didn't want to have this discussion right now, when she was trying to figure things out in her head and her heart. The thought of not seeing Bernie this week crossed her mind and she didn't like it. He made her laugh and they had such fun. And she wasn't done with her degree. Did mastering relationships mean she had to be in only one?

Before she answered, he said, "I can see by the changes in your expression that your answer is no." He paused.

She still said nothing as she couldn't figure out what to say. Then she tried, "Owen…"

He cut her off. "El, it's okay. I'm ready. You're not. As I said this morning, I've fantasized about you for years, and not just in a spank bank kind of way." He stroked the back of her hand with his finger. "But getting to know the grown-up El has blown away my fantasies. I can't stop thinking about you. I want to be with you all the time, and get to know every little thing about you, what you like, what you don't, what each of your expressions means."

El felt warmth return to her heart. What he was saying was so sweet and sincere. She wanted a guy who wanted to be this much a part of her life. But despite the calls from her mom expressing joy that El was seeing Owen, the encouragement from Teresa, and Mr. Fluffy's apparent enthrallment, El needed to make sure for herself that Owen was the guy she wanted to be with. And she wasn't sure yet.

"Owen," she began again. "I love the time we spend together. I love the way I feel in your arms. And the sex, well, wow."

"I know, we fit together so perfectly," Owen said.

"We do," El said. "And we have great chemistry. But I'm just not sure I'm ready to commit."

Owen frowned.

Just then El worried that he might "break up" with her even though they weren't "together." El added, "I don't want to stop seeing you, getting to know you better, and exploring where this might go." She squeezed his hand. "I care so much for you."

"El, I love you," Owen said, staring into her eyes. "I only want to be with you."

"I love you, too, Owen. But I'm not sure I'm in love. Hell, I'm not even sure what that feels like. I thought I knew before, but after listening to Teresa and Leticia, I just don't know."

"I can be patient," Owen said.

El was feeling a whole barrage of things: loved, curious, worried she'd hurt him, worried she'd end up alone, proud for staying honest and true to herself.

She leaned towards him and kissed his lips. "Thank you," she said. He kissed her again but deeper, probing her mouth with his tongue.

When they broke apart, Owen removed Mr. Fluffy from his lap and gently set the cat on the floor. He said to El, "I can also be persuasive. Let me show you how," and he picked her up and carried her into the bedroom, placing her on the bed, and pinning her down underneath him.

Over the next hour and a half, Owen busted out moves El had only read about. By the end, her mind was mush; she thought her body might be permanently turned on, albeit a bit sore; and she was sleepy. Owen curled around her and they feel fast asleep.

At five on Monday morning, Owen let himself out of her apartment. The note he left in the kitchen said, "I meant it when I said I love you. And Mr. Fluffy, too, of course." He had made coffee and it was still hot when El padded into the kitchen at five-thirty and saw the note. She smiled, but then thought, This could all end very badly. Until she thought back to last night. OMG. Love or not, I've never had so many orgasms before, she thought.

While she showered, she consciously pushed thoughts of Owen and the sex from her mind. She needed to focus on work, and to schedule a call with PJ (hopefully for today) and to circle back to Bernie and Keith about getting together. She also wanted to e-mail all of those couples from before and find out how they knew each other was the one.

She typed and sent that e-mail while she ate some fruit, toast, and cheese for breakfast. And she texted PJ, who said she could video conference with her tonight at seven.

After work, El ate a quick pasta dish as she jotted some notes for PJ. At seven on the dot, PJ's picture popped up on her screen and El happily answered. PJ looked relaxed with her hair pulled back into a ponytail and a yellow and purple tank top.

After a few minutes of chatting, PJ asked, "How is the degree going? What are you learning?"

El told her about focusing on herself and some of the books she was reading. She also mentioned her study group with Keith and Teresa's wedding.

PJ smiled and said, "It doesn't seem like you need any help from me. You seem to be doing just fine."

"Thank you," said El. "It's been really interesting and a lot of fun, but…"

"But?"

"But now I feel I need to go to the next level. How do you know when someone's the one? I'd love to hear how you knew Shayla was the one for you."

"Good question." PJ looked off to the side while considering it. "It's funny when I was in relationships before, they always seemed like so much work. I thought you had to work hard on relationships. So when there was a lot of drama and problems, I thought that was normal. Then I met Shayla and it was much easier, and at first I thought there was something wrong with that. But then I realized when you're with someone who's right for you, it is easier, you're not fighting all the time."

She smiled and said, "Of course, we have problems and disagreements, but we behave respectfully." She tipped her head to the side. "Getting back to your question, I first started to think that she was the one on an afternoon that we were sitting around my apartment. I was reading and she was watching TV and we weren't doing anything special, but it felt nice and comfortable. And I remember thinking how great it was that we could both just relax together. It felt so right. Soon after that, we had a fight about going to visit her family. I had something else I wanted to do instead and I explained that. And she didn't get nasty or critical or passive aggressive; she explained why she wanted to go and why she wanted me to come along with her. She really tried to understand my point of view and I really tried to understand hers. In the end, I didn't go, and even though she was disappointed, she understood."

PJ frowned. "I was concerned that we'd have a big fight when she came back but instead, we had another good talk. That's when I thought she was the one. I didn't have to change for her. I could be me and she was fine with that. She didn't have to agree with me all the time but could support what I wanted to do. And I could support her." PJ smiled again, "And that's made all the difference. I found someone who could love me for who I am."

"Wow," said El. "That sounds great."

"Yes, she's terrific." PJ grinned. "If you're looking for the one, the other thing I would consider is how does the person make you feel about yourself? When you're with the other person or think about the other person do you feel good about yourself and who you are or do you feel bad about yourself? To me, the person who is right for you lets you be yourself and supports you and helps you be the best version of yourself. And you do the same for them."

El thought back to Derek and how she felt unsure and never good enough around him. "I see what you mean."

"Is there any particular reason for asking that question now?" PJ took a sip from her mug.

El told her about the conversation that she'd had with Owen and said that she wasn't sure she wanted to be exclusive.

PJ nodded. "It sounds like he took it well."

El smiled, "Yes, he was really sweet about it. I appreciated that."

"What are you going to do about it?"

"That's the problem. I just don't know."

PJ paused. "What's really bothering you here?"

"What do you mean?"

"Everything you've said about Owen sounds great. What's holding you back?"

El took a sip of her tea as she thought about her answer. "I don't know. Part of me is worried that he's crazy about some fantasy he has, not the real me. I want him to care about me not some dream he had in high school."

"Okay. And?"

"Also, sometimes he seems too perfect. I mean he's sexy and handsome. And he's really nice and sweet and attentive. I mean the first dinner he cooked for me blew me away. But…"

"But?"

"I keep waiting to see the real Owen. He can't be that wonderful." El sighed and lowered her voice. "Sometimes I wonder how soon is this going to fizzle out?"

"So you're convinced it's not going to work out?"

"No, no, not at all. I just worry. I mean things started off well with Derek. Of course he was never as attentive as Owen has been, but we had a great time in the beginning. I just don't want to have another Derek situation."

"Then don't date another Derek."

"Ouch."

"Do you think Owen is like Derek?"

El looked into her mug and thought for a moment. "No, he's not at all like Derek. I guess I'm just a little nervous."

PJ shook her head. "Understandable. But don't let worrying about the future mess up the present. You should have a picture of what you want the future to be, but you need to enjoy the present. Think about how you can be really present with Owen and enjoy what you have and build on it."

El nodded. "Good point. If I'm too scared what might happen in the future, I'm not going to be able to enjoy what's going on now."

"Think back to the mind movies that we discussed when you wanted to ask for a raise. Picture in your mind your happy relationship movie. What does it look like? How do you look? What do you look like together?" PJ paused and sipped her water.

El thought back to how happy her friends looked. That's what she wanted. El smiled and thought about how Owen looked at her and how she imagined they looked together. "Thanks," she said. "I hadn't thought to use mind movies to picture my ideal relationship."

"It works for business, why not for relationships? And it doesn't need to be your ideal relationship. That might be too hard to imagine. Instead just focus on creating happy mind movies."

"I like that. I tend to focus on the negatives and I need to remind myself to play happy mind movies."

"Good," PJ said. "Now, let's take it back to your degree. Besides creating positive mind movies, what homework do you need to do?"

El smiled. "Well first, I need to stop worrying that Owen is Derek because he's not. And I need to relax and enjoy what's going on now without worrying that he's too perfect. I'm sure I'll see more of the real Owen soon."

"And how much of the real El have you showed him?"

"Good question. Probably not much. I've been on good behavior, too. I guess I need to be willing to show the real authentic me if that's what I want from him."

PJ nodded. "Yes, that's fair. What else do you want to do?"

"I've already started. I sent out a message to people I know asking them how they knew their partner was the right one for them."

"Now, let's forget about the degree. What do you need to do to find out what your head and heart say?"

"I think I need some quiet time."

"Remember, there is no deadline. Stop trying to rush things."

El nodded. "Yes, it's just been so strange lately. With Teresa's wedding and with Leticia and Jack moving in together, I feel like everyone else but me has this figured out."

"Wait, back up. Leticia and Jack?"

El explained.

PJ said, "Good for them. But don't let other people's timetables determine yours. Not your friends and not Owen. This is about you and how you feel."

El thanked her and they talked a little more before ending the call.

As El tidied up the kitchen, she thought about what she wanted to do next.

She texted Owen, "Thanks again for this weekend. I can't wait to see you again. What about Saturday?"

The response made her frown. It said, "Sorry. Can't see you on Saturday–I'm helping a friend move. Maybe Sunday." She immediately started worrying that he was upset with her because she hadn't said that she would commit to being exclusive. Maybe he was going to break up with her. Maybe…She stopped herself. That was ridiculous. It was nice that he was helping a friend move. She'd see him on Sunday. She pictured the wonderful way he'd looked at her. She closed her eyes momentarily and smiled.

She also got a text from Bernie asking about the wedding and checking when they could get together again. They agreed to dinner on Wednesday night.

Before she went to bed, she looked at some of the responses that she'd received to her question. One friend said that she knew he was the one when she was in a car accident and he was the first one at the hospital and visited her every day. Another friend said she knew he was the one when he started walking her dog with her and it felt really comfortable. Her cousin said she knew when she realized that they both had the same sense of humor and loved doing the same silly things. El enjoyed reading them, but they didn't give her the answers she was looking for.

Chapter 28

Bernie had suggested a local Thai restaurant by his house and said it was his treat as a thanks for when she had taken care of him. When she arrived, he was already waiting and jumped up from his seat to give her a hug and kiss. He wore a fedora and blue shirt with tiny salmon and starfish on it. He put his hand on hers when they sat down and said how nice it was to see her. El smiled and said the same. She felt comfortable with Bernie and he made her laugh. She thought back to what PJ had said. "Stop trying to analyze everything," she said to herself.

The evening was fun, and Bernie told stories about what was going on at work. He asked again about the wedding and wanted to hear all about it. Throughout the meal, he touched her arm and smiled at her in a sweet way.

After dinner they walked down the street to window shop. El liked the way his arm felt around her and how comfortable he felt against her. When they said good night, she closed her eyes and enjoyed the feeling of his lips on hers and his arms holding her close.

In bed that night, as she thought about Bernie, thoughts of Owen interrupted. She decided she needed to read and reached for the mystery novel on her night stand. She remembered that was the one he had started reading when he'd spent the night. Ugh, she thought, I can't get him out of my brain. She tossed and turned before falling asleep.

All week long, Owen had work commitments in the evenings because he had team members that were visiting from South America. El and Owen exchanged some texts during the week but it seemed like he was focused on entertaining his visitors. El was also busy at work so it was fine with her. Though once or twice, she wondered if he was purposely creating space between them.

She had hoped to see him Friday night, but instead she sat alone in her kitchen talking to Mr. Fluffy. Owen told her he was helping his friend with packing that night so they could get the move done on Saturday. She thought it was nice that he was so helpful to his friends, but she really wished that she could see him. She debated showing up late at his apartment to surprise him on Friday night but then decided that probably wasn't a good idea.

On Sunday morning, El got a text from a number she didn't recognize. It said, "El, this is Owen's girlfriend. I know he's been seeing you on the side but he's not interested in you anymore. Leave him alone."

Owen's girlfriend? She was in shock. "Who's this?" El texted back quickly. And how did this person know her name and number?

"Owen's girlfriend. He gave me your number. It's over. Leave him alone. He loves me."

El sat down and felt nauseous. This could not be happening. She put her head in her hands and tried to calm down. She took some deep breaths. She obviously needed to talk to Owen. She spent a few minutes trying to figure out what to do.

Another text came in a few minutes later from the same number. "He told me all about you. But it's over. He loves me."

El's hands were shaking so she put the phone down. After a few more deep breaths, she texted Owen. "Hi"

He quickly responded with, "Hi."

She spent a few minutes typing and retyping, trying to make her message as neutral as possible. "I just got a text from someone saying that she's your girlfriend and I should leave you alone."

The phone rang. Owen's name showed on the screen. El took a few more deep breaths. She wasn't sure she wanted to answer and considered letting it go to voicemail. She decided to be brave.

"Hello?"

"El, I don't know what's going on. That's crazy. I don't have another girlfriend. Honestly."

El tried to sound calm. "I'll forward the messages to you, but here's the number they came from." El switched them to speaker phone so she could navigate to her texts and read the number.

Owen was silent for a second, and El realized that she was holding her breath.

"Shit, El, I'm sorry. That is my ex, and she's obviously nuts. Nothing she texted is true. I think she wants to get back with me. But I only want you. Please believe me, El. I'm so sorry."

El felt her shoulders relax slightly. "This is not how I wanted to start the day."

"I know. I know. I can't believe this happened. I'm sorry."

"How did she get my number? And my name?"

There was silence again until Owen cleared his throat. "Well… I did tell her about you. I thought she'd be happy for me. After all, she was the one who broke up with me. But maybe she—"

El interrupted. "You talked to your ex-girlfriend?"

"Yeah."

"And you told her about us?"

"Yeah."

El tried to sound calm. "Why were you talking to your ex-girlfriend?"

There was another pause. "Taylor called me because she needed help moving and…"

"Wait, that was the friend that you helped move the past two days?" El could not believe what she was hearing.

"Yes, she needed help and…"

"Your ex-girlfriend was the friend that you moved yesterday?" El repeated.

"Yes but…"

"And somehow she got my number?"

"Maybe she looked at my phone when I was in another room and got your number from my contacts. I had told her about you. She was probably jealous."

"I can't believe this. You told me that you were helping a friend, not your ex-girlfriend. That's a big difference. Why didn't you tell me that's who you were helping? And what happened to that guy she left you for?"

There was another pause. "Well, I thought it might upset you."

"You think?" El's comment dripped sarcasm.

"I only helped her move. That's it." Owen sounded irritated and defensive. "And we're not exclusive. Remember? Why are you reacting

238

like this? What's the big deal?"

That stung. El tried to speak calmly. "No, we're not exclusive, but I expect the truth from you. You deliberately lied to me because you thought I would be upset."

"But…"

"And yeah, you're right, I wouldn't have liked it and I would have talked to you about it. But calmly. Now I'm upset because you lied to me. How can I be in a relationship with someone who won't tell the truth?"

"El, I'm sorry. I screwed up. I should have told you. Can I come over now? Let me make it up to you."

"I don't want to see you or talk any more about this right now. I'm going to block her number. I need time to think."

"Please, El, let me explain."

"Owen, I'm too upset to talk. Let me calm down and sort it out."

"Okay, I understand. I love you. Please call me later."

"I will."

"Okay, El. Again, I'm sorry."

After El disconnected, she put her head back, closed her eyes, and tried to re-arrange her thoughts. She asked herself what was she so angry about. So Owen had a crazy ex-girlfriend who wanted him back when she realized he was dating someone else. That wasn't a big deal, really. But he lied by omission. That thought kept going around and around in her head. Maybe she was overreacting, but trust and truth were really important to her.

She texted Leticia and asked if she had time for a call. A few minutes later, they were on the phone.

As El talked, Leticia interrupted her with comments of "no" and "uhuh".

"Am I being too sensitive?" said El.

"No way! He's a total jackass! I can't believe he lied to you like that!"

"I thought you liked him."

"I do but that was really stupid. Now you can't trust him. What else is he hiding?"

Even though El appreciated her friend's support, she felt bad for

Owen. "Yeah, but he said he didn't want to hurt my feelings."

"Girl, that's just an excuse. A real man would have told you and discussed it with you. Hell, a real man would not be helping his ex with anything. I don't care if he was trying to be nice, she's an ex! He's never said they had an ongoing friendship or any kind of relationship."

When El hung up a few minutes later, she felt supported but had no idea what to do. She looked at the clock and realized that she had to jump in the shower and get to the bookstore to meet Keith.

When she got there, Keith already had his coffee and oatmeal. She said hi and went to get a cup of tea.

When she sat down, he looked at her and asked, "Are you okay?"

She forced herself to smile. "Yeah, why?"

"You look upset."

"Crazy morning." She waved her hand as if to brush it away. "But now I get to enjoy myself in study group. How are you doing?"

Keith talked about some of the reading he'd been doing, and they discussed the books.

He asked about the wedding and what she had learned. She admitted that she had not done a great job of researching at the wedding. She quickly said that she'd met with PJ and had sent out a request to find out how people knew they had met the one. Then she said, "How important do you think honesty is in a relationship?"

He looked at her. "Foundational. You have to have honesty."

"I agree. But honesty about everything?"

"What do you mean?"

El took a breath. She hadn't planned to tell the story to Keith. She had been feeling a bit awkward with Keith because she sensed he wanted something more between them but she needed to unload. She told him about the texts and call with Owen. "So is that a guy thing? That it's not a big deal?"

Keith sat back and breathed out. "Hmm. Not sure how to answer that." He paused and then said, "Okay. Let me talk about me. Back when I was married, there were certain things that I knew would upset my ex and I wouldn't bring them up. I wouldn't lie about them but I thought it would be better if she didn't know because I didn't want to hurt her feelings. The truth is though that it was easier for me. I just used that as an excuse, because I didn't want to have that discussion or fight. Not talking was easier."

He shifted in his chair and leaned forward. "Of course, the more we didn't talk about things, the more they got bottled up and you know where it ended." He tapped the books in front of him. "This material is helping me to realize that honesty needs to be at the base layer of relationship-building. The tough stuff has to be talked about. And you need to set that as an expectation at the beginning of a relationship. I want to know the good, the bad, and the ugly from the person who's my partner."

El was nodding. "Yes, yes. Exactly. Otherwise it all feels like it's built on a bunch of lies."

They talked more about it, and El told Keith how much she appreciated his comments.

He smiled. "Does that mean I get a gold star for today?"

She returned his smile and laughed. "Absolutely. You are my favorite student."

They continued to joke and agreed to meet again next week. Before they ended, Keith looked serious and touched her arm. "Are you going to be okay?"

"Yeah, I'll be fine, thanks."

"Okay, let me know if you need anything."

When she got back to her house, she saw a text from Leticia. "Just talked to Jack. He said don't be so hard on Owen. That his heart was in the right place (protecting your feelings) even if his actions were misguided. Seriously? Men!"

El frowned. She didn't want this to cause a problem with Jack and Leticia. She quickly texted back. "Don't worry. I'm feeling better. Thx."

As she straightened her apartment, she thought about what she wanted to do next. She considered avoiding Owen and thought about what was authentic for her.

She texted Owen. "Hi."

He quickly texted back. "Hi."

"When can you talk?" she texted.

"Now."

She closed her eyes, took a deep breath, and called.

"Hi El, how are you doing?" Owen sounded nervous.

"Hi, much better than before."

"Oh good. Listen, El. I am really sorry. I never meant for this to happen."

"I'm sure that's true. Here's the thing. I'm feeling hurt right now and I need some time to think about all this. I realize that you didn't want to upset me, but I'm bothered that you didn't tell me the truth. I feel confused and need time to process what happened and then we can talk about it, okay?"

"Okay. I understand. I'll be here. Let me know when you want to talk."

"Thanks, Owen."

After she hung up, she closed her eyes. She thought back to her conversation with PJ and next steps for her degree. This felt like she was taking her exams. She just wished she knew what the answers were.

El spent the afternoon reading, doing yoga, grocery shopping for the week, and meditating. She thought about the men in her life. Bernie was so funny and charming, and their relationship was so easy-going. She cherished that. But she also acknowledged that while they touched and kissed occasionally, she couldn't really see herself having sex with him. Neither of them had attempted to take their relationship there and she was pretty sure he was actively sleeping with other people.

She thought about Owen and how hurt she felt, but somewhere in the back of her mind, a voice said that she hadn't exactly set any expectations with him and had made assumptions about his relationship with his ex. Had he ever said they weren't talking? Had El even asked? Just because she and Derek were over and done with and had no communication since the break-up didn't mean that every couple acted the same way.

El jumped on to Facebook and put a quick poll on her wall. "Are you still friends with any of your exes?"

Within seconds, posts started pouring in with answers like: one, some, two of them, all of them, nope. But the majority of people claimed to still be friends with at least one of their exes. El was astounded but also realized how valuable this information was. And it made her think of Bernie again. He seemed to be on great terms with his exes, including the doctor and Stuart. But he also seemed to be *that guy*, the one who befriended and stayed friends or acquaintances with everyone.

El didn't think she could do that. She wasn't that easy going. She had no desire to ever see Derek again.

But Owen...she pulled up his social media accounts and scrolled through his photos. No recent pictures were of him and his ex. In fact, it looked like all but one of the photos with his ex had been removed from his account. His most recent photos were of the marathon and of Mr. Fluffy, with silly captions like "catnapped my heart" and "catalyst for change." El chuckled aloud. The third photo showed Mr. Fluffy snuggled up against Owen's chest, like the furball was nuzzling him. El thought maybe Jack took the photo two weekends ago. Owen had titled it, "These snuggles 'catapulted' me to my true love."

El's breath caught in her throat and tears formed in her eyes. The depth of Owen's love reached her through that photo. And PJ's words echoed in her head about having respectful discussions and disagreements. That's what people who loved each other did. She owed him that. She picked up her phone.

When he answered on the first ring, with "El, I'm so sorry. I promise—"

El cut him off. "No, Owen. I'm sorry. And I'm ready to talk. May I come over?"

"Of course," Owen said. "Or I can come to you and Mr. Fluffy. Either way, I'll be so glad to see you. Do you need dinner? I can grab some on the way?"

El said, "I'll call the Chinese place on the corner near my house. Please pick it up. And Owen, thank you, and see you soon." She ended the call and jumped onto Lucky Cat's website to place the order and to pay for it.

And then she sat on the sofa with Mr. Fluffy and did a few deep breathing exercises while she waited for Owen's arrival. She still felt a bit emotionally tender, but Owen was worth working things out with; she planned to talk to him about her hopes, her fears, her expectations, her desire for him to peel back his layers and show his true self, and to lay out her real feelings, and she wanted him to do the same.

She felt nervous waiting for Owen. She tried to distract herself by thinking about Byron Katie's four questions. Is it true, she asked herself. Did Owen lie to her? It felt like he had lied to her but was that really true? She thought about the second question, can you absolutely know it's true? The reality was no. He'd never said he wasn't seeing his ex-girlfriend. When he said he was helping a friend, maybe he really believed that. Though she could never refer to Derek as a friend maybe Owen did stay friendly with his exes. She said to herself, but he did admit that I might be upset so he… Then she shook her head and asked herself, how do I react when I believe that thought? Shitty. I feel just awful. I feel betrayed. She took a deep breath and thought, Who would I be without this thought? She smiled. That was easy. She would be much happier. And more relaxed. And not so stressed out.

She paced around the apartment thinking about what to say. She thought about how she might have reacted to something like this in the past. She might have gotten upset and either sulked or gotten angry. Or maybe she would have glossed over it and made excuses for him. Instead, now she knew she needed to talk to Owen about it. She wanted to share how she felt about it and talk about what she needed. And she wanted to listen to him to understand him better.

She smiled as she thought back to something she had learned from PJ about work, if you don't ask you don't get. Yes, she needed to ask for what she wanted in this relationship. She didn't want to assume. She wanted to be clear.

She meant it when she said she wanted to keep seeing him. But what she knew now was she wanted to intentionally invest in them creating an us. Because at the heart of all of her research, that's what she learned: mastering relationships hinged on two people creating and investing and loving an "us"—though in their case, their "us" involved a third, Mr. Fluffy, who seemed to insinuate himself into their relationship, or maybe it was really he who let El share his relationship with Owen. El laughed and shook her head. "Silly cat," she said, just as the intercom chimed and Owen's voice asked to be let in.

Chapter 29

Mr. Fluffy perched himself on the back of the sofa ready to pounce as soon as El opened the door, and El smiled, thinking maybe the cat had the right idea and that would be one way to break the ice created earlier.

When she opened the door and saw his face, she smiled and reached up to put a hand on each of his cheeks and kissed him. He put one hand on her back and awkwardly held the other hand with the take-out food bag by her side.

Mr. Fluffy meowed behind her. She ignored him and continued to kiss Owen and moved her fingers through his short black hair.

When she finally let him go, he said, "Wow, I'll bring over Chinese food any time for kisses like that."

She laughed and said, "Sounds good to me."

As he walked toward the table he said, "Listen El, I'm so sorry."

Mr. Fluffy followed them and jumped on the chair next to Owen and rubbed against him.

"Owen, I'm sorry. I shouldn't have gotten so upset."

He put his arms around her and held her close. "No, it was me. I should have told you. I didn't think it would be such a big deal, and I certainly had no idea she would contact you. That was nuts."

El nodded. "It was awful." She leaned her head on his chest and breathed in deeply. "I was so upset thinking that you were seeing someone else. That's not what I want." She looked up and into his eyes. "I want you."

He looked at her surprised and said, "You do?"

"Yes. It made me think about how I would feel if you weren't in my life. And I didn't like that feeling. I like the way it feels when we're together."

He hugged her more tightly.

She continued, "And I like thinking about you and knowing you're there for me." She moved her head back to snuggle up against his chest. "Being with you at the wedding was wonderful and scary at the same time." She paused. "The situation with Derek really hurt and I don't want to go through that again. Relationships are scary. It's hard for me to trust someone else after that." She hugged him tightly. "But I want to."

"Me too," he said kissing her hair. There was silence. "I've been there, too. I promise I will do everything I can not to hurt you. I care too much about you."

"Thank you." She sighed again. "And I care too much about you."

They talked more about what happened. El said that when there was a problem, she wanted to talk it through. In the future, she wanted better communication.

"Does that mean there is a future for us?" he asked gently.

"Yes," she nodded. "I want us to work together on a future." She paused. "But to do that, I also want something else."

"What?"

"I want to know the real you. Sometimes you seem too perfect and it worries me."

He started to laugh.

"No, seriously." She smiled. "I mean it. I feel like I've been dating the perfect Owen. You're sweet and cute and hot, and sometimes I feel like I don't know the real you."

"You mean I'm not really sweet and cute and hot," he teased.

She shook her head. "No, you are. But there's more to you than just that. I want to get to know the real you. The you that is nice enough to want to help your ex-girlfriend move and silly enough to think that she won't want to get back together with you."

"Hey!" He smiled.

"Come on, of course she'd want to get back together with you. She'd have to be stupid not to!"

"Well thank you, I think."

"But that means that I really want to know you, and I want to hear the good and not so good."

"Does this mean I can fart in front of you now?"

El tipped her head back and laughed. "Ewwww. That's not what I mean."

"You said you want the not so good."

"But…"

"Kidding. I get it." He put his mouth on hers and kissed her deeply. He then kissed a trail to her ear. "Does this mean I get to be with the real El? The good and not so good?"

She took a deep breath, and said, "Okay. Here's something that you need to know about me." She paused and saw his warm brown eyes look concerned. "I'm not sure how to say this. I guess I'll just say it. I'm not interested in running a marathon with you." She shook her head. "I know it's important to you and I'll be happy to cheer you on at the end of the finish line but I don't ever want to train with you. I'm really not interested in working out like that."

Owen looked at her intently and then hugged her. "Oh honey, I don't care about that. You don't need to like it or do it with me. Were you really nervous that I would be upset about that?"

She held him closer and spoke into his shoulder, "You've suggested that we work out together a bunch of times and I didn't want to tell you 'cause I know it means a lot to you."

"El, we don't need to do everything together or agree on everything. I'm sure there's stuff you want to do that I don't care about it. It's okay." He squeezed her. "I care about you."

"Thank you. You're so sweet."

"Is there anything else?"

She pulled back and looked into his eyes and said, "I really appreciate that. I was a little nervous about talking to you and about saying that but I want to be able to talk to you and not sugar-coat things. I need to know that you want to be here not just for the wonderful dance nights but for the next morning when we have to clean things up and the other nights when it's not so great and maybe it's boring. Will you be here to talk to me? And to listen to me when I'm upset? And tell me when you're upset before it gets too far and things blow up?"

He took her hand and kissed it. "Yes, yes, and yes."

"I want something real. I don't want the fairytale."

"That's what I want, too." They kissed again.

The dinner grew cold as they went into the bedroom.

When they later re-heated the food, El told him some of the things she'd learned about communication and relationships. He asked how the degree was going.

"I'm hoping you'll work on my thesis with me," she said.

He stroked his beard and smiled, "I've dreamt of taking classes with you."

"I'm not sure what kind of classes you're thinking about, but I meant helping me work on some ideas that put it all together."

"I'm all in as long as it's with you. What's your thesis about?"

"I'm thinking it's something about how to build a great relationship."

He put his hand on hers and looked at her. "Let's do it together."

She talked to him about some of the books she had read and he asked to borrow her copy of *Attached* so he could read it and take the quiz. She was glad Owen was interested. Based on what she knew about him, she thought he would score with a high Secure Style. She looked forward to talking with him about it and learning together.

When they got into bed that night, she snuggled up behind him and held him close as he fell asleep. She enjoyed his warmth and the rhythmic feeling of his breathing as he softly started to snore. He left at five. so he could get home and take a shower before going to work.

That morning at work, she got a text from Leticia asking if she was okay. She realized that she hadn't let her friend know what had gone on with Owen. She texted back that she had seen Owen the night before and they had worked things out.

She waited to text Teresa to see how she was doing. She and Jordan had gotten home from the honeymoon late the night before. Teresa texted that afternoon saying she was back and the honeymoon had been wonderful.

"Gecko?" El texted to both her friends.

"Yes! Too tired tonight. Tomorrow night!" texted Teresa.

Leticia responded with a snarky comment about why Teresa needed more sleep and she answered with happy emojis.

El traded texts with Owen that night and she went to sleep thinking about him.

The next night, El was the first to arrive at the restaurant and as she waited she thought about the night when Teresa had shown off her engagement ring. She recalled how sad she'd been feeling about her split with Derek. She hated to admit how envious she'd felt about Teresa's engagement. El had learned so much since then. So much about herself and so much about relationships. She almost felt like a different person. Someone who was much more in touch with who she was and what she wanted.

Then she thought about Leticia and how mysterious she had been during that time. She shook her head slightly thinking about Leticia and Jack moving in together. Things had really changed.

She remembered her initial ideas about working on her Master's Degree. When she'd thought about working on relationships, she hadn't really thought about working on herself. She'd been more interested in understanding how guys thought and how to meet the right one.

Leticia arrived and interrupted El's thoughts. She started to grill El about what had happened with Owen and just when El launched into the story, Teresa arrived. The friends hugged and El marveled at how happy and relaxed Teresa looked.

They ordered drinks and appetizers and Leticia and El wanted to hear all about the honeymoon. Jordan had kept the location a surprise so she didn't know until the night of the wedding where they were going. The next afternoon they went on a cruise to the coast of Mexico. Teresa sighed when she talked about how amazing it was and how much fun she had.

"Seriously, did you ever get out of the cabin?" asked Leticia.

Teresa smiled. "Yes, of course. We had to eat at some point." They all laughed and she told them more details and showed photos on her phone.

When the margaritas and loaded veggie nachos arrived, El proposed a toast. "To my dearest friends. I love you both and I'm so happy to see you happy!"

"To us," toasted Leticia.

After taking a drink, Teresa raised her glass again. "To my best friends who helped make my wedding the most special day of my life."

They all took another drink.

El said, "Thank you! Probably Jordan had something to do with it, too."

At the mention of her new husband's name, Teresa grinned broadly. "Oh yes he did." She told them about the cruise excursions that Jordan had planned for her. She dipped her cheesy chip in guacamole. "And I have to thank you for taking the pole dancing class with me."

El laughed. "Did they have a pole in the room?"

Teresa leaned in and said, "No, but remember the sexy dances they taught us to do up against the walls and on the floor?" She smiled. "They worked out very well." She declined to give any more details, but her smile told the story.

El thought back to those moves and realized that she had not shown them to Owen yet. That could be a good idea for the weekend.

As they caught up, El mentioned that she had spoken to PJ and she had said "hi" to both of them.

"That's great! How is she?" asked Leticia.

El told them about their conversation. "She was impressed with what I had learned so far."

Leticia and Teresa raised their glasses. Teresa said, "You've certainly come a long way from the way you acted with Derek."

El nodded. "You know it's funny. I realize now that Derek wasn't the right one for me."

Leticia gave Teresa a look that clearly said "duh." She said, "Hear hear," as she raised her glass.

El smiled. "But it's not right to just blame him. Good relationships should be a two-way street. I should have been comfortable enough to discuss it with him but I wasn't. I was afraid that I'd lose him and instead I lost who I was. I felt like I didn't have a voice in that relationship." El looked down and sighed. "I mean it was never going to work with him but it always felt like he was in control and that's not what I want. I want a partner, someone who's in the relationship with me."

Teresa and Leticia nodded at their friend.

El said, "I thought about something we talked about one time about writing our own stories. I started to think about what kind of relationship story I would want to write for myself."

She looked up at Teresa. "I remember what you said about when you were finally sure Jordan was the one when you were standing next to each other doing the dishes. That's what I want–someone next to me, working with me on the relationship. Not someone who wants to control everything."

Teresa patted her arm. "Good for you. That's what we want for you."

El smiled at her friends. "And now I'm feeling much better about being in a relationship and I appreciate all your help and support."

Leticia smiled and said in a high voice, "But Cinderella does this mean that you don't need to be rescued by a handsome prince?"

El laughed. "I don't mind dating a handsome prince but I don't need any rescuing."

"Glad to hear that. That sounds like my kind of a happy ending." Leticia took a fully loaded nacho chip and asked, "Give us an update then on the Master's Degree."

"Well, I'm doing some research about how people knew that their partner was the right one." She shared some of the stories she had been sent.

El said, "I've learned a lot and it's funny, I feel like I just went through midterms or finals with Owen."

Teresa said, "Wait, what happened?" El filled her in on the issue with Owen and his ex-girlfriend and then told them both about the conversation on Sunday night.

"I even proposed…"

"You proposed?" interrupted Leticia with a smile.

"No, no," she said quickly. "I mean I suggested that he and I might want to work on my thesis together. I told him about the degree and he was really interested and asked to read one of the books."

Teresa frowned. "You're not really writing a thesis are you?"

"Oh no, definitely not. But I did like the idea of talking it through with him and figuring out how we could both work on developing a good relationship together."

"Okay, that makes way more sense," said Teresa.

El turned to Leticia. "Do I need to lend you and Jack some of my books?"

Leticia tossed her head back. "I think the only things I want to read right now are about how to manage a construction project. But I'll let you know if I need them."

Teresa asked Leticia about the plans for their condos and Leticia started to share her ideas.

As El looked at her friends, she thought even though their relationships with the men in their lives had changed, they were still her best friends. She knew their lives would continue to change and they would be there for each other.

Chapter 30

The next weekend, El sat on the couch snuggled next to Owen with Mr. Fluffy nearby. He stroked her hair. "A penny for your thoughts."

"Just a penny?"

He hugged her. "Okay, lots of pennies."

"I'm thinking how lucky I am."

"Because you found me?" Owen joked.

She laughed. "Oh, you're so humble. Yes, I found you and that makes me very happy. But I also found me. And I needed to find me in order to be comfortable to have an us."

Owen smiled and said, "I'm lucky, too. And I'm glad you found yourself so I could get to know the real El, too. I love us." And he sealed his declaration with a long and passionate kiss.

EL'S LITERATURE REVIEW READING LIST:

Attached: The New Science of Adult Attachment and How It Can Help You Find—and Keep—Love by Amir Levine and Rachel Heller

Catering to Nobody (Goldy Schulz Book 1) by Diane Mott Davidson

I Need Your Love—Is That True? How To Stop Seeking Love, Approval, and Appreciation and Start Finding Them Instead by Byron Katie and Michael Katz

Mindset: The New Psychology of Success by Carol S. Dweck

Talking From 9 to 5: Women and Men At Work by Deborah Tannen

That's Not What I Meant: How Conversation Style Makes or Breaks Relationships by Deborah Tannen

The 5 Love Languages: The Secret To Love That Lasts by Gary Chapman

The Gifts of Imperfection: Let Go of Who You Think You're Supposed to Be and Embrace Who You Are by Brene Brown

Wedding Cake Crumble by Jenn McKinlay

You are A Badass: How To Stop Doubting Your Greatness and Start Living An Awesome Life by Jen Sincero

You're Wearing That? Understanding Mothers and Daughters in Conversation by Deborah Tannen

AUTHORS' NOTES

Laura would like to thank her wonderful family for their support—especially her Aunt Fran and Camille. She thanks her amazing daughter, Julianne, who is a special person and a talented writer. Laura wants to give a big thanks to her friend Ian, who helped her to better understand and value honest, heartfelt communication. Thank you also to her friend Chrystal, who is a kind and thoughtful person, as well as an amazing cook. Laura appreciates the coaching and guidance from her friend Davina Lyons, who is the Founder and Facilitator of TRIBE Authentic Woman and educates and inspires women to embrace their authentic selves (www.tribeauthenticwoman.com). She also wants to thank the team at Express Mie Pole Dance Studio in Chandler, Arizona, for a fun and empowering experience (www.expressmie.com).

Jill would like to thank everyone she has ever gone on a date with for inspiration for this book. In many ways, we are a compilation of our experiences, which serves as mechanisms for growth. For that, she is grateful. Thank you also to the readers have supported us on El's journey and who have asked for more. Jill never would have thought that ten years of teaching children's literature and the origins of fairytales would have influenced future books, but here it is, and what a fun journey it has been. We look forward to what the future has in store. And lastly, Jill is grateful to the two main men in her life: Nacho the red heeler and Rick. Thank you for the love, support, and giving me the space to write.

AUTHOR BIOS

Laura C. Browne is the voice of Careertipsforwomen.com, a business coach who has worked with hundreds of women in all stages of their careers, a corporate trainer, and the author of nine books. She can be reached at laura.browne@careertipsforwomen.com.

Jill L. Ferguson is an award-winning writer and the author of ten books, one ebooklet, and thousands of published articles. She is the founder of both Women's Wellness Weekends and Creating the Freelance Career, and she regularly coaches entrepreneurs and people who want to be published or write books. She can be reached at jill@jillferguson.com.

www.ingramcontent.com/pod-product-compliance
Lightning Source LLC
Chambersburg PA
CBHW020634260626
47157CB00008B/2741